LOCKHART

D1640664

RALPH BLAND

LOCKHART

RESOURCE *Publications* · Eugene, Oregon

LOCKHART

Copyright © 2021 Ralph Bland. All rights reserved. Except for brief quotations in critical publications or reviews, no part of this book may be reproduced in any manner without prior written permission from the publisher. Write: Permissions, Wipf and Stock Publishers, 199 W. 8th Ave., Suite 3, Eugene, OR 97401.

Resource Publications
An Imprint of Wipf and Stock Publishers
199 W. 8th Ave., Suite 3
Eugene, OR 97401

www.wipfandstock.com

PAPERBACK ISBN: 978-1-6667-1324-4
HARDCOVER ISBN: 978-1-6667-1325-1
EBOOK ISBN: 978-1-6667-1326-8

04/07/21

I long to talk with some old lover's ghost,
Who died before the god of love was born.

—John Donne

How strange when an illusion dies.
It's as though you've lost a child.

—Judy Garland

Even a man who is pure in heart and says his prayers by night
may become a werewolf when the wolfbane blooms
and the moon is full and bright.

—Curt Siodmak, *The Wolf Man*

PROLOGUE

McClellan, Alabama
December 30, 1972

He was finishing off the first of several planned forthcoming pitchers of Miller High Life when a fire truck rumbled down Moss Road with the engine roaring and its siren shrieking like a banshee at high decibel. As was his custom Thomas Lockhart was seated at the front window table at Dixie's Pub looking out at Moss, which was the most traveled route in the city of McClellan. He'd first heard the siren in the distance wailing and shrieking its ghostly tune, high above the sound of the Rockola from wherein Neil Young was telling everybody in the joint that moment how only love could break their hearts. He set his mug down on the tabletop and watched as the truck passed by and sped on to the light at the intersection and turned right on Rainbow Hills. He knew there was no other place it could be headed except toward the Covington campus, because there was nothing back that way but the school and U.S. 80 heading east out of town.

He walked to the counter and paid his bill, pushed the glass door open and stepped outside. He didn't have his car at the moment—the Fairlane was broken down again, waiting for him to have the money to fix it—so he would have to hoof it if he wanted to get to the campus, but it was only two miles, and he could do that with his eyes closed. When the day came when Tom Lockhart couldn't run a measly two miles to get somewhere, even with a pitcher of beer gurgling in his stomach and the remnants of a joint dancing in his head, well, that was the day the powers that be could call the National Guard down from Kent State to travel south to McClellan, Alabama, and aim their carbines and open fire and put him out of his misery.

He broke into his patented long-distance run over to the turn for Rainbow Hills and followed the fire engine up the road for a half mile, running at a pace steady and controlled, that gait that people were always so surprised at the efficiency of it and how long he could maintain such a steady speed. Practice, he always tells them. I've been running somewhere since I was a kid. I've always ran to anyplace I needed to be. I never had patience enough to wait for somebody to take me somewhere. And when I was old enough to get a car I still used my legs, maybe not to sprint, but if it was a faraway place I knew how to make good time to get there. I could beat anybody driving a car and get there first every time. I was always the winner.

The streetlights illuminated the way as he made his way to Henderson Street and then to Lee Avenue. He is sure of his footing and knows his way without having to use his eyes or any artificial light to navigate the darkness. Years of experience, he thinks. It also helped when he looked over the roof-tops of the apartment buildings lining the western border of the campus and saw the orange almost pinkish glow in the night sky, and he knew that this was the fire and this was where McClellan's lone fire engine was headed and this was why he was running because there was a fire at Covington College this night and he had to be there to see it.

God required him to be present.

He turned the corner by the Fine Arts Building and crossed the lawn to where the Education Department and the Music Department shared a building, and when he came to the center of the square he could see the two girls' dorms and the one boys' dorm standing dark and desolated—because this was Christmas break and everyone was gone, the students, the faculty, the administration, all of Covington—and he saw the fire engine parked with men scuttling about unwinding hoses, and another fire truck from a neighboring town joining them, and a crowd of neighborhood people standing back a safe distance watching Peterson Library burn. Soon there were police cars and newspaper and television reporters and photographers with heavy cameras slung over their shoulders, all awaiting the time when they could approach the flames to get closer and take pictures and describe the sight so it could be on the news later that night and read about tomorrow morning.

Thomas Lockhart stood and watched the fire lick at the corners of Peterson and poke through the roof and envelope the third-floor balcony like clasped fingers ready to say a prayer, and he knew there was no stopping any of this now, just as there was no stopping what had happened in this same place a month before, that Peterson Library was going to go away and leave no trace or reminder of what had happened here in this spot, that it was time for it all to end before the new year came around.

(A few minutes past four on Wednesday afternoon Faith Mercer went over the railing of the third-floor balcony of Peterson Library and landed on the walkway below. There was no one around to see her fall because it was the Wednesday before Thanksgiving and Covington College was deserted with the students gone home for the holiday and the teachers leaving for the four-day break and the administration office closing at noon. The only people left on the grounds by this time were six members of the janitorial crew and one private policeman who served as security during the school's peak times, which at Covington were few and seldom. Sergeant Bill, as everyone called him, was busy closing out his shift going behind the janitorial crew checking buildings for locked doors and closed windows, and was close to finished and ready to go home when he came around to the front of Peterson and saw the girl's body on the sidewalk. The position she was in, with her head twisted around and her legs sprawled in different directions, left him no doubt she wasn't going to be getting up and she wasn't going to be walking away. He knew she was dead, so he called the police and the paramedics and sat on the bench of the library porch and waited for someone to come. He kept looking at the girl's body wondering if there was anything he could do for her, but he knew enough from his days as a policeman to not go over and touch anything and mess up whatever evidence the detectives and the coroner might find later. He knew there was nothing he could do to help the girl, but he hated seeing her all wrought-up and tangled and twisted like she was with people coming to see her this way. He thought about the girl's parents and how sad Thanksgiving was always going to be for them from now on.

Word traveled fast, and it wasn't long before Tom Lockhart knew something was going on that late Wednesday afternoon. He was standing on the deserted sidewalk of the shopping strip in downtown McClellan, looking into the storefront window of Hinkle's Pet Shop at the empty cages where there were usually puppies on one side and kittens on the other, wondering on this Thanksgiving Eve exactly where the cats and dogs and fish and parakeets and such went to on the holidays when the store was closed. Was there a holding cell downstairs where they all got locked up until Monday, with only some lone employee coming by during that time to feed them and give them fresh water, or did they get farmed out somewhere to some big animal orphanage where they had to eat gruel and feel lonesome and rejected while the rest of the world counted their blessings and gorged themselves on turkey and dressing and slabs of pumpkin pie? He was weighing these thoughts in his head and giving immeasurable regard to them, for the most part because he'd seen fit to smoke the remnants of a nice fat killer joint a half hour before, and under its effects this sort of heavy thinking and pondering came to him pretty regularly. He felt acutely akin this moment to the animals of Hinkle's and their holiday plight of being forsaken and abandoned, seeing how his own parents were now two years dead and departed and how his older brother, Sam, had seen fit to confiscate the bulk of the family estate for his own, seeing as Sam was the executor and had friends down at City Hall to boot. With a lack of funds at his disposal, it had been difficult for Tom to travel the four hundred miles from McClellan, Alabama, back to his hometown of Rhodes, Tennessee, to contest any legalities about the will, seeing how his 1965 Fairlane was not truly a road warrior or highway-ready and preferred staying parked and immobile most of the time. There was only the Trailways bus to catch to get home, which cost more money than he wished to pay, and so, as he had the past two Thanksgivings and Christmases and Easters, he had remained in McClellan over the holiday break in his tiny apartment with the one room and the kitchen and the shower where the past summer there had been a baby copperhead waiting for him one morning, a dwelling he paid for by working in the school bookstore carrying boxes and ringing up orders because he seemed to be one of the few students around who could master the ancient NCR cash register at the front counter checkout.

He was looking in the empty windows identifying with the abandoned animals and feeling the sinking holiday feeling settling in when he saw the ambulance and the police cars racing up the hill. He got in the Fairlane and followed them, and when he arrived he was in time to see the policemen draping tape across Peterson's porchway and steps. There were more police cruisers and cops milling around that he'd ever known existed in McClellan, ambulances and vans and men everywhere. Three attendants in white set a stretcher down and lifted a body upon it. From where he was behind the police barriers he couldn't see clearly, but someone in the crowd said it was a girl.

In a few minutes the ambulance with the body inside pulled off without its sirens turned on, and Tom knew that meant no one inside was in a hurry to get anywhere. Whoever was getting carted away was dead. He wondered how it happened. Then he heard someone say the girl had fallen from Peterson's third floor. Maybe she'd come outside for a minute and slipped on something, lost her balance and fell over the railing. Or it could be she'd jumped. Whichever way it happened, the voice said, she shouldn't have been in there. The library was closed, been closed and locked up since noon, so she had to have been in there when they locked the doors and left. Wonder why that was? I guess they'll find out sooner or later.

There was only a small column about it on Page Three in the morning edition of the McClellan Register on Thanksgiving Day. It said the victim was unidentified pending notification of kin and police were still investigating what happened. Further details had not been available at press time.

On Friday the deceased was identified as Faith Mercer, a student at Covington. Lockhart read the story sitting in the McClellan McDonald's eating a sausage and biscuit and drinking a cup of coffee. He focused on the article and the name and wondered if any of this had anything to do with him. Faith Mercer had worked at the bookstore. She was from Birmingham. Her father was a preacher. She was an English major like him and some others he knew. She'd been in several of his classes over the past three years, and she'd liked him. She had a boyfriend, sure, but he could tell it was him, Thomas Lockhart, she really liked. She would have dropped the boyfriend for him in a second, he believed, if only he said the first word, but he hadn't done that. He at least had never lied to her or led her on about that. He'd done other things to her, sure, for a while, but it was all by mutual agreement. He had never told her to leave her boyfriend for him, and after a while he stopped doing those things with her because he sensed there might be trouble. He went away. He even told her it was because he was in love with someone else, which he thought sounded like the right thing to say at the time. He also told her that because it was true.

Over the Thanksgiving break he thought about Faith Mercer and wondered if he should make the trip to Birmingham for her funeral, but then the talk started up when people returned from the break, questions and conjectures about Faith Mercer and how she was into drugs and how the possibility existed she might have been pregnant, and how the two of those states factored together to probably make her delay going home for Thanksgiving because she was trying to work out what to say to her parents, her father the preacher, and to her boyfriend, who maybe was or maybe was not responsible for her condition, how she would tell everyone, or maybe it was the boyfriend had refused to marry her and take responsibility for what he had or hadn't done. It was a lot of things and it was a lot of talk.

Because a lot of people knew how wild she'd become over the last couple of years. There were a lot of stories of how Faith Mercer carried on.

And because of the talk and the fact that perhaps he might be linked to Faith Mercer in a negative connotation, Tom Lockhart decided not to catch a ride with any of the other students going to Birmingham for her funeral, because he remembered the times he had been with her in the night, in the dark in his small apartment that was just this side of being condemned, and he wondered if maybe it might be true she'd been pregnant and maybe it might be him who was the father. He had never really known what Faith and her boyfriend did when they were together, what she did with anyone else either, but he for damned sure knew about him and her and what they had done for a time, and the idea of it crept inside his soul and took up residence there. He knew from the start he was never going to be rid of her entirely. He knew himself. He was going to be guilty of this act whether he was or wasn't. He knew from that moment on he would never be able to forget.

But it wasn't just the fact that maybe he was guilty of this crime and maybe he was sorry about it, for it did not stop with that. There was some anger attached to it too. He felt like he was perhaps having to pay for this after he'd been driven to it by something else, by someone else. He knew he wouldn't have jumped into these doings with Faith Mercer if there hadn't been something pulling him into it, if something sad and unfair hadn't turned him into the creature he'd somehow become. He remembered the person he'd been growing up in high school back in Rhodes, how he had been in love with all the things in the world and the world had been in love with him. He had come to Covington then on his own, not traveling to any of the nearby colleges or state schools with the friends he'd grown up with, but instead taken the partial scholarship Covington offered him and come all the way to McClellan in the state of Alabama to study English and Creative Writing and learn the skills necessary to become a writer himself, and when that was done he would write books like Wolfe and Fitzgerald and Salinger and show the world the error of its ways. Life would open for him like some immense doorway leading to his own form of Paradise. There would be love and happiness and great riches in this land of promise to come, and he felt himself balanced on the doorway preparing to enter.

He was where he wanted to be, the world was his to take.

Then the girl named Maribeth McAllister came along, and after a short time the girl Maribeth McAllister told him goodbye, and the world went dark after that.)

He stood for a time in a drizzling cold rain in the darkness, watching Peterson Library disappear a little at a time, the ancient bricks charring and the wood glowing orange and white, until at last the flames went out from the water from the fire hoses and the falling rain and all the light was gone and it was dark wet ash with grey-blue smoke rising from the rubble that could only be seen from the headlights of the gathered vehicles. The crowd had gone home, and Tom found himself the only one left watching. There were still a few firemen poking the ashes of what was left of Peterson and spraying the area with endless streams of water, wetting down what would never be dry again, and Tom wondered how long they would keep on doing it before they were allowed to stop.

How long does a fire burn, he asked himself? Is there a scientific point where a temperature degree is reached that is considered completely out and non-combustible? Or is it all just a matter of opinion, where one person says that is it and it is out and it is done, while another looks at the cold wet remains and is not so sure, that something may look like it is dead and gone but still might retain that certain something, that spark, that force of ignition that is waiting for the clock to tick and time to go by before it suddenly finds the wherewithal to become a fire again and burn what is before it and around it until it turns orange within its red and yellow flame and somehow becomes so hot that nothing can put it out, that all that can be done is wait and allow the flame to burn itself out, to curl and blacken and ride up into the waiting sky and drift off in the wind, never to be seen in its burnt place again, to be gone and vanished but never completely forgotten despite its disappearance, but remembered as a fire that started once that never truly came to an end.He wore no hat and his hair was wet with rain. His jacket was drenched and hung heavily on his shoulders, and he thought about removing it and shaking the water off, but it was cold and he knew he would freeze and it wouldn't do him any good. There was no warming up from this, he thought. This was a chill he was going to have for a long time.

He could hear the downtown McClellan First Baptist Church clock striking twelve. It was midnight and the hosing down of Peterson continued. He looked at the library in its dark ruin and thought about how long it had stood in this place, since before the Civil War and through Reconstruction, and now it was gone. He had first spotted Maribeth McAllister coming out the front doors of Peterson, and now those double doors would never open or close again. He thought of the third-floor balcony, how on spring days students liked to come outside and sit in chairs or gather at the railing and watch the pedestrian traffic of the school go by below them, reading their books and talking and watching squirrels and birds jump among the branches and fly and flit from the tops of the oak trees and magnolias back and forth from the rooftops of the dorms and the department classrooms. The balcony was gone now too, the roof had caved in, and he turned his eyes to where it all once was and saw a vision of Faith Mercer leaning against the now-consumed railing, thinking of someone or something, trying to decide how she was going to live or how she might die, and he wanted to tell her to stop, but it was too late for that now.

It was always going to be too late.

And it came to him how he was always going to be present in this moment he was now in and how he was never going to leave. He saw how he would come back to this place in all the years to come even when he was truly not here, and he knew what he would leave behind this night would not stay here in the ashes and the ruin and the rubble but would find him wherever he might go, would seek him out and abide with him for all the years to come, and no matter what he did or where he ended up it would always be with him and it would never leave.

It was going to be a long time to live with it all. He would have to somehow learn how to endure what was now and what was yet to come.

ONE

April 18, 2003
Good Friday
Rhodes, Tennessee

It was spring, but it for damn sure didn't feel like it. It had been officially spring for a week or more now, and people were joking about how spring had simply passed by Rhodes this year, that it had been winter or something close to it for a while with all the gray skies and north winds and only a glimpse of the sun here and there, and then when March ended and April came around all at once the sun had come out hot and orange and it was a race to store away the sweaters and jackets and stocking hats and pull out the tee shirts and shorts and sandals. The temperature bypassed the usual middle-seventies and skipped over the gentle breezes that were supposed to be around and climbed instead into the eighties and stayed like that for two weeks, until it was time for spring break from school and Easter. All that time the sun had beaten down and the nights were humid, and everyone was convinced that summer was already here to stay.

By the time noon came around on this Good Friday, what businesses that had bothered to even open were closing at noon. Schools had let out the day before, so the students and their families had been free to leave Rhodes early to go on vacation, to visit with relatives in distant cities for Easter or take an early trip to Florida and the beach. From mid-afternoon on Thursday until noon on Friday there was a steady stream of cars and trucks and minivans on South Main and Highway 231 heading for Asheville or Gatlinburg or back south toward Gulf Shores and the Florida beaches, people migrating for the weekend and the week afterward, with only the unlucky souls left behind who had to be at work on Saturday and back again early on Monday morning whether the Savior had risen from the grave or not.

On South Main on the east side of Rhodes, the road cut through the business district and kept ambling northward to the apartments and suburbs and on to the far expanses of the county where the elite white-collar business owners and professionals of the city lived in sweeping homes set far back from the asphalt and the rabble. In the strip of businesses that ran through town, the Bank of America had a long line of cars at the drive-thru, folks depositing paychecks and drawing out extra cash for the days ahead. Polk's Polka-Dot Piggly Wiggly's parking lot looked like it was Christmas Eve or a big snow scare or some sort of crisis, cars filling the spaces and circling around looking for a place to park, some of them giving up and heading for the Kroger four miles away on the west side. The talk was Kroger was thinking of building another store somewhere on South Main, but nobody knew exactly where it might be, everything was hush-hush, and no bulldozer had broken any ground for a building yet.

The Tiger Market at the corner of Tucker Road had all its bays in use, and across the street the Mapco was going great guns too. Little Caesar's was open for lunch, and three doors down from them the Olympia Grill was serving today's meat and three. No one was wandering around the Auto Bargain shopping for a used car; there was too much to do and too many places to be to worry about getting a new set of wheels today. Wheeling and dealing would just have to wait until the start of business Monday, when there'd be plenty of time to dicker.

A half mile down South Main, at Lane's Chevrolet/ Buick/ GM, the new car business was running slow too. Danny Lewis was returning in the company van from Little Caesar's with pizza for all the sales staff, himself, Herb Watson, Johnny Castle, and Gail Belden, who was the receptionist. There hadn't been but two customers all day, and Michael Hoover, the Sales Manager, had already left for the holiday to go out of town. The two customers had both informed the sales crew how at the moment they were only looking, so about the only thing that had been accomplished on this Good Friday was taking a few names down and handing out brochures and business cards in case those people who were only looking decided to get serious later on. As slow as it was it was going to be a long night until closing time at eight, but everybody knew that was the way it was going to be. Matt Lane wasn't going to close the dealership early just for a holiday. The business would be open regular hours Friday and Saturday. The staff considered it to be a bonus to even be off on Easter Sunday, since Matt usually stayed open Sundays too, because Sunday was a day when people liked to wander in and look at what might strike their fancy in a new ride.

Danny parked the van by the front door, but didn't get out right away because he had the radio turned up listening to Lynard Skynard. He leaned back in the seat and let the guitar riffs take over his being, closing his eyes to the world around him and escaping from the dealership for a blessed while. Everybody would just have to wait a few more minutes on their pizza. Sometimes a guy just has to have a little "Free Bird" simply to keep on living. When the song ended, he opened his eyes and peered off into the sky over the showroom rooftop. It was looking dark, and when a commercial came on he gathered up the two boxes of pizza and hurried inside before the clouds cut loose and he got soaked.

"It's fixing to come a good one," he announced. The salesmen were all leaning on Gale's counter waiting for him to get back. Friday was always pizza day at Lane's.

"Maybe we'll have a damn big storm and the power will go out," Johnny Castle says. "Then we'll have no alternative but to lock up and go home." He walked over to the front door and opened it, stuck his head out and looked up. "Yeah, it's getting dark, all right. Maybe we ought to all go back to the waiting room and huddle up and be safe."

"If you're in the waiting room I'm staying here," Gail says. "I'm not about to huddle up with the likes of you anywhere."

"Don't knock it until you've tried it, Missy," Johnny grins.

Danny fishes in his pocket and brought out some bills and coins and laid them on Gail's desk.

"There's everybody's change," he says. He walks away but keeps his eyes peeled seeing if anybody rushes over and picks it up. Usually they don't, so he waits a minute or so and goes back and pockets it himself. It's not like he's stealing it.

Herb takes his usual two slices from the two boxes, one pepperoni, one sausage, grabs a napkin from the pile, and goes over and sits down at one of the desks. If he goes off by himself to eat he won't be tempted to snarf down more than two slices and get sleepy and suffer acid indigestion and have to keep popping Rolaids until closing time. He's getting too damn old to keep throwing crap down into his stomach night and day. He's also fat enough already without doing anything to compound it.

Johnny is getting a Pepsi from the courtesy cooler when a flash of lightning illuminates the room and a loud blast of thunder follows it up. It sounds like a bomb with echoes and vibrations and reverberations, and the lights flicker two times, then come back on.

"Whoa," Danny says. "That was close."

The rain moves in, fat drops at first that hit the windshields of the parked cars outside in the lot like water balloons, splatting and spreading on the glass and bouncing and pinging off the roofs and the hoods. Like they are watching a snake swallow a rat, entranced, everyone walks over to the front windows and looks out to see how hard it is raining, to see the lightning and secretly wonder if the wind that is whipping the telephone wires and the traffic light out on South Main up and down and sideways is going to be one of those storms people talk about later and never forget where they were when it happened. They stand at the windows munching pizza and watch the rain come down and the wind blow, like none of them have ever seen a storm before.

All of Rhodes keeps getting darker, and shoppers hurry to check out at Polk's and deposit their checks at the bank and finish their lunch at the Olympia and get out to their cars and get home before the weather gets too bad. This is one of those things about living in Rhodes; they all agree on this. One day it will be like winter and then all at once it will be summer, one minute the sun is shining and then the storms come at you just like that. That's the way it is in Tennessee—if you don't like the weather right now, just wait a day or two and you'll get something entirely different.

It's Good Friday in Rhodes, but all the preparations for Easter will have to wait.

A heck of a storm is on the way.

Dewey Eberhart had finished for the day already. He'd really had nothing but the Saab from the professor from Murfreesboro to work on this morning—a new plug and a cable to get the speedometer working again— and that had taken a little under an hour, so basically he's been sitting in his lawn chair listening for a good while to the classical music station coming from the old RCA console he has propped up against the garage wall. The console had been his mom's and dad's back in the day, and it was a part of the house and he couldn't get rid of it. It had an AM/FM band and a turntable that played 78s and 45s and LPs and an adaptor to stick on the spindle so you didn't have to fit a plastic piece in the hole of a 45 every time you wanted to play one. Everything on the RCA still worked fine as wine these forty years later, so Dewey had never seen the need to go out and get anything new. Maybe one of these days he might need a new needle, but so far the original one was holding up fine.

The classical station was located in the public library on the other side of Rhodes, and when it wasn't playing longhair stuff that Dewey really appreciated whenever he was high or pleasantly inebriated or both, it also aired political programs and public interest forums and news from NPR, which Dewey liked going on in the background while he was working during the day. He'd developed an interest in political happenings since back when

Tricky Dicky was in office and liked expressing his disdain for Republicans to his pet squirrel Phyllis, to voice his disgust for Democrats and his distrust of mostly anyone who held an office in D.C. or in the state of Tennessee or even in the city of Rhodes, even if there was precious little corruption going on in Rhodes these days, since years of past underhandedness and dishonesty had already stripped the city of whatever treasures it had once possessed and there wasn't much pillaging left to be done..

Since it was technically lunchtime, Dewey sat in his lawn chair on the pavement of the driveway with the garage door over his head providing shade. He had a cantaloupe crate from the Polka Dot Piggly Wiggly sitting beside him serving as an outdoor table, providing a place for his bottle of Mateus wine and a glass for him to sip on while he perused his daily dose of James Joyce and *Ulysses* the same way he'd been doing at lunch for the past thirty years. On the other side of him Phyllis, who he was not actually certain was a female squirrel or not but just seemed that way to him by the way she was always demanding things from him, nuts, cheese, sometimes potato chips if he was feeling generous, Phyllis, who had been around for a while now, since the morning Dewey had found her cowering under a Volkswagen Rabbit he was working on—he had picked her up and held her and fed her and let her sleep in the garage for a while so the hawks and the foxes wouldn't get her, until finally letting her come in the house and sleep in the kitchen or in the den or his bedroom or after a while just any old place she wanted to—was sitting, Phyllis was, on her hind legs accepting shelled peanuts from Dewey while he had his regular lunch of Oscar Mayer bologna and white bread—a Rhodes Special, he liked to call it—a few tokes on a roach from last night, and a glass of Mateus to read by. He always looked at his watch and limited himself to one hour for his luncheon escape from the bonds of the work world, but today, being Good Friday and with no auto-mobiles present to repair, he allowed himself to keep sitting and sipping and toking and reading and feeding additional peanuts to Phyllis and permitting the long weekend to get started early. He listened to Offenbach and relaxed and thought to himself how this was exactly the reason he had never tried to go out in the world and find a real job.

He paused reading about Bloom and the Glasnevin funeral and looked toward the west, thinking of the Dublin cemetery and how he had spent three days walking through it when he visited Ireland twenty-five years ago and wondering if he was ever going to fulfill his vow of going back there to live. The sky had increasingly turned a deeper shade of blue, and Dewey could see how the world was getting darker by the moment, like somebody was dimming the lights before the beginning of a play. He felt hot wind blowing in his face like it was trying to tell him something. He knows something is coming and is not far off.

Coming down River Road he sees the figure making its way toward him. The figure doesn't speed up the way most sane people would when there's a storm coming, but just continues on its steady gait, walking along in the grass at the side of the street like nothing is going on any different now than anytime else. It is like this body has experienced lightning and rain before and just isn't that impressed with it. There's no fear in this person; anybody can see that. He's just somebody getting to where he wants to be and sees no reason to worry or hurry, because he's always made his way before this and he'll for damn sure get there this time too.

Lockhart, Dewey thinks.

Only that damn fool Tom Lockhart would stroll along in front of an approaching thunderstorm like there's all the time in the world. The thing that tickles Dewey so much is he knows if Tom Lockhart wanted to—even at the advanced age both of them have arrived at—he could take off on a dead run and be here at the garage lickety-split before the first raindrop ever hit the ground. But Lockhart walks at his own pace, and Dewey knows it has nothing to do with any coming storm or the Easter holiday or anything the rest of the citizenry of Rhodes is concerned with this afternoon; no, Tom Lockhart is walking and thinking and working something out in his head, and Dewey knows by the time Tom gets here and comes up the driveway he'll have it all figured out.

It's always been hard as hell to separate Tom Lockhart from his game plan, no matter how preposterous it might be.

Actually, Tom Lockhart is not involved in any sort of mental plan that will help him negotiate high seas or rocky roads presently in his path, but is instead in the midst of editing his second novel—which went to press thirteen years ago—and trying to eliminate a couple of scenes and passages which, as he thinks about them now in this year of 2003, made no sense either then or now. Perhaps if he had never written them or swallowed his pride and eliminated them from the manuscript like his editor had suggested, then perhaps he could let the book rest in peace now. It is not like he can do anything about it anyway; heck, his editor is dead and the press that published his first two (and only) novels is out of business now, gone under back before everyone believed they were going to die from Y-2K, when they should have known if it wasn't that it was going to be something else.

He lifts a hand in greeting to Dewey when he starts his climb up the steep driveway, watching his footing so he doesn't step in one of the ruts or stumble on a wayward rock and tumble back down the hill like a human avalanche. Dewey waves back with his wineglass in his hand, and Tom is glad to see all is normal here right now at Eberhart's Foreign Car Repair, or whatever Dewey is calling his garage these days, since Dewey changes the name about once a year, whenever he gets tired of the way it sounds.

Tom hears a long rumble of thunder and wonders if a storm might be coming.

"You know," Dewey tells him as Stravinsky floats out from the garage, "you're about the only person I know who has a car and leaves it parked so he can walk back and forth to and from work every day. What is it—two miles each way? You're also the only knucklehead who does it when a storm is on the way and the chances are multiplied he gets struck by a bolt of lightning before he makes it home."

"I've dodged lightning bolts before," Tom says, "plenty of them. Sent down by Thor because I did something to piss him off. I've always seen them coming and got the hell out of the way just in the Nikodemus. Anyway, Dewey, I haven't a home to go to around here yet, just your happy abode until I find somewhere to live where I don't have to listen to babies crying or neighbors playing Black Sabbath to all hours of the morning or gunshots going off outside the window that make me take up residence under the bed."

"You lived too long in downtown Chattanooga is what your problem is. You think every place is the same as that."

"You're probably right. There were certain sections in that town where peace was hard to come by."

A flash of lightning hits somewhere too close to shrug off, and thunder follows it in a series of vibrating booms. The noise is like a line of bombs being dropped up and down River Road and all the way to South Main. Phyllis stops munching on a shell long enough to freeze in an upright position and twitch her nose to make sure she is still a part of the planet, while Dewey decides that sitting here in the open in his lawn chair with the metal frame and the metal garage door over his head is possibly not the best place in the world to be right now, so he gathers up his Mateus and his roach clip and his copy of *Ulysses* and folds up the chair and moves inside the garage. Another flash of lightning comes along and the RCA stops in mid- "Rites of Spring" and the lights go off along with it. Up River Road Rhodes looks powerless too, its paltry skyline faded and gray and the traffic light at River Road and South Main unlit and swinging like sixty in the breeze.

The wind starts gusting and the treetops sway. Power lines dance. A metal trash can rolls and tumbles through the grass from some neighbor's yard over the rise, and rain falls like all the needles in all the syringes in the world, sharp and slanting and deadly, pointed so a grown man will yelp if he's dumb enough to stay outside uncovered in it for too long.

Tom Lockhart is stupid a lot and backward sometimes and ill-informed in a lot of different ways, but he is not dense, or at least not dense so much that he's going to stand outside braving the elements simply to see if he might die or not from the assault. He takes fast steps inside the garage for shelter. The sky is dark like the sun has clocked out for the day and won't be back until Monday, and the rain advances in sweeping battalions across the yard and onward down River Road, blown by a wind that howls like White Fang and shrieks like a phantom and tries to take everything it passes with it on its journey to Hell.

"We could be looking at a tornado right here, Dewey," Tom says.

"Maybe it's a tornado. For all we know it's the end of the world." Dewey takes another sip of Mateus, glad he didn't panic and leave his glass out on the cantaloupe crate. If he had, the glass would be gone now just like the crate is gone, which he watches as it scoots along end over end past the side yard and down the slope to hit River Road and continue on to god knows where. "Of course," he continues, "it could be we're living right this minute in biblical times. You do remember from your Sunday School upbringing how on Good Friday the world got dark when they crucified Jesus, so maybe we're getting a good dose of symbolistic forewarning right now from Our Father Who Art in Heaven."

"Do what?"

"Just saying, Tom, it might be more than a coincidence that our fair city is blacking out on Good Friday. Maybe it's Jehovah's way of telling this town how fucked up it's becoming on a daily basis."

"That's everywhere, Dewey. God would have to destroy the entire planet if He was setting standards like that. Rhodes is no better or worse than anywhere else."

"So you're saying we're all in this together?"

"Exactly. We are the world, we are the children."

They stand several minutes watching the wind and rain pelt the ground and move trees around and transport whatever's not tied down from South Main toward them to stop and rest a handful of seconds and then get lifted up to swirl some more and fly away somewhere else. After a few minutes the lightning stops and the thunder pipes down to a low rumble, and all that's left in the semi-darkness is the sound of the rain continuing to fall, harder for a while like it's a drummer practicing next door, then calming down to a patter and a hiss and finally a drip. The clouds open and the sun peeks out little by little, and all at once it is so quiet and peaceful it is like no storm has ever happened. There is still no power, however, and there are sirens in the distance running up and down the streets of Rhodes, so it's not like what has just happened was a figment of either of their joint imaginations.

"That was quite a show," says Tom. "Wonder what the encore's like?"

"I would venture that now is when we have to wait two days for somebody to come back from the dead. Only thing about that is if that's what's supposed to go on here then it's already happened. That back from the dead guy would be you, buddy boy. You're the only one I know of who's arisen from the tomb around here lately. You were as good as buried in everybody's mind for a lot of years, and now here you are, walking among us again. Do you mind if I feel your side to make sure you're real?"

"Not Our Heavenly Father, but circumstances beyond my control have me standing beside you now."

"Yeah, I know. Good old Sam threw himself a seven and you had to come back for the funeral. He was your older brother and you were supposed to show up—I understand that. But nobody expected you to stick around for good. We had you penciled in as a permanent resident of Chattanooga, happy in your life there as teacher and writer. Now I did have an inkling that maybe things weren't always rosy with you all the while, just by the news that trickled in from time to time. You know what I mean, little insignificant things like no more novels after the first two came out about a hundred years ago, news of your divorce, and then that tiny little rumor of how you weren't teaching high school anymore, that you'd been banished and had to leave over one petty little thing or another. I even heard you were driving a bread truck for a while."

"Doughnuts, Dewey. Cinnamon buns and snack cakes and goodies galore. I ran a route for six months and gained close to twenty pounds sampling the menu. I had to quit before I became a dirigible and floated away untethered. Then came word of Sam dying and I came back for the funeral, like I was supposed to show my respects to the asshole or something. I don't know where that idea came from. Then, instead of leaving, I let Matt talk me into taking a job with him, so here I am, gainfully employed and a resident of the old hometown once more."

Tom takes the joint Dewey has fired up and draws a thoughtful lungful, then hands it back to Dewey quickly, because he has learned over the years that, for him, once is always enough. There is no need for him to stumble around anymore with an eternal smile hearing instrumentation in music he'd never previously heard or having great insights about life and love and philosophy that have all packed up and been gone long before he awoke any sad morning after. Been there, he thinks, done that.

He climbs the basement stairs to go into the house, takes a left by the kitchen and heads down a hallway to the room Dewey is letting him crash in until he finds a place to live. He's been back in Rhodes three weeks now, been on his new job for two of those weeks, but the pickings have been slim

in finding an abode. There are three apartment complexes around populat-
ed by wild singles driving jacked-up pickup trucks and souped-up Camaros
and motorcycles, single mothers in halter tops and newlyweds duking it out
and peeling rubber and police cars, scenes Tom Lockhart has been privy to
plenty of times during his Chattanooga sojourn and decided a while back
that enough was enough, that it was time for some order and peace to soften
the pounding of his soon-to-be faltering heartbeat in these declining years,
that he simply could no longer tolerate the whims and impulses of the outside world much anymore, so he is looking now for someplace to be away
from the hustle and bustle as much as possible.

At least here at Dewey's there's not a lot of craziness going on. By the
time Dewey climbs the stairs at the end of the work day he is pleasantly and
completely higher than Ben Franklin's favorite kite, and all he wants to do
then is flood the house with music from the scores of reel-to-reel tapes he's
recorded over the past thirty years and cook salivating dinners from scratch
using all the faculties and self-taught methods and recipes he's garnered all
these decades of living here alone. Tom has learned in the past couple of
weeks that Dewey is possibly the greatest cook on the face of the earth, or at
least it must be so in Rhodes.

He kicks off his shoes and lays down on the bed. There is nothing to
see on the ceiling above him, only a bare surface that could have stood a
coat of paint about a decade ago. There is, in fact, nothing much in this
room whatsoever to actually gaze at and study—no books in a bookcase or
pictures on the walls or even curtains with a design at the windows, only
plain shades on a roll that can be raised or lowered according to whether
one wants to look out at the desolate stretch of River Road running down to
River Grove Cemetery or not.

But he is happy this moment, settled here among all this nothing and
lack of substance.

It seems to him, positioned here in the peace and calm of the room,
that this moment has been a long time coming. He thinks of Covington and
all that had gone wrong there those lifetimes ago, and he remembers leaving McClellan after graduation, unable to return to Rhodes by the middle
of his sophomore year because there was no home here for him anymore;
everything he thought was in some way his had been taken away. Good
old Sam, his older brother who'd decided through his executor powers that
their parents' estate should simply go to him—the house, the investments,
all the family mementos and pictures and keepsakes. Being a lawyer, Sam
had knowledge of how to perform certain screwing-over procedures, but
Tom had never been able to understand the stealth that had been involved.
Sam didn't have to go to extremes to have everything, for it had been such

a handing-down that was already done long before Jimmy and Elizabeth Lockhart met up with a wrong-way drunken driver on the interstate coming home from a baseball game. When Tom received his portion of the inheritance—a check made out to him from the estate, signed by his brother—he did not realize that what he had received was merely a form of hush payment, something to satisfy him for a time while everything else that had been a part of the family was busy being sequestered over to Sam.

But he had never been truly surprised by the turn of events, for he had sensed being on the short end of the stick in the family dynamic for a long time already by then. If he'd been asked, he probably would have stated he expected nothing different, for he was accustomed to this version of the status quos by now. It seemed normal. He just didn't understand why Sam had to be so diametrically mean and sneaky over something that was already a foregone conclusion before it happened.

He had no real home, then, starting with that point in his sophomore year and continuing to the summer after graduation. What friends he had were gone after the graduation ceremony, and staying around McClellan didn't seem to be too much of an inviting option. There were no real jobs for real adults, only the kind of cheap wages businesses like to dole out to students, and Tom didn't believe he wanted to try and find a teaching position at the two schools within the city limits. He had this sense that it was time to move on somewhere, but he had no notion which direction to go. That was when his Covington friend Ray Miles called him and wondered if he might be interested in coming to Chattanooga. There were a couple of positions open in the high school where Ray had started teaching, and Tom Lockhart, knowing there was nothing in McClellan, Alabama, but the ghost of a romance with a girl named Maribeth who was gone from him forever, and the memory of Peterson Library going up in flames, and the recurring thought of Faith Mercer falling from a balcony on the day before Thanksgiving, falling to her death with what may have been a part of him inside her to the sidewalk below, and so he packed what possessions he held, filled his Fairlane with gas from the Phillips 66 by the interstate, and left for Chattanooga to see what the future might hold, leaving Covington College with its fire and smoke and icy despair behind for what he figured would be forever.

He'd gone to Chattanooga and impressed the principal so much on the interview he'd been offered the job on the spot. Later, he amended his self-congratulatory feelings from him being so wonderful that he had to be hired to the realization that the actual reason he'd been offered a position so fast was because Collier High School was at that time desperate. They needed an English teacher badly and the start of school was on the horizon, and he had been lucky enough to walk right into it.

It had been a good ride too, he thought, one that had lasted twenty-three years. He had taught his classes and sponsored the school paper and managed to write two novels during that time. His life had looked good. He'd found companionship with a few of the lady teachers and had his share of dalliances and hot whispers and angry words of parting. He'd even married once—a Lynda, his first colossal mistake—and become a father, possibly, to Mitchell, even if he had never spotted much of a resemblance between him and this perhaps son that had totally convinced him he was for sure the boy's father. Divorce had come (as he knew it would) after two years, yet he'd still managed to maintain his footing at school, and all had looked good and smooth until he stepped into the affair with Dr. Rose, Amanda, his principal. When that came out into the open it was all over, because Dr. Rose happened to be the wife of the superintendent of the Chattanooga school system, who was fast to decide that something like this could not be associated with him and his wife, and so the chips had fallen and it had become time for Thomas Lockhart to depart, as in vanish. Conduct unbecoming to the profession; Tom remembers the wording. He had known immediately they had him dead to rights, had known he couldn't win in a game like this, so he had offered up his resignation in exchange for no mark being denoted on his record. He wanted to keep his pension, so he didn't fight the decision. He would simply disappear and make it easy on everyone, especially himself. He figured if he could salvage his reputation and work history and not get tarred and feathered for his sins, he could live with it. It was much like what Dylan said. He would not die and it wasn't poison.

He spent two years trying to find something else to do. He drove trucks and stocked shelves and ran cash registers at liquor stores on Friday and Saturday nights. He wondered if he would ever rise from the basement of Chattanooga back to a penthouse with some kind of a view. He was a man of fifty-two still searching for gainful employment. It was not a pretty sight to behold.

That was when the word came that Sam had died, and so he had come back to Rhodes for the funeral. He couldn't have explained why he bothered to make the trip.

And that was when Matt Lane offered him a job.

TWO

Birds chirping away, even in the dark before the sun comes up. Tom Lockhart in his usual place this pre-dawn, sitting half-asleep in Dewey's den, hard-pressed to recall just when and what he had been dreaming when he'd left his bed and migrated downstairs during the night. Within the fog of his waking brain he remembers filling a glass with water, draining it down like he has been thirsty for days and not been granted the right to hydrate, and then stumbling around in the dark to knock the bejesus out of his shin on a coffee table, collapsing into a chair the Salvation Army would refuse to take, then laying back his head and falling asleep like he'd been hit by a poison dart from a headhunter hidden behind one of Dewey's mammoth stereo speakers, six of them by last count in this one room, all the size of Volkswagens.

He decides to drive to work this morning rather than walk. In his two-week history of employment at Matt Lane's dealership he has hoofed it most days back and forth in the mornings and afternoons, preferring the fresh air and the quiet of his thoughts to the radio and the ear bugs he obtains from hearing some song he never liked in the first place and having it stuck in his head for the majority of the day until something worse pops up from the satellite radio at work and takes over with another in a line of atrocious melodies. The parts and supply office he operates for Matt is generally closed on Saturdays along with the Repair Shop, but Matt had made mention of how a customer or two might want some vehicle part on a holiday weekend, some shade-tree mechanic changing a fan belt or a battery, and maybe if the office was open they would come here to get it rather than drive to the franchise places on the other side of town. Tom, figuring he owed Matt something for hiring him for this job, decided to cheerfully volunteer to open this Saturday before Easter and make some extra money on the side at the same time. Besides, it wasn't like he had anything else to do, and he for damned sure didn't want to sit in front of a computer screen waiting on words to type that were not going to come no matter how long he imprisoned himself there hoping inspiration might possibly come by for a visit.

Jim Morrison, deceased for longer than Tom cares to remember, is in the middle of asserting that people are strange from the speaker in the ceiling of the parts office, which inspires an agreeing grunt from Tom as he walks around turning on lights and signing on the computer and switching on the overhead television in the corner, muting it when he sees it is only the news of the world right now and therefore nothing of importance. He spoons out coffee into a Mr. Coffee basket and fills the cannister with water, wondering how he has made it to this place without caffeine in his system so far. Dewey doesn't drink coffee, preferring chocolate milk as his morning drink, and Tom's coffee maker is still packed away in one of the boxes stuffed in the Fairlane's trunk. He bought instant coffee to tide him over until he finds a place to live, but it is so bad he hasn't the heart to warm it after the first three days of enduring the taste. This morning he has engaged in showing some moxie and waiting for coffee until he gets to work, another in a long line of trials and tests he forces upon himself from time to time just to keep himself rugged and tough and fit for whatever mysterious race he's running or secret competition he's trying to win.

He is taking his third sip of coffee when the door opens and Abigail comes in. Abigail is no customer, but is Matt's younger sister, not exactly an employee of Lane Chevrolet/Buick/GM but more of a semi co-owner, even though her real job is as an art teacher at Rhodes Middle and not here in any capacity other than she is the youngest of the Lane family and thus has been bequeathed a part of the family business as part of her inheritance. There are other businesses in the Lane legacy too, too many for Tom to number, car washes and convenience markets and satellite used car lots and other ownerships, so Abigail could never work at all of them even if she wanted. Sometimes, out of the goodness of her own heart, she uses her clout at the dealership to get sizeable discounts for her friends and fellow teachers when they need a new automobile.

Abigail is currently a Williams, in the final stages of getting a divorce from husband number three, Garland, a city council member and head of Rhodes Parks and Recreation and a lawyer on the side. Abigail is forty-eight these days, but eternally looks fifteen years younger, so the wear and tear of failed marriages haven't done harm to her likeness whatsoever. Tom is of the conviction she is a vampire, since there seems to be not too many discernable differences in her appearance over the years. When he left Rhodes back in the distant past for Covington, Abigail was still a freshman in high school, already a beauty and making a habit of driving boys crazy, and when he came back to visit before his sophomore year at Covington, he and Abigail had a summertime fling that bordered on tempestuous. Tom is still not certain who had been the major aggressor at the time, him or Abigail, but he suspects if he was going to court to be tried for high crimes he would likely be found innocent of any sins other than being a red-blooded American boy.

Because the truth of it was what guy in his right mind could have ever resisted her?

Abigail is wearing a sleeveless green dress that is cottony and cool and clings to her in all the right places, places Tom has fond memories of clinging to several times himself in the past. Black hair cascades down her back like she is Liz Taylor's first-born, and her blue eyes dance and wink and make him become instantly and fully awake. She walks behind the counter to the coffee machine, and as she passes he sees how her lips, even this early in the morning, are glossy and pink. She pours coffee into a Styrofoam cup, mixes in sugar and cream until the concoction is light-colored and hardly coffee anymore, then inches closer to Tom and grazes his hip with hers. This has always been Abigail's way of saying hello to him, like it is her way of saying they can start getting intimate any time he wants, now that he is back and she is here, just a little hint of what might be currently on her mind.

Abigail has always liked him. Tom knows this as a fact.

"This is an unexpected surprise seeing you here this morning," she says. "I came around the corner and saw the lights on and was shocked to see the parts department open for business on a Saturday. I thought no wonder Matt has hired this fellow—he is really such a stellar employee, going over and beyond the call of duty, here when he really doesn't have to be. I was so impressed, and pleased too, because I thought I was going to have to drive all the way over to Dewey's house just to get the chance to jump your bones today."

Such a speech elicits another hip bump from Abigail, and were not Tom still embroiled on his first cup of coffee he would probably be inspired enough to send a bump back, but instead attempts to politely stand his ground and pretend at this early hour of the day there are no gutter-like thoughts already galloping through his head.

"Maybe I ought to be the one asking why you're here on a Saturday morning," he says, "since I've yet to notice you being an early riser as long as I've known you. And on a Saturday too. Something must be up."

"I've got a friend from school coming by to look at a car this morning. I told her I'd meet her here and get her a good deal." She takes a sip of her coffee-like substance and Tom sees the trace of lipstick left on the rim of the cup. "We were all out late last night at Thompson's partying down, so she may not make it in as early as she said she would." Abigail smiles, white teeth and eyes that make her nose wiggle and reminds Tom just exactly how goddamned cute she can be when she wants. "I tried to call you last night and invite you to come join us, but you had your phone turned off again. Too bad. You would have had a good time, but I guess that's not the kind of thing you like to do these days. That's the signals you keep sending out."

"It was a school night for me. I had to get up early, so I tucked it in at a decent hour. You'll get old like me one of these days, Abigail. Then you'll see how it is."

"You keep telling me how decrepit you are, but I'm not all that inclined to believe you. If you were as bad off as you keep saying you are, you'd be planted out there in River Grove already."

"I'm pretty sure I'm due for a fitting pretty soon."

"So, you're just going to work all day on a holiday weekend? I'm disappointed, Tom. I would have never believed you'd become such a money-grubber in your old age."

"I'm only keeping the place open for a couple of hours, just in case some enterprising soul decides today is the day to fix up the family station wagon and wants to come in for all his necessary supplies. If there's nothing shaking by mid-morning, I'm out of here."

"How about we have lunch together?" she suggests. "It's nice outside. I could take you for a ride and re-acquaint you with the old hometown, show you what's changed and disappeared since you left and what's still around. We could have some fun, Tom. Or are you going to keep putting me off forever? When do you plan on giving a poor girl a break?"

She twinkles her eyes at him and settles her hip into his again. She is hard to resist.

"You're not poor and you're certainly not a girl. But okay, I give you permission to give me the grand tour."

She sets her unfinished cup on the counter and walks to the door. She is still smiling at something unsaid and turns to give him a goodbye wave.

"I have to see if my friend is here yet," she says. "See you in a little," and then she is gone.

Tom makes an attempt to get busy doing something, but there is really nothing to do but look at the TV and the morning news from CNN or play Pacman on the computer (which he is getting pretty good at) or lean on the counter and drink more coffee and have visions of sugarplum Abigail dance through his head. He tells himself if there is no action in the next two hours he will indeed close up shop for the day. He may even leave before Abigail comes back to appropriate him, for he thinks it might be good to avoid harm's way for as long as possible. She is, after all, technically still a married woman.

Because he knows how it is with him when a woman makes herself available. Something happens. Something there is in him that overcomes any words to the wise or cautionary modes of behavior. Even with the hard lessons of the past and his vows to himself and the sun and moon above him to never stray again or to be foolish no more or to keep himself from taking a path where he loses control and good sense and becomes that shapeshifter he once was, that form who ruined lives and threw away trust and maybe sent someone who didn't deserve such a fate over a railing to an early end. He does not like constantly suspecting and mostly knowing that because of him the world is at times a mean and ugly place, and happy endings have been canceled and foregone for those who had possibly once dared to love him. He has told himself the meanings of the words no and never, but somehow they've had a way of escaping him and not allowing him to hold them in his mind, leaving him alone to do unforgiveable damage to a human heart again.

He is not fast enough in his resolutions. As he is locking the door at ten-thirty Abigail is coming down the walk with her bag slung over her shoulder and her car keys dangling from a finger. In the spring sunshine she is something to see, and despite the fact he doesn't really like her that much he is happy to take the vision in. She is a sight for sore male eyes, that is for certain. He thinks if he did not feel this way that he would be dead, and so he is glad that in his ancient age of fifty-three he can still be stirred like this. There are worse things, Lockhart, he reminds himself. You ought to know that by now.

"That's what I like," Abigail says, "a man who's on time for an appointment."

She leads him to her car, a shiny blue BMW convertible, sitting with the top down already and awaiting the two of them to get in so it can take them on their pending getaway. This is quite a car, and Tom eyes it desirously, thinking how wonderful it would be to have such an automobile to wind around roads and avenues each day with the wind in his face and hair, then he remembers how such a machine as this probably costs more than he has ever accumulated in a savings account in his lifetime, and so reconciles himself to the fact that this is why Abigail is driving and why he is a passenger. Once more he is reminded of the great truths and verities of the world. The rich get richer and the poor drive high-mileage used Hondas.

"Have you talked to Matt today?" she asks. She is in the midst of winding the BMW out in third gear, squeezing the RPMs out to make certain she's at least twenty miles above the speed limit.

"No, I didn't think he'd be awake before noon on a Saturday. I know how you filthy rich people are, how you all like to sleep in just to flaunt the fact you can in poor people's faces."

"I told him to call you and make sure you know you're invited to Easter dinner tomorrow."

"He mentioned it the other day. I'm not so sure I'm totally up for a gala banquet with the royal family, though, me being a commoner and all that."

"You're his old friend, you have to come. You're also my date for the day. You can't expect me to be around Matt and Sherry and William and that insufferable wife of his and their kids all by myself. I'd die before it was over with. I suppose the adults are all right in small doses, but when you throw in two children running around raising all sorts of hell that's when I have to call in reinforcements. That would be you, Thomas. You can tell me entertaining stories and hold my hand and keep my teeth from grinding down into a fine powder."

"Why not just go somewhere and avoid the whole scene?"

"Mainly because I live there, sweetie. Where else am I going to go on an Easter Sunday? Everything in town will be closed and everyone I know will be at family gatherings. I enlisted you to keep me from being lonesome and to help me ward off those mean old holiday blues."

Abigail drives through the Saturday streets of Rhodes like she is in a Grand Prix contest, cornering and accelerating, down-shifting and speed-ing. Tom thinks how if he was the one driving this way he would have al-ready been pulled over by now, ticketed, breath-analyzed, read his rights, and driven in the back seat of a cruiser over to the pokey. But he is not Abi-gail, high-cheek boned, tan and slim, black raven hair flying in the breeze behind dark glasses. He cannot blame the authorities too much for their inaction. If he was on the force and saw such a species of female as Abigail pass him by, he would also be too damned awe-struck at the sight to even consider enforcing the law.

She motors down old avenues pointing out locales where his high school once stood, turns corners and jets past the old Baptist church where once he accepted Jesus, even when at the time he wasn't so certain Jesus accepted him, passes stores and strip malls that house businesses he's never heard of. She stops at a drive-in Sonic and they eat hot dogs and sip milk-shakes while he studies her ankle and knee and all that they connect to, all those parts there within reach by the gearshift. Good grief, he thinks, she knows I'm looking. Better snap to immediately. Trouble this way.

"Matt told me you're now living out at the family estate too. I didn't know that until the other day."

"I am. I moved in a couple of months ago, right after Garland and I broke up. I didn't want anything more to do with that house of ours other than get it on the market and sell it. It was easier for me to move back home again. The guest house out back was just sitting vacant, so it's a perfect fit for me, out there away from the main house with a private driveway and garage. I come and go as I please, which is peachy. I'll give you a tour tomorrow."

"I saw it. Matt pointed it out to me when I came out after Sam's funeral."

"Well, you have to come inside to really appreciate it. It's got a really cozy floor plan." She smiles across at Tom and pokes his knee with her finger. "Three bedrooms, dearest. We can be like the three little bears and find one that's just right."

After a long excursion through some neighborhoods and cul-de-sacs Tom didn't know existed, Abigail pulls back in to the dealership lot, idling there beside his faded Accord in her gleaming roadster with her smile and her eyes beneath her glasses that he imagines are doing a Salome dance plotting some kind of fate for him. It is probably a good thing he is getting out now. A few more glances and touches and comments will move him past any rules and regulations for his new lifestyle and back into the goings-on of the past he's been trying to avoid. He keeps telling himself he is going to be a grownup one of these days very soon, but he keeps encountering blips and setbacks.

"Make certain now that you don't pull one of your classic no-shows on me tomorrow," she says. "One-thirty sharp. You stand me up and make me go through this dinner all by my lonesome and you can rest assured there will be hell to pay for it later on."

"I'll be there."

He watches her back up, throw the car into gear and drive away with a wave, the radio blasting with George Michael vowing he is never going to dance again. The BMW disappears down the road and Tom stands beside his sorry Accord watching her departure, waiting for his thoughts to return from the labyrinthian gutters, where they seem to frequently abide these days.

Against his better judgment, he has made plans this Saturday night to capitulate from the self-imposed exile from his old Rhodes friends and acquaintances he's imposed upon himself since his return for Sam's funeral. He has seen a few familiar faces on the fly here and there over the past few weeks, coming and going on his tiny journeys around town trying to get settled, but so far he's resisted spending appreciable time with any of his old pals other than Dewey for conversation and sharing ancient memories and providing clues to any of them toward solving the mystery of why he has never returned to Rhodes until now, where he has been and what he's been doing for such a long stretch of years, and if he is the same person he was those lost decades ago or is he the way the rest of the world has turned out to be, changed and unrecognizable from the sunny days of the past, a stranger now among them? Tom Lockhart knows the answers to most of these questions; he simply wants to keep them to himself for as long as possible. Too much information spilled out in the public grasp can wind up harmful.

It is mid-afternoon, and he has three hours before he is supposed to present himself at Thompson's Tavern for a Saturday night of fun and reunion. A part of him wishes to get into his poor excuse for a car and drive back to his borrowed room at Dewey's and take a nice nap, but he knows the possibility is great that if once he quits the scene here in Rhodes Proper where he stands this moment, he will be hard-pressed to return due to a lack of motivation. In his new pose as a decent human being, he is attempting to not go back on his promises or to not make excuses to forestall normal human interaction. He thinks it will be a nice gesture not to disappoint those who knew him from way back when by not appearing when and where he has said he would.

He enters Pocket Billiards, climbing the steps beside the dinky salvage store that is currently closed up, where once there was a television repair shop and a Blockbuster after that and a used bookstore after that. Tom remembers the last time he was home for a visit, maybe fifteen years past, when he went in the bookstore and happened upon his first novel filed away in the middle part of a shelf, alphabetized by his last name, looking pristine and new amid other tomes with ragged spines and torn covers. The novel was at least ten years old by then, but it was easy to see it had never been read. It might as well have been released that very day. And whatever day it had arrived at the bookstore, from wherever it had been and purchased in some kind of trade, the fact was clear that it was unread from its prior home and unread at this new home too, and Tom was willing to bet the ranch that if the old bookstore was still here right now, his novel would be right there with it, unread, unchanged save for the thin veil of dust accumulated on the cover because of all the time it had reposed on the shelf untouched.

The pool hall looks the same as when he left it last, back in September of 1968, when he and Dewey played Snooker on the night before he left for Covington. He buys a can of Coke from a machine and chalks up a stick. He plays Rotation by himself for hours, hearing the clack of the balls and the radio station playing every classic rock song that has ever been recorded.

At six o'clock he places his stick back in the wall rack and drops his empty can in a trash bin by the pinball machines. He goes down the stairway and walks up the sidewalk past the Olympia Grill and Ace Hardware and

Subway, crosses over South Main at the light and pushes through the doors of Thompson's. He is three minutes past due, fashionably late so he won't appear anxious on this initial night of social mixing. He again wonders why he is so ill at ease being back among people he has known from the long ago, then remembers there are reasons why he feels this way. He has not forgotten what it was like all those years past, why it was he left town in the first place rather than remain with his safe peer group and going off with them to school and war and marriage and occupational life with no possibility of parole. He was going to be somebody back then, he thinks, he was going to accomplish wonderful feats, and now here he is for all to see his magnificence and behold his mighty works.

He is not Charleston Heston. He is not Moses. He is here, he is Tom Lockhart, and he is who he is.

Thompson's has changed since the last time he was here. First of all, the owner and namesake, Wayne Thompson, died some twenty years ago, and the business has been gobbled up by an anonymous franchise that likes to pretend it's operated by real individual people with names and faces and personalities but is really just another in a series of shams and fictions created by a corporate entity to make its faithful clientele think they are a part of a big happy family instead of merely being sheep coming through the wooden doors with the frosty glass to get happy and inebriated and comfortable enough with alcohol and the décor to not care that they are making some multi-faceted business richer by the day. The walls are brick, lamps hang down like pale globes above the dozen tables and four booths in the place. A long bar stretches across a side wall, and a flight of stairs leads up to a half-balcony, where three tables with two chairs each await those in romantic courtship with a desire to be alone with their current one and only. An ancient Wurlitzer stands against a wall downstairs between the two restrooms for atmosphere and adornment, not functioning for years now, replaced by a modern throw-off CD wall box that gives one play for a dollar or twelve for a ten-dollar bill. When paid music is not engaged, a satellite radio plays through hidden speakers in the nooks and corners of the walls and ceiling. Tom can remember the old speakers that sat in the four corners of the first floor in the Mesozoic Era, all as big as Brontosauruses with visible wires from an amplifier stretched across the baseboards. *Tripped over one of those wires one night on a drunken stroll to the restroom, pulled it out of the speaker when it wrapped around the toe of my Hush Puppies. Thought a gargantuan snake had me in its grip. Kicked and stomped and wrestled it off. Knocked the speaker over and wires and fuses spilled out everywhere. It took about a year before somebody finally figured out how to get it working again.*

He spots his friends back in the left corner, two tables pulled together so everyone can hear each other over the music and the surrounding laughter and the fact that they may be going deaf in their old age. Doug Burke sees him immediately and raises his hand to beckon him back. Linda, Doug's wife, sits beside him, engaged so deeply in conversation with Judy Malone she is unaware Tom has arrived. He takes a moment to size up the scene before taking his first step forward, trying to determine if he knows everyone he is looking at or if the people he thinks he knows are actually someone else. Unidentifiable friends. He finds this happening a lot lately. Folks change and don't much look like they used to when one isn't around watching them deteriorate daily over the years. Probably for damn sure don't act the same way either. He wonders if he appears the same to them as they do to him, if they think he's slipped several notches toward geezerhood and maybe insanity too.

John Malone leans back in a chair holding a mug. John is Judy's husband, a Kingsport native who first came to Rhodes with Judy after they met at UT-Knoxville years ago, to marry her and coach high school football while Judy taught fourth grade and had babies. Tom wonders how many little Malones are in the world by now. Five? Six? He has lost count. He will have to ask and find out, so Judy and John might somehow believe he really gives the first hairy orangutan's behind about it, since probably by now any sires are close to being eligible for Social Security. Vic Hale and some woman Tom does not know sit at one end of the joined tables, and Charlie Polk and a bimbo who is probably not his daughter sit in the middle. Charlie is the owner of the Polka Dot Piggly Wiggly, inherited from his father after flunking out of college, so if all holds true to form the bimbo is another of Charlie's hired hands, one more in a long line of sweet curvaceous young things who drink up Charlie's profits nightly while keeping a job without doing any work until a better gig comes along. How long, Tom wonders, has this sort of thing been going on with Charlie Polk, hiring girls half his age, spending money on them and bedding them and then watching them leave just before he gets tired of them and decides to fire them? It's been a while. It's been going on since before old Mr. Polk kicked the bucket and left him the store. Charlie was screwing any woman with a Piggly Wiggly name tag on even back when he and Tom were in high school.

"I was just about to call you," Doug says, "to see if you were going to show up or not. I thought you might chicken out because you were afraid we were going to bring up some of those crimes from yesteryear everyone knows you're guilty of."

"The statute of limitations has run out by now, so I don't have to worry anymore. I can show my face in public anytime I want."

"I guess I lose the bet this time," Linda says. She sits with a margarita in front of her, her glasses balanced on her nose so she can read fine print and see who is across the table from her at the same time. "I was going with the odds that it was just a rumor you'd actually moved back to town. There have been some people who said they've seen you, but I wasn't so sure. You certainly didn't ever stop in to say hello or anything, that's for sure. I'm getting old and forgetful, but I would have remembered if you had. Tom Lockhart home and in the flesh isn't something to be easily forgotten."

"I'm back," Tom says, "or at least what's left of me is back that the vultures haven't picked off my bones all those times I got left for dead in the middle of a lost highway."

Everyone is shaking his hand and pounding him on the back. He is unaccustomed these days to this kind of attention, having folks act like they are glad to see him and all, and he basks for a moment in the feeling. He reminds himself to try and be charming and friendly and halfway civil for a while, that simply because he has learned so well how to alienate people and have them wanting him dead after a fashion there is no damn reason for him to showcase such skills tonight. These old chums recall him as a good guy, a friend, someone who'd walk the extra mile for any of them back in the wondrous days of yore, and it might be nice for them to continue to regard him the same way. There's plenty of time in the coming days and months when they'll no doubt discover the fangs he's grown while he's been missing. They'll come to learn how good old Tom Lockhart sometimes ducks around a corner these days and escapes, and all they'll ever get to see is something running off in the moonlight, some shape they've not seen before, some figure definitely not one of them. And how he in turn will begin moving away from all that is safe and good and disappear into whatever darkness he can find, to rend and tear all the good from whatever has tried to give him shelter, rip everything into pieces and throw it down and break it into jagged fragments, because there is something somewhere that has told him this is how it has to be in this his lifetime, this is the path he must travel at times, to ask no questions because it is what it is and can never be explained.

Judy hugs him and looks him in the eye.

"You don't look a damn bit different," she lies.

"You're absolutely right," he says. "I've always had gray hair and sagging eyelids. All you have to do is look at my annual picture and you can see how I haven't aged a single day in all these years."

Charlie Polk leaves his hot little number and walks over to Tom with his familiar evil-fun smile.

"I can't believe somebody hasn't shot your ass by now," he says.

"It's not like it hasn't been tried."

Charlie is six foot six, but somehow looks even taller tonight. Maybe it's because everyone else Tom is looking at all seem to have expanded in width, while Charlie, if anything, is even leaner than he once was, so it could be his height is an optical illusion. Maybe too it is that Tom may not be as big as he once was. It could be he is not so much of a big man now as he was when he took off from Rhodes thirty-five years ago.

"Have a seat," Doug says. He is sunburned and windblown despite the fact it's just now spring. Doug is the head caretaker at the cemetery, commander of a crew of mowers, diggers, and general day laborers, all looking to make enough in one day to drink up that night. "Here's a menu if you want something to eat. Different management around the place these days, but they still make a pretty good burger. They haven't managed to screw that up yet. Here's a fresh mug if you want beer. I don't know what a stranger like you drinks anymore, but I do remember you once could put some draft beer away if you got inspired enough."

"The reason you remember is because you were usually sitting beside me cheering me on. I seem to remember you doing the same thing I was."

"Right the first time," says Doug.

"Why in the hell haven't you been down to see me?" Charlie asks. "Hell, if I'd known you needed a job I'd have hired you in a New York second doing something. If nothing else you could sit in my office all day and night with me. I've got a heck of a whiskey collection back there we could take turns sampling."

"That's exactly why I didn't come. I already know how to abuse alcohol without getting instruction from you."

Charlie grins rakishly, curling back his lips and showing his teeth, which makes him look like a predator getting ready to spring. Glad, Tom thinks, to see that nothing much has changed around here in the old behavioral studies department.

He relaxes in his seat and allows these voices and faces from the past to ebb and flow with the songs he hears around him, lets them make their familiar joyful noises in his presence that make him feel like he is in a place where he belongs once more. He takes a soothing sip of beer and surveys the room. His group is the one with seniority; everyone else in the place is younger, experiencing nights like this for maybe the first or second time, thinking of them not as he does, as being repetitive, time-worn, but magical and fresh and totally new. He sees a young woman standing by the end of the bar, talking to three people seated on stools, motioning with her hands as if she was describing a big fish that got away, a dazzling-white smile on a stunning face, hoop earrings and bracelets and necklaces that dance and clatter and jingle.

He studies her for thirty seconds and falls in love with her.

"Matt was supposed to come tonight too, but he called this afternoon and canceled because Sherry had them hooked into going to some banquet and hadn't let him know about it." Linda picks up a chip from her plate and looks it over for faults before popping it into her mouth. "They had to take a rain check for tonight. In the last ten years or so, those rain checks have been piling up pretty regularly. You never see them around much anymore. Sherry seems to be always out of town, and about the only way to get a glimpse of Matt is to go invest some money or buy a new Buick."

"I know what you mean," Tom says. "I've been working for him a couple of weeks now and I haven't seen him but once, and that was on my first day there. Since then, he's been invisible."

"He's probably locked away at home spending somebody else's money," Doug says, "or out of town on a cruise. As far as the dealership, he just has his managers download the profits and funnel them into his account. It's a tough life old Matt lives."

Linda smiles at Tom.

"I thought you might be bringing his little sister with you tonight. I don't mean to be the town snoop, but the word is you've been seen out and about with her a few times in the past few weeks. Not that I'm nosey or anything like that."

"Somebody told her I was abandoned and she was trying to rescue me from the shelter."

"Still squatting at Dewey's?" Doug asks. "I've been leaving messages on your damn phone for three days now, trying to let you in on a little deal I think you might be interested in."

"My phone's buried in a box somewhere. I can't find it. Now, as far as deals go, as long as it doesn't require me investing my life savings into something huge and grandiose that can't possibly go wrong, I'll be interested to hear it."

"Do you remember that old stone house down by the cemetery entrance, the one the caretakers always lived in?"

"Sure. Sits at the end of River Road right at the cemetery entrance."

"That's the one. It's been sitting vacant for a few years now, since the last guy that lived there died. Worked for me about ten years cutting grass and stuff, and then one day he just conked out on his riding mower over in the Pleasant Valley section. I kept passing by in my truck and seeing that mower going around in circles. I finally stopped to see what was going on and he was dead behind the wheel, making doughnuts for I don't know how long between the tombstones. I had to jump up on the platform and turn the ignition off to get it to stop, and the whole time I was trying to get up there

Melvin was sliding off the seat like he was trying to leap on top of me." Doug shakes his head and takes a soothing drink from his mug, as if it contains a reward he deserves for the perilous ordeal he has gone through. "Anyway, what I'm getting at is I really need somebody to live in that house again. Things aren't as quiet and peaceful around this town as they used to be, and I'm getting tired of working all day and then having to go back two or three times a night to run off people making out in cars or kids drinking and doing drugs or devil worshippers dancing around in the moonlight trying to call Satan up from Hell so he can help them get even with the folks in town who've pissed them off and done them wrong one way or another."

"Man, I didn't know a cemetery supervisor had such a stressful existence," Tom grins. "I'm surprised an old fart like you is still alive to talk about it."

"Well, if I keep having to make trips out there every time the moon rises I might as well go ahead and dig a hole for myself and climb in, because it's going to be the death of me sooner or later if something doesn't give. That's the reason I'm bringing it up, to see if you might be interested."

"You want me to move into the house and scare off the crazy people every night so you can stay home and watch *Magnum P.I.* in your pajamas? Does that sum it up?"

"All you have to do is pay for your utilities and get the cable hooked up and you'll be set. No rent money required. When the Devil's Brigade sees a car in the driveway and a light on in the house they'll know their privacy's been breached and they'll go somewhere else to sacrifice their cats."

"I don't pay rent?"

"No. Utilities is everything. All you have to do is move in. If you do happen to see something weird going on you just pick up the phone and call the police. It's not like you've got to put on your damn jeans and go out and tell them to leave. I would tell you to lock the gate, but that won't work. The son of bitches just drive around it and tear up the grounds. I leave it open so they'll stay on the pavement and not make a big mess I have to spend the entire next day cleaning up."

"Why has it taken so long to find somebody to move in?"

"Probably because half of Rhodes thinks the damn place is haunted. Hell, I don't know. Maybe because there hasn't been anybody around crazy enough to want to live there with the Manson Family likely to drop in at any time. There's ghosts and snakes and racoons and coyotes and all sorts of critters in those woods. I had to wait for you to show up before it came to me you were nuts enough to be the perfect candidate for the job." He scratches his ear and smiles. "What do you think, buddy? Free room and board for as long as you stay? You're not going to find a better deal than that anywhere. You'll pay out your ass for an apartment here in town."

"That's true. I've been looking around."

"You can start moving in tomorrow if you want. Or if you want to wait a day or two I'll have the place cleaned up for you. I just happened to bring a key with me if you want to take a look at it. I can call the folks at Corporate tomorrow and tell them the problem is solved and they don't have to lose sleep anymore worrying about getting sued for somebody's grave getting desecrated. They'll be overjoyed."

"I would say I'll think about it and let you know, but considering that I'm desperate I'll take you up on it. Dewey and Phyllis are getting tired of my company, so I need to make a move. You know the saying, fish and company stink after two days."

Doug fishes in his shirt pocket and hands over a chain with two keys on it.

"One's to the main house," he says. "The other goes to the shed where all the dead bodies are stored."

He screws up his face and looks at Tom.

"Who the hell is Phyllis?" he asks.

When it is ten Tom pleads weariness and gets up to go. He reaches for his wallet to throw in his share of the night's festivities but a chorus of voices tells him to put his money back in his pocket. This is your welcome home party, Judy says, and it's our treat. We're glad to see you.

Down this holiday sidewalk to the Accord. Every place closed up now except for Little Caesar's with their lights blazing. Smells and scents waft into the air. Feel like opening the door and telling them they can go home now. No more business tonight, I could say. Everybody out of town or in bed already, sleeping so they can get up for sunrise service, somebody trying to get sleepy under the sheet, moving over closer, let's play around some here in the dark. Me, I'm on my way to sleep alone. Again. In Dewey's house for maybe one last night. Close the door so Phyllis can't come in. Don't want her rooting under the spread or taking a nip out of my leg. Seen those claws. Could be scary dealing with in the dark.

Tomorrow coming up. Have to go to Matt's for dinner. Easter fixings. Can't stand up the boss. And Abigail. Says I'm her date. We'll see about that. Probably going to have to teach her a little lesson. Let her know Thomas Lock-hart is no easy mark. Married woman still anyway, in case I forget. Sometimes a fellow can be too nice for too long. Women start expecting it to go on forever.

Here's the Honda sitting beneath a streetlight. Dents and scratches and faded paint. Lets me know it's mine. Don't know if I've ever owned a car I despised as much as this one. Souvenir of bad times. Can't make it break down. Something tells me it is my own personal curse and it's going to run forever with me behind the wheel.

Teach it a lesson too. Whole world gets damn impertinent if you don't watch it.

Not a bad night this. Mile, maybe two, from here to Dewey's. No full moon, but enough to see my way. Nothing to worry about anyway. Only thing out here with teeth and a heartful of murder is me. Anybody sees me coming better run. Walking upright through Rhodes. Dark deeds and bloody thoughts, heading for what is home now, alone this Easter Eve.

THREE

A few moments before sunrise on Resurrection Sunday. Tom Lockhart up and walking with the set of keys Doug gave him last night in his pocket. Down River Road with a scattering of houses on each side before finally falling off to open fields approaching the river. Floods sometimes through here these days, Dewey says; construction and cleared land and the water has to go somewhere. You'll have to watch it because you're right on the river. Still, that house has been there for years, sitting on that little rise like it does. I guess if it was going to go under it would have done so by now. So you'll probably be okay.

Something else to think about other than ghosts and lunatics on the loose and snakes spitting poison. Tom wonders if this is such a good idea after all, down here with the elements by his lonesome while the rest of Rhodes sits in recliners watching HBO without worrying about possibly dying or being the next to get mangled. Might be worth the price of rent or mortgage to live like a real human being. But tried that for years, he reminds himself. It didn't work. At least in this house of stone he'll have time to think and perhaps write and come to some sort of decision about who he wants to be when he grows up.

Only a half mile from Dewey's house, so it is not like he is that far removed from civilization. Jiggle the lock and the door opens with a push. Sticks a little like maybe it doesn't really want his company, like it's happy enough just sitting empty here by itself, which makes Tom think maybe he and this place are going to get along after all.

There's a living room with a fireplace. Not the place for a convention, for sure. Wonder if the chimney works and I'll have enough energy to chop wood? A small dining room and a big kitchen with a nook on the other end. Also a washer and a dryer which may or may not work. Look like fire hazards to me. Up some steps and there's a bedroom and a shower, a balcony that runs off the back that looks out toward the river, which is out there but can't be seen because the trees are blooming. Deep dark woods, even in the morning light. Varmints and flying hungry winged creatures with teeth. Have to keep an eye out or perhaps get swallowed. Look off to the left and there's the shed Doug told me about. Big enough to be a garage if I had a car I wanted to keep from the elements, which I don't. Pull the Honda in there and it would fall apart from lack of nature's onslaughts.

This will do. Need to move in as fast as possible. Get it cleaned and call some movers and get my worldly possessions out of storage. One trip will do it. Not much to show for a fellow on the downhill slope of a century.

Out the door and through the gates. River Grove Cemetery, established 1804, that's what the sign says. Walk up the hill and get off the pavement, cross over the pedestrian bridge past the creek that runs down to the Crockett. Property all mowed and manicured, flowers on graves, the place looking fairly welcoming even if one has no thoughts of expiring just yet. Doug and crew doing quite a job. Last night he said he'd hire me for the ground crew if I decide I don't like working for Matt. I said I don't like working, period. At least with Matt I'm alone most of the time. Nobody around giving me orders or telling me the story of their life.

Down in the Serenity Garden section, next to the funeral home and the florist shop and the mausoleum out back, about twenty cars are parked by a tent, where a crowd is gathered for Sunrise Service. Could go and join in with them on some up-from-the-grave-He-arose refrains, but in a hurry to check some things out and get back to Dewey's to clean up. Have to be at Matt's by one, and it's a stretch of the legs from Dewey's just to get the abandoned Accord, then it's a journey to Matt's estate or mansion or whatever the term for spaciousness is. Not used to having such a hectic social schedule.

Hear them singing as I pass and curve around to Sunnycrest, the ground where my family is pushing up daisies, tulips, and the occasional dandelion. Dirt and the remnants of withered flowers cover Sam's new plot, a month here now and still awaiting a marker. Probably in the process of being chiseled, since, knowing damn Sam, it's going to be large and garish and impressive and let anyone who comes across it know that the man buried here was a mighty pillar of this earth when he was around and it's best not forgotten, even if he had to royally screw over his brother back in the day just to assure he'd arrive at the top and never have to cast his eyes upward again.

But this is old resentment and not why he is here. He is just in this place on Easter morning to have a little peek into what it's like on the other side, seeing how everyone much kin to him is planted in this place, and he's the only one left now clocking in and out among the living.

Behind Sam's grave is his mother's and father's, Jimmy and Elizabeth. Tom's parents have been gone thirty-three years now, victims of a drunk driver going the wrong way on 40-East. He remembers getting the call at Covington in the middle of finals sophomore year. Took an exam and drove the Fairlane home. Early November, the world drizzly-gray with no sign of sky. Blanket of dismal clouds. Stood inside the funeral home not knowing what to do or say. Seemed much like a dream, but was already used to having no family. Dad thought I was turning into a hippy; my mother couldn't be bothered because she was making sure Sam got through law school with no worries or hitches. Learned his lessons well, it turned out. First thing he did as executor of the estate was give me the shaft. And I was far away by then, fighting the world and soon to fall in love with Maribeth McAllister. A check in the mail from the estate the only thing separating me from poverty. I thought it was some kind of mistake and it would get resolved later down the road. Didn't really believe Jimmy and Elizabeth would have wanted things turning out this way, Sam with everything and me bought off like a downsized employee. Thanks for your years of service, but times have changed. Hope this sees you through to better days ahead.

Hard even now to hold my folks responsible. They'd gone all those years being so proud of Sam, he with his honor roll status and First-Team All-State tight end and pretty girl friends and going to Vanderbilt on an academic scholly. It was almost too much to fathom, even for me. I was overwhelmed and intimidated from the time I could spell both the words, and I balanced those dual feelings of awe and admiration for Sam with small unspoken feelings of envy and resentment and a pervading sense of wondering in this world of which I was a member when would it actually be my turn?

Time went by and I found out.

Never, not in Rhodes, not in this family dynamic. Because there was only room for one at the top, and Sam had arrived there first. But I was an accommodating soul in those days. I accepted what was and came to terms with what in this world I couldn't change, and so I decide to move on. I left for Covington and left everything behind while the planet spun and days went by, and thought that one day I might return to claim a part of what was mine.

I never figured then that there would be nothing left to come back to.

Lockhart doesn't know how long he stands looking at tombstones and re-living ancient history, forgiving his parents who didn't know any better and forgiving Sam even though he did, but after he feels the too-warm April sun begin to beat upon his neck he turns away and begins the hike back to Dewey's. The sunrise service has dispersed, and only a few cars are left in the lot, their passengers maybe making their own graveside visits to nearby relatives, or ponying up with other worshippers in one car and motoring off to Cracker Barrel for Easter breakfast. He guesses they are probably correct in their practicality on this day. By mid-morning they will be rid of all troublesome holiday trappings. They will have worshipped and prayed for their own dead, honored Jesus in song and prayer, had fellowship with friends and loved ones, and be back home to rest or read the morning paper or maybe cut the yard before an afternoon nap.

It is all so cut and dried. Sometimes Thomas Lockhart wishes he was so lucky.

But he has places to be, and so he starts back. When he crosses the bridge he cups his eyes from the sun so he can view his new abode from afar. The gray rock stands out in the morning sunshine, and despite the fact the majority of Rhodes thinks it may be haunted and considers it a dilapidated shamble, Tom looks it over and decides he likes what he sees. He'll get moved in and take it from there, but the good thing is he'll have a place where it's him and only him, and it will be home for as long as he wants it to be, and he'll take some time and a few deep breaths and see what happens next.

After he gets ready he bums a ride into Rhodes from Dewey to get the abandoned Honda, not because he is lazy and doesn't want to hike another mile, but because it's damn hot for what is supposed to be a tranquil spring day and he doesn't want to sweat through his clothes and feel dank and clammy the rest of the afternoon and night, even though he has the feeling that in such a social situation as he is fixing to enter there is a good chance he will feel dank and clammy anyway and those two things will probably be the least of his worries. He remembers growing up with Matt and going over to his house after school, to shoot basketball or maybe spend the night, and how he would always look at the big rooms with upscale furniture and pictures on the walls, the pool table in what was called the playroom and the plush rugs where his feet sank down into them and he'd think how he might have trouble freeing himself later. There were always luxury cars parked in the drive—Cadillacs and Continentals and Rivieras—and along a back patio were tables and chairs for entertaining alongside a pool with two diving boards.

That house from the past seemed like a hovel compared to what Matt is inhabiting these days, Tom having been introduced to the current dwellings his first week back. Matt had attended Sam's funeral and invited Tom out to dinner the next night, hinting he had something to talk over with him at the time. After what had seemed like the journey of a lifetime, past the Rhodes city limits and around winding country roads and thickets of woody fields with deer darting across in defiance of the Honda's approach, he came upon a road with spacious houses separated by rocky and knotted wood fences, searching and finally finding a stone mailbox with Matt's name etched upon it. He turned up a long asphalt drive and rode another quarter of a mile to the house. It was a tall structure with a wide soaring door so Mighty Joe Young wouldn't accidentally bump his head when he entered, and fifteen yards of porch stretched both ways to the left and right, strewn each way with gliders and swings and rockers and tables and chairs for the taking of tea and coffee and maybe something alcoholic. The drive made a circle with enough space for tour buses and presidential caravans, so Tom made the arc like he was driving a go-kart at the state fair and rolled to a stop. He'd spent a minute looking at the place and wondering if once he got in there if he'd ever be able to find his way out.

He doesn't have the time to knock on the door when he arrives this day, for it swings open and Abigail stands before him in a yellow clinging dress that makes her look like she's stepped out of some Technicolor epic for a spell so she can meet Tom and dine with him this afternoon. She is, of course, her usual knockout self, and this dinner, Tom believes, may not be for the faint of heart.

Like a magnet she immediately hooks her arm through his and leads him into the living room.

"You're right on time," she says. "I'm impressed!"

Abigail has had a few drinks already, imbibing in earnest on mimosas after breakfast in preparation for the Easter banquet. This is no big surprise to Tom, since only perhaps twice since he's returned has he seen Abigail without a glass in her hand. Dewey says there are abundant rumors around that Abigail has had to go dry out a time or two down through the years, but no one can really confirm it for a fact. A woman like her, Dewey says, good-looking as hell and filthy rich to go along with it, can pretty much do any damn thing she wants and not worry the tiniest bit what anybody thinks about it.

"I'm still amazed at how far out into the wilderness this place is. I thought my car was going to keel over before I even made the property line."

"You should have called me, lover. I'd have been more than happy to come pick you up."

"No thanks. I got a good dose of your driving yesterday. You not only don't observe the speed limit, but you're into some daredevil stuff I want no part of."

"I was just warming up," she says. "You should see what happens when I really get going."

He follows her into the den, where Matt rises from a leather chair and greets him with a handshake and a pat on the back. Matt is also drinking, fumes being emitted from a glass of whiskey which might be mixed with ethanol. Tom turns down any of the varieties of alcohol offered and asks for water instead.

"I thought you were going to come by and visit more often," Matt says. "I didn't mean to just hire you on for a job and then have you disappear back into the legions of the ambiguous workforce. I was hoping we could have a few laughs about our sordid pasts a couple of times a week now that you're back in town to stay."

He jiggles his glass and watches the cube of ice go around in a circle a couple of times.

"You haven't even let me know if you like your new job or not. I told you to call me and keep me up to date. You must be doing all right, though, because I haven't heard anybody gripe about it yet. If you were screwing stuff up too much I'd be getting phone calls from morning to night right and left with everybody in the sales and service departments bitching about it."

"Well, it's not that difficult, Matt. You sell a part, you re-order another. When you're out on the shelf you order something to replace it. If you don't have what they want in stock you tell them to take a number and take a seat, you order it and you call them when it comes in."

"One thing we do know," Abigail says, "is this boy Thomas Lockhart is one smart cookie. He comes from a smart family. He and Sam are the only ones in town who ever got scholarships to go to college because of their brains. Everybody else either had to pay for it or throw a football a mile and a half or be able to jump over the courthouse to dunk a basketball, otherwise they were out of luck. They were on their way to Viet Nam or tying up their apron down at the Polka Dot Piggly Wiggly getting ready to punch the time clock and go to work."

"We'll eat in a little," Matt says. "Let's sit and talk a while before the kids get here and we can't hear ourselves think anymore."

Sherry materializes from some unknown room with a glass of white wine in her hand balanced among bracelets and rings. Along with lots of jewelry Sherry has put on some additional weight since the last time Tom saw her. She is no longer the fleshy buxom sight she was in school or in the early years of her marriage. She is the mother of two children, one son who is upstairs and will soon be down to join them for dinner, and another boy who never returned from his senior year at the University of Virginia, where he overdosed a couple of weeks before graduation. It was a lot of years ago, and Matt and Sherry don't speak of it much.

"Tom, it is so nice to see you. It's been a long time since you left town, and it's nice to see you home again."

It's good to be here, he wants to say, but he doesn't. He doesn't really want to start spinning lines of bull about the good old days and he doesn't really know why he is here this Easter Sunday at all, but he guesses he could feel that way about a whole slew of things these days. For this moment, he is simply on the cusp of feeling incredulous, since the last time he was around Sherry in a social setting she was throwing up at the side of the school gym after drinking too much cherry vodka after the baccalaureate service the night before graduation. Two days later he'd left for Covington and she'd gone away to Knoxville in the fall, and even with her marrying Matt those thirty years ago their paths haven't crossed much since.

But past times are discussed and laughed over for a few minutes, who married who, who went where, who was over at River Grove with the worms playing pinochle on their snouts, who was a grandparent already and how such a thing could be, how time slips away so fast. Tom sees how Abigail is not joining in on the conversation much, since she is younger than all of them and would like even better to be so young that she does not even recognize any of the subjects being discussed, but she is forty-eight whether she likes it or not or has it in her mind to ever act her age, so she believes the best thing to do is be quiet and perhaps this part of the afternoon will go away. Tom sees how she is being silent and waiting for all this talk of age and school days to dispense. Despite his efforts to avoid her, he still knows her like a book. He has been aware of her for a long time now.

William and his wife and two children come down the stairs and enter the den, all smiles for Tom, the stranger from another place and time. William is the oldest son, now a partner in Matt's financial office, and his wife is Avery, a slinky blonde who works in the mayor's office as his press manager. Avery is certainly nice to look at in a Rhineland kind of way, but Tom senses something hidden in her that he would not like being around on a continual basis, a quality much like Eichmann had when he continually went around telling everybody what a good boss and a great guy Hitler was and how wonderful the country was going to be in the coming days. The two children, boys, Matt and Sherry's grandsons, are both dressed in smart outfits that probably cost more than the sport coat Tom is wearing and the sorry car he has driven here combined. He watches them immediately begin circulating and disrupting what peace was once present in the room, guesses their ages to be perhaps six and four, the pair seeking out anything in the house they can get their hands on and destroy. He has seen them thirty seconds now and already knows them to be insufferable. William, Tom recalls, was a little asshole in his time, so how could his offspring not be any different? He has to caution himself to stop passing judgment on everything and everybody on the spot right this moment, so early as it is in the afternoon, or this could be a long ordeal before he can get out of here and away.

A black woman in an apron comes and whispers in Sherry's ear, and Sherry stands up and says that dinner is ready.

Tom attempts to lag behind and allow everyone to go to the dining room first, which he thinks is good manners and protocol on his part, not to mention the fact that they all know the way and he does not and he doesn't want to take a wrong turn and end up in the torture chamber or someplace out of the way like that, but Abigail again comes and hooks her arm through his and guides him past the kitchen proper and into a dining room with lace curtains on the windows that look out on the vast back acreage of the house, the pool, a pasture with grazing horses and burros, several garages where Tom knows any number of expensive automobiles are parked, and a narrow road that leads up to another house a hundred yards off.

"That's where I live now," Abigail points out.

"So I've been told," Tom says. "Looks like West Egg to me."

"West what?"

"West Egg. Gatsby, my dear. Remember him from high school English? He wrote about people like your family."

"I don't remember," she smiles. "I must have used the Cliff notes."

Food gets brought in by three people, a man, a woman, and a younger version of the woman who is probably her daughter. They are black and of some undetermined nationality, cooks and servers and general help, and Tom can't help wondering if they live in the basement when they are not on duty, some kind of upstairs downstairs kind of arrangement, or if perhaps they are banished out to the servants' quarters somewhere out beyond the trees.

He's doing it again.

The Easter ham is sliced and platters and bowls of vegetables and bread are passed around. Some comments are made on how good everything tastes, but what appears to Tom to be the most important segment of this meal is that the glasses are kept full of wine for Sherry and whiskey for Matt and William and mimosas aplenty for Abigail and Avery. He thinks he should perhaps get up and go sit with the children, who are drinking grape Kool-Aid. He would at least be more at home with them, he and his water glass making certain to stay nice and well-behaved and not say or do anything he is going to regret later on.

No damn slipups, he thinks again. Had enough of those in the past to last a lifetime.

By the time late afternoon gets around, after portions of ham and choices of five vegetables and turning down cake and ice cream for dessert (who are you, he hears a voice ask. Who is this person turning down ice cream? Must be careful, he tells it. Have to watch it and stay light on the old feet or could maybe get bogged down.) he stands with Matt on a second-floor porch taking a gander at the back yard. The two boys are searching for Easter eggs, squealing like piglets on their way to slaughter, Avery and Sherry are clapping their hands, and William is standing off to the side on his phone while pretending he is enjoying every second of this gathering. Tom studies him in his faked elation and recalls holiday moments such as these in his own life, when he was thrust into a situation where he had to be a father to his own son, even though he considered Mitchell to be perhaps someone else's child who wasn't present to take the responsibility. He recalls what it was like to have to go through all the polite public motions of being a father, even while knowing Mama Lynda was either just returned from screwing someone else or winding up this segment of the family interlude so she could leave and go screw another willing soul before the night was through. Before and after, that was the way it was with good old Lynda, Lynda with a Y, finding romance in every tense and nook and corner almost as soon as Tom had made the mistake of saying I do, uttering such an oath because he was told a child was on the way and it was his, and he had not then known that he should question his ownership in the part.

Matt is talking away.

"The dealership is always going to be there," Matt is saying. "It's served the family well down through the years, but I'll tell you, if I had to be down there to deal with it on an everyday basis I wouldn't last too long. I had my time selling cars during the summers in college, and I knew even then I'd be moving on to something else as fast as I could. I couldn't deal with people all the time, not with the way they act when they're buying a damn automobile. It always seemed to me that people wanted me to give them a car, like I was supposed to feel sorry for them because my daddy had money and they were all so poor. Two summers of that and I knew I had to go in another direction, so it was on to law school and then to finance."

"Too bad I didn't know about you selling cars back then. I could have traded in that old Fairlane I had for a Sting Ray. I could have used your employee discount to whittle the payments down to size."

"The only reason that didn't happen was because you stopped coming home from Alabama the whole time you were there, and then you started teaching in Chattanooga and you didn't come home then either. You just stayed away and wrote a book or two and taught and made the mistake of marrying some girl you shouldn't have, and then getting into god knows what all those years when everybody lost track of you."

Matt grins at him like this is something between two old friends that needs some serious broaching.

"You never did tell me why you left Chattanooga so fast. What did you do, shoot somebody? Flunk some crime boss's son and he put a contract out on you? I'm betting there's a woman involved in it somewhere. I say that based on your past record, my friend. There's a part of me that believes deep down that Tom Lockhart may have been gone and out of sight for quite a long time, but it doesn't mean he changed much while he was absent. I think it's hard for a wild animal to ever give up hunting, for a leopard to change his spots, for an old dog to learn new tricks. I could go on, but I think you catch my drift."

"Let's just say I'd worn out my welcome and decided on a change in venue."

"I still say there's a woman in the mix somewhere."

There's just so much Tom can talk about with Matt these days—maybe it's not just Matt, maybe it's just about anybody—so he's growing a little tired of this polite bantering and uneasy conversation he's been listening to and offering up the last three hours, so all at once it occurs to him that he would be in a much finer mental state on this Easter evening if he were to make his goodbyes and get on the road. The idea of cruising back with the radio tuned to some non-harrowing classical music seems like a good way to put a cap on this block of required social intercourse. He needs to find a way to get out the door and leave the Lanes behind here on the plantation to ponder their holdings. And the sooner he gets back to Dewey's the sooner he can put into motion his plans for getting moved out to the caretaker house.

He escapes Matt fairly easily, mostly because Matt has had a goodly amount of sipping whiskey trickle down his throat over the course of the day and is ripe for some recliner time now with his feet raised on a platform, so Tom is out the door and on the porch and feeling pretty good about making such a smooth escape when he hears a voice speak to him from the twilight.

"I was wondering how long you and that damn brother of mine were going to exchange the truckloads of endless bullshit before calling it a night?"

Abigail is sitting in a wicker chair with her legs crossed and her arms behind her head, a glass of what can only be another mimosa sitting on the table in front of her. There are no lights on the porch, but between the lingering sunset and a few lightning bugs in anticipation of summer making their entrance to sniff the evening air Tom can see her just fine. Especially he sees her legs, one crossed over the other and dangling like bait before his eyes, making him feel like some gulping fish in a pond suddenly spying what could be a nice morsel for dinnertime. He tries not to look and to certainly not take a step toward her to get any closer, but realizes he's failing when he's already doing what he's telling himself not to do. He's right up on Abigail before he knows it, and no manner of common-sense rationale is keeping him from noticing one more time what a great-looking woman she is.

"It looks to me like you were planning to leave without even telling me goodbye. That's so very rude of you, Thomas Lockhart."

"I thought you'd already made the trip up the road to your cozy Mc-Mansion for the night. Since you've had about a cargo carrier of hooch this afternoon, I was hoping you'd called a taxi to get you there."

"I was holding out on you being a gentleman and escorting me there yourself, but I guess I should have known better than that, since I've never seen you act the least way in that fashion in all the time I've known you."

She gets up and walks toward him without the least hint of a wobble from her alcohol intake. She's pretty tough, Tom thinks; I'd be under the table by now.

"Do you realize we've known each other almost forty years, Thomas Lockhart?" She inches up and stands in front of him with her eyes in the shadowy light, takes her fingers and places them on his arms. One finger slides up and down his sport coat sleeve, making its presence known through the fabric and the shirt beneath and his skin waiting there suddenly standing at attention. It is a good thing I drank water all afternoon, he tells himself, for this could get dangerous if I'd gone ahead and taken a dive off the wagon with everybody else.

"I was in fourth grade when I saw you the first time," she says. "I remember it. I had the biggest crush on you. You'd come over after school with Matt, the two of you shooting basketball or you spending the night sometimes. I thought you were the handsomest thing back then, right from the very start. I'd sit in my room down the hall and write your name in all my notebooks. I'd even make up stories and write them down on paper about how it was going to be when the time came that you were my boyfriend. I had it in my head even way back then that you and I were going to one of these days live happily ever after together."

"So I'm supposed to believe you've been patiently waiting for me to come courting for the last forty years, forsaking all others and whispering a little prayer for me each night before you go to bed?" Tom grins. "Damn, I'm flattered, Abigail, even if you did have to interrupt your undying devotion to me to get married a time or three. Despite those diversions, I truly do believe you've been thinking of me all the time and counting down the hours until the day I returned. Oh yeah, I believe in the Easter Bunny too. I forgot to mention that."

"Well, the good thing is you're here now, aren't you, so it looks like it's going to work out fine." She is against him in the shadows, wrapping her arms around him and looking up into his eyes, her own eyes shining in the blossoming moonlight. "We're the both of us right here together in the flesh at last."

Fingers moving along my neck as she draws even closer. Smell perfume under the mimosa-tinged breath, drifting out like a southern breeze from the mouth of her. Lips glossy shining like stars above. Body that won't stop, everything in its right place. Wonder where all this was back in my days of tribulation and woe, suffering for a night and a moment like this. And those times when I took them for myself without asking. Just went ahead with what I figured a man had to do in the blackness of evening so he wouldn't be longing for it later when it was gone, even when he knows he'll regret it someday. Something, though, he has to do, else be beaten. And I couldn't allow love to beat me one more time. Maribeth was gone and the world had to pay for it somehow. Because I wasn't going to go through the rest of my life broken and beaten. In love with a dream, a memory. If it was going to happen to me this one time, when I thought I'd been everything I thought I should be, if I was going to carry it with me all my life, then the world could carry something of me with them too. I had it in my mind I would never stop until I'd made it where it was all a part of yesterday and I was in the present and future in a world I'd built where nothing could ever get to me again.

He finds himself kissing Abigail, just like that, like it is the old days again and this is exactly what he ought to be doing even if she is still somebody else's wife, and then he sees Peterson Library burning inside his head again and he thinks of Faith Mercer and the maybe-baby she carried down to the sidewalk with her.

He pulls away from Abigail and her lips and feels her go limp against him. She lays her head against his chest, breathing heavily, as if she's been running a race and she's taken the last step in her energy bank. He realizes she is almost unconscious, ready to pass out from all the liquor she has drank this day.

"You need to go to bed," he tells her, and she makes a sound that is a cross between a sigh and a moan and falls closer into his arms. It is not like he can sit her down in one of the chairs on the porch and get in the car and drive away. As much as he hates it, there is still some iota of gentlemanly behavior left in him. Whether Abigail being three sheets in the wind is his responsibility or not, he still feels like it is up to him to get her situated and safe for the night before he leaves.

He could knock on the door and let Matt and Sherry and William handle this, but something in him says he has seen enough of the Lane clan for one night and he will take care of Abigail himself.

He is not Errol Flynn, and he is not some Universal monster carrying a fair damsel in distress around the countryside, but he somehow gets Abigail into his arms and takes her to the Honda. He deposits her in the passenger seat and drives around the house to the paved road leading to Abigail's place. He is hoping the doors aren't locked and he can get her inside and in bed, and somehow God hears him and the door is open and he doesn't have to go around jiggling knobs or attempting to pry windows open. Or come down the chimney like jolly old goddamned St. Nick, Lockhart, you damn fool, I'm glad you don't have to do that. He miraculously lifts her from the seat without rupturing a disk and gets her inside. He supposes her bedroom is up the stairs but decides not to push his luck, either with the physical strain of getting her up there or the very real temptation of what he might do once they are there. No, this couch will have to do. Lay her down and cover her with this blanket. Turn on this lamp in the corner and close the door as I go. Stand on the porch with that part of me saying to go back in, to not let a night such as this go by.

You are old, the voice tells him. How many more times do you think moments like this are going to come your way?

He studies the doorknob a moment and then walks down the steps to the car. He winds down the drive to the street that leads back to the highway, careful not to take a wrong turn somewhere and be forever lost in this congregation of the rich. When he is sure he is going in the right direction and actually homeward bound he relaxes a minute and drives along in silence peering out at the pavement before him and the thickets of trees and shrubbery that line the road, wondering what sorts of wildlife are watching him pass from their safe shelters. It is odd to him how he feels infinitely more comfortable somewhere out in the darkness without light to see than he would if he was back among the living with their voices and their thoughts and their artificial light keeping them from darkness. He thinks how moving into the caretaker's house where he is surrounded by the silent dead and creatures beyond polite society will be a good thing for him. He will be by himself. He has convinced himself that this measure of solitude is what he needs for a certain term or perhaps forever.

After a few minutes of abject silence, he switches on the radio and punches the buttons for something to make the half hour trip home peaceful. He foregoes New Country and Classic Rock and a syndicated call-in talk show discussing how good life could be if only the entire Democratic Party would take a voyage on the Titanic and sink somewhere, and instead settles on the local public library radio station, classical music that plays twenty-four hours a day. Tom rides along and lets whatever is playing soothe him. He doesn't know any of the titles of anything that comes on, but three selections play by the time he turns on River Road, and he finds himself totally cleansed of all prior human contact, cooties, and germs he's had to endure this afternoon and evening. It is like he is a human being once more, which has been a long time coming these days. He'd been wondering if he was ever going to approach such a status again.

"You're listening to WTRN," a female voice says. "We've just finished hearing Puccini, 'Turandof—Nessum dorma.' Before that, 'No. 4 in B flat minor', by Fredric Chopin, and leading off the top of the hour was 'Symphony No. 1 in C major, Opus 88 II. Adagio', by Georges Bizet. It is now 9:31 PM in Rhodes, Tennessee. The temperature is currently 74 degrees. My name is Martha Jane DeMars, and I will be with you this Easter evening until midnight."

By this time Tom is sitting in Dewey's driveway with the engine idling while a new musical selection begins to play, and he realizes he's been staring at the garage door for an indeterminate amount of time. It was the music that transported me so, he thinks, took me away from the tired tunes I sometimes hear and the dreaded yesterdays that get provoked in the old think box when they are played, and it was the voice of the woman who spoke in such a way I was leaning forth to listen. What was her name? She said her name. How could I have already forgotten it?

He sits and listens for a few more minutes to see if the voice comes back to speak to him again, but the selections being played are all too lengthy; he cannot enjoy them while he is thinking of the voice he heard not so long ago, not while he is waiting to hear the voice again.

The garage door light comes on and the door raises. Dewey appears with a wine glass in his hand. He is in his bathrobe, and Phyllis skitters to a stop beside him, the two of them looking out to see what is going on in their yard.

"I thought you were too drunk to get out of the car," Dewey says. "I came out to lend you a hand."

"I'm okay," Tom says. "I'm so sober and straight I'm dangerous, so you and Phyllis better let me pass. Neither of you make a false move and everything will be all right."

"Sober and straight?" Dewey asks. "No wonder you're feeling unhinged. How many times have I told you it's not a good idea to neglect your vices?"

FOUR

Getting moved in takes close to a week. By Saturday afternoon Tom stands in the living room and knows there is nothing more he needs to do to make the move official. The utilities are turned on and he's liberated his sofa and wooden table and chairs from a Chattanooga storage unit and paid to have them transported the three hundred miles to Rhodes. The house is small enough that it appears filled. He is almost satisfied until he gets to the kitchen and it comes to him that he needs to make a trip to the store and stock up on some food, otherwise he's going to drop dead of starvation here among his many riches.

Whatever important event is going on that requires every living citizen of Rhodes to cram into the Polka Dot Piggly Wiggly this afternoon he can't say, but he joins the throng and pushes a bascart through crowded aisles trying to negotiate his way through the store and up to the check lanes. Until this moment, he hasn't been aware that Rhodes is in the process of becoming another crowded town with families and children, imps and rascals darting and impeding progress everywhere while he tries to snatch bottles of ketchup and mustard and meat for the grill and soda and beer to wash it all down by. It doesn't help any that by the time he enters Aisle Five and is loading bags of charcoal and lighter fluid into his cart Charlie Polk himself appears from wherever he has been hiding and stands by Tom's side grinning that same smile Tom remembers as a preamble to trouble from thirty-five years past.

"Come on back to my office," Charlie says. "We can have a drink or two and do some catching up."

"Man, I'm just here to get some food. I don't make it a habit to go into a grocery store and get juiced. I've got an empty refrigerator at the house and it would be nice to have something in it besides empty shelves."

"Hell, you can shop any old time," Charlie grins. "Come on. You've got to see my headquarters. I promise you'll be impressed."

Push this cart through a swinging door and follow Charlie past coolers and compressors and stock loaded on pallets against walls. Sign that says Employees Only. And I once worked in this store for over a year. Bagging groceries and stocking shelves and looking at women through the one-way glass in the Meat Department. Charlie and Dewey and me peering out on Friday nights when we were supposed to be working. Charlie's dad our boss, so we knew we could get away with anything. And on one of those nights in the summertime Dewey with a joint. Said, here. Try this. And the show we were watching through the glass got a lot more interesting.

All the way back to the far-right corner is a door that says No Admittance. Charlie jiggles his keychain until he comes up with one that fits the lock, opens the door and we walk down a short hallway. Restroom on the left. My private chambers, Charlie says. Opens another door and there's a big room. Used to be where we stored returnable pop bottles in wooden cases. Walled in now and painted ivy-green. Desks and chairs and cabinets and an intercom. Television balanced on a shelf. Coffeepot and a water cooler. Refrigerator in the corner beside a cabinet of glasses and plates and bowls. Microwave and a tiny bar. Shot glasses and bottles of assorted spirits. Air conditioning blowing on Low. All the comforts of home.

"Jesus, Charlie, do you live here? All you need is a bed and you'd be all set."

"I got beds all over this town for sleeping and other stuff." He pushes open another door and there's a recliner sitting there. "But if I happen to get desperate to consummate a deal I've found out this baby works pretty good."

"God, you haven't changed a bit."

"True. That's why I've got two ex-wives to my credit. Old habits, buddy boy, die hard, even when you tell yourself all the time that someday you're going to change your ways."

He rummages around behind the bar and comes up with a bottle of Jack Daniels. He takes two glasses out and sets them on the bar, opens the freezer compartment of the refrigerator and brings out a bowl of ice.

"No thanks," Tom says. "None of that for me."

"Who are you?" Charlie asks. "I thought for sure I'd invited my old friend Tom Lockhart back for a drink or two." He takes a step closer and looks into Tom's eyes, like he's examining them for a medical report. "Who goes there?" He cups his hands into a megaphone. "Has some alien come down to earth and commandeered my old pal's body?"

"Your old pal can't take crap like this anymore, not even on Saturday nights. I'm an old man, Charlie. My spring chicken status expired about twenty-five years ago."

"Could have fooled me. I can't tell any difference. I thought you were as young and carefree as I was, but maybe I'm not as old as you. That's confusing, since I remember you and I being in the same class."

"You've been pickled so often your body is preserved in alcohol and doesn't age any."

"One little drink. Come on. One's not going to hurt you."

"One and that's all."

They drink for a minute, Charlie leaning back in his chair and elevating his feet on the desk. He picks up a remote and points it at the TV, and the set comes on during a segment of "SportsCenter." He fiddles with the buttons and the images change to the checkout stands up at the front of the store, cashiers beeping items and customers standing in line like sheep to be shorn, waiting for the final total so they can lay their money down or write their check or swipe their plastic cards. Mellow Lite Rock plays in the background among the beeping and the clatter, and Tom wonders if this noise is being transported through the broadcast or if it is simply so goddamned loud on the front end that the sound waves are carrying all the way back here to Charlie's bunker. Charlie hones in on one particular cashier, a bleached blonde with hair down her back in her red Piggly Wiggly polo shirt and a pair of jeans that were obviously painted on right before she clocked in for today's shift.

"Thought you might want to take a quick gander at some of the local talent," Charlie says. "I hired her two weeks ago, but I can tell already she's going to go far in her career here."

Tom shakes his head and looks into his glass. Trouble down there. Charlie has poured too much whiskey and added too little ice. Tom is not going to fall for such tricks as this.

"Yep. Same old Charlie," he says.

"Yeah, don't I know it?" Charlie says sadly. "Not much I can do about it now."

Charlie presses more buttons and images of the stockroom and the meat department and all the individual shopping aisles pop into view, men loading bags of dog food and women studying labels and a shifty-eyed soul leaning on the meat counter eying Porterhouse steaks, looking very much like he is thinking of slipping a few under his shirt to sell down the road and have money for drugs and fun tonight.

"Watch this," Charlie says, and he presses another button on the remote, and on camera a red light starts flashing by the steaks and the fellow standing beside it studies the light for maybe three seconds and then turns and walks away. Charlie follows him with the camera up the aisle and all the way to the electric doors leading outside, where the guy takes one more look around and then walks out.

"I just love doing that," Charlie says. "I like watching the look on their faces when they realize they're being watched. The only thing better would be to have some kind of cattle prod running through the case that would shock the hell out of them whenever they picked up something they weren't going to pay for."

Lockhart looking deeply into this whiskey he refuses to drink. On his face is a slight smile at Charlie and the world Charlie lives in, but there is also the thought going through his head of how time has gone by and everything has changed but a whole lot of that everything has somehow remained the same. Round and round it goes. Life a circle. He thinks of all the old faces he's seen since returning to Rhodes, how once one squints and studies the features of those of the long ago past there is that moment of recognizance. Listen to the words being said and all at once a voice becomes familiar. Amazing to think that people have lived their entire lifetimes going from one set of experiences to another, spinning gray hair and maladies of age and the emptiness that comes when the realization dawns that dreams get crushed beneath the boot of passing time and aren't ever going to happen. Or come anywhere near true. Matt is still in love with privilege and money. Charlie sitting in this shelter forever seeking flashy young girls and endless laughs. Dewey drinking Mateus and studying *Ulysses*. Watch them all going around on the carousel. Think they're so much wiser now. Know what the world's up to and how to get by without bruises or scratches. On their way to some kind of content. Happiness. Hate to be the one to tell them none of that is out there anywhere. All behind you now. Growing smaller in the rear-view mirror.

Charlie continuing to regale him with tales of chicanery and sexual conquest until it's enough and too much. Tom rises and says goodbye and goes to finish his shopping. When he gets to where he parked his cart earlier it is not there, and Charlie says one of his employees must have thought it was an abandoned order and put it back on the shelves. This convinces Tom to leave and walk over to the Dairy Queen and eat a burger sitting at the picnic table outside, since there are no mothers and children or young lovers having splendor in the grass out there at the moment to bother him. He wolfs everything down and decides to head home and complete this worrisome shopping task another day, for right now the karma is just not right.

He has to laugh out loud when the Accord won't start, because he always has to hand it to the dealer of fortunes when he knows he is beaten and there is no way to mount a comeback. As much as he enjoys walking, he is not crazy about the idea of hoofing it home this night. He weighs his options on who might give him a lift, but after considering Charlie back at the store full of whiskey and Abigail looking perhaps not for love but in all probability lust in her BMW, he decides walking is not the worst fate he's ever endured. He's halfway down South Main when he hears a horn honk behind him, and he turns to see Doug in his Silverado with the window down.

"My guess is you've robbed Little Caesar's and you're on your way to Mexico with the loot."

"I'm hiking home because my goddamn car decided to clock out for the night."

"Does it need a boost? I've got cables."

"How about a ride to the house instead? I don't feel like messing with anything right now. Anyway, maybe if I leave it sitting the city will spot it and tow it off and I can do myself a favor and let them keep it."

"Sounds like you may be in the market for a new car," Doug says. He turns Garth Brooks off on the radio and eases out on the road. "Good thing you're working at Matt's. He might give you an employee discount if you're lucky enough."

"He probably would if he was ever there. Matt's like the Great Spirit, invoked in name only, never to be seen in the flesh."

"How's life at the Haunted Mansion? Are you all moved in yet?"

"Finished today. I was in town to stock up the refrigerator and the pantry, but I made the big mistake of going into the Piggly Wiggly when Charlie was there. Between being taken on the grand tour of his back office and hearing how many bimbos he's hired, screwed, and fired over the past month I never managed to make it to the checkout lane. I had to let it ride until another day."

"I've had that happen to me too. Damn Charlie gets to talking and you can't get away."

Doug turns on River Road. When he passes Dewey's house he slows a little to allow some animal to scurry across the road.

"Boy, that was a big one," he says.

"What was it? I couldn't see."

"Coyote, man. Come all the way up from the river to here, looking for food or a stray cat or something. Son of a bitches are getting bolder all the time. They get used to people and they're not afraid of anything. I'm surprised you haven't seen any of them where you are. Hell, they're all over the place."

"Well, I haven't been there but a day. They haven't introduced themselves yet."

"They will. Don't worry."

Tom is halfway rude and doesn't invite Doug in for a beer or anything, but the truth of it is he only has three beers left in the refrigerator from the move from Dewey's and he doesn't feel like sharing. On this first night here he needs as much refreshment as he can muster. Anyway, it's not really his fault he wasn't allowed to shop. God knows he tried, but it simply wasn't meant to be.

He watches Doug's taillights disappear up the road and feels a parcel of guilt for his lack of social graces. Doug did give him a ride home, and Doug was the one who got him into this house. Tom shakes his head for being such an ungrateful bastard.

Three beers under the moonlight on this first night. Thomas Lockhart leans back in his deck chair looking out into the darkness of the woods. Spooky silent here, but not to worry. He's been in worse places than this before.

Spring becomes almost summer. Memorial Day there on the calendar. Schools letting out. Long summer vacations already planned with swimming parties and barbecues and maybe a week at a beach. Cut the yard weekly and drive to Atlanta to watch the Braves.

Downtown a stage is set up where live music can go on for the four-day break with groups and bands and singers from all over. Booths and picnic tables and a carnival troupe in for tilt-a-whirls and Ferris wheels and hot dogs and caramel corn. Beer and wine so the world is not only respectful of the dead but a fun place too.

Thomas Lockhart is a month in residence at the cemetery estate, feeling now almost like a regular townsperson.

It was determined the Accord had seen better days. Whatever was keeping it from starting on Tom's foray to the Piggly Wiggly for supplies had acted as a blessing to keep him from driving it any further, since when he and Dewey finally did get it to turn over a loud explosion sounded down deep in the block and black smoke rose up and made them abandon their positions until they were certain no more blasts were to come and they weren't going to get obliterated. They hauled it off to one of Dewey's business acquaintances and sold the whole damn thing for junk. A hundred dollars in his pocket that Tom transferred to Dewey in exchange for a rust-bucket El Camino that had been sitting for a couple of years and a day at the side of Dewey's house. Abandoned by its owner after bringing it in to be repaired. Vapor lock and a fuel-line leak, Dewey said, all stemming from a wreck where somebody plowed into it from the back and then put it in reverse and left the scene. Once I got it fixed I called the guy and the number was out of order. He never came back and it's been sitting ever since. Yeah,

I had the title transferred to me. Got a friend down at City Hall. Give you a new battery and some recaps and you'll be ready to go. Radio works just fine. I'll be happy as hell not to have to see it every frigging day.

So, the El Camino is twenty-eight, which is two hundred and twenty-six in dog years, but is okay by Tom as long as it starts when he asks it to, which so far is not a problem. On this Friday afternoon, Memorial Day weekend, he parks in his yard and carries provisions for the long holiday inside—cans and packages and cartons and bottles—arranges them in cabinets and inside the refrigerator and checks the air conditioner to make sure cold air is coming forth. Sun is setting and all seems right, so he doesn't even turn on the television to hear the network news of the world, because why give the world the opportunity to depress, frighten, infuriate, and bewilder you when you really don't need to hear about anything crappy going on elsewhere?

He doesn't know why he becomes tempted enough by the thought of barbecue plates and cold beer being served at the Memorial Day picnic, but by four on Saturday afternoon he is obsessed by the idea so much he decides to take a stroll up the road and see what he can find to eat and drink. And look at too, he reminds himself. Don't forget that. You may have spent a good month holing up in the house and being a good boy and keeping to yourself, but you can't deny there is something inside you now stirring to get out. Best to be aware of such inclinations and make prior plans to keep them safely tucked away, where they're not making that unseemly effort to get out and nip, bite, and take a plug out of whatever morsel happens to go by within reach.

He walks up River Road toward South Main and the festivities, walks mainly because he has the idea in his head that he might just sample several brews and partake of assorted firewater, and if the expected result occurs it will be good to not have to worry about driving. He can engage in one of his favorite pastimes, that being the initiation and commencement of the Intoxicated Hike, from which great mental observations are seen and future philosophies planned. Not to mention lifting up the old voice to the heavens and belting out a familiar tune or two. All good for the soul once in a while, but one must not get too carried away and jump into the pit of teeth and human snares. Have to keep an eye out for those doing their best to always spoil one's fun. Woods full of them these days.

He passes by Dewey's house on his right. There's no sign of Dewey or Phyllis sitting out back, and Dewey's truck is absent too. Tom wonders if by any chance Dewey has gone into Rhodes for the carnival, but no, that would not be like Dewey. Dewey is not one to enter the gates of society like that. Maybe before, back in the long-ago days he might have done such a thing, but that was in the past, that was when Dewey had his own hopes and dreams and enchanted visions of what might befall him some magical evening in the future. Tom remembers Dewey leaning back in his chair and telling him a story of a departed time, the story of Linda before he went off to Vanderbilt and she to Knoxville at the University of Tennessee. This was all pre-Doug, Dewey said. Do you remember? We hooked up at a party and it was one of those things and we spent a bunch of nights together. Then I left for school and she went off with everyone else to Knoxville, and Doug was there and she got immediately knocked up and that was that. She married Doug and they had the kid and we've never much spoken to each other since. And you know what, Tom? It just could be I might have been in love with her then. Because I couldn't stand it at school without her. First time I ever felt that way about anyone. I dropped out and came home. But by then it was too late. She was with Doug and it looked to me like it was going to be forever.

Everybody has something like that in their head, Tom thinks. He wishes Dewey was home. He would walk up the drive and tell him so, but Dewey is gone and it's none of his business anyway. Everybody has their own drama taking place. The trick is learning how to work it out in your own way.

On out onto South Main where the cars are lined up with people trying to get into town and find a place to park. Tom hears the sound of guitars jamming out undecipherable licks from a stage on past the intersection at City Walk, which is almost a park and almost a trail but is not truly either, and from where he is he can see an audience standing before a stage, and on both sides are booths serving food and drink, crafts and clothing, and in the backdrop carnival rides go up and down, swinging wide and turning over, machinery and levers and engines that roar and thrill and might possibly make it through the entire holiday without throwing a bearing or popping a bolt and killing a person or seven. There is barbecue and hot dogs and burgers and all the food Tom remembers from every fair and circus he's ever been to in his life, and for some strange reason he wants to make a circle of the square and order everything there is to eat and drink, and then he wants to walk home in the dark with the noise and the music over his shoulder and hear multitudes of coyotes howling as he lays down in his bed to sleep.

For a long while he sees no one he knows. He is surrounded by a great crowd of strangers, unfamiliar faces and voices he has never heard before, and this is fine with him. He likes walking along with no one asking anything of him, questions or favors or how he feels about the current state of the world, who's to blame for what and what's to be done about it in the end. He sees the big Ferris wheel turning and watches its passengers take their turn at the top, the earth below them and the sky close enough to touch, and he hears the laughter and the sounds of happiness drifting down toward him, and he wishes that he could freeze this moment and make it stay forever, the smiles and the happiness and the total acceptance that, for one budding summer night at least, all is well and the troubles of the day and ages past have vanished.

He sees the woman walking with another man. She is eating popcorn and smiling, her light hair soft on her neck, the hoop earrings large enough for a lion to jump through, her baubles and bracelets tinkling and skittering across the air to come into his ear and have him hear only the intimation of her presence above the music and screams and shouts of glee coming from the crowd. It is the woman he saw in the bar those six weeks ago, walking by him as the fairest of this fair and this city of Rhodes, and all he can do is watch her pass with this faceless man at her side who doesn't deserve her like he, Thomas Lockhart, does, and disappear among the ball caps and sunglasses and eyes and ears attuned to the world he wants to steal her away from.

She is gone, and so he orders a beer and a foot-long with extra onions and sits at a table by himself to watch what's left of the world go by, knowing the highlight of the parade has already passed and thinking how this is like the story of his life. No magic around to last, but you can always have a hot dog.

He is sitting and watching the sun go down and keeping private score in his head when a man in a black Hawaiian shirt walks up and peers down at him.

"Thought I might introduce myself," he says. "I'm Garland Williams."

Being not entirely stupid and also being not very much interested, Tom looks up from his beer and nods politely, knowing already any words he says will be wasted. He sits and waits for what is to come, because he knows what's on the way.

"Abigail Williams happens to be my wife," he begins.

"You mean your soon-to-be ex-wife, don't you?" Tom says.

"She's not my ex-wife yet," Garland Williams says. "She and I may not go through with this divorce, as a matter of fact. Last I checked this morning we were still officially married."

"I don't know about that. But then, I haven't had that many conversations with Abigail lately. I came back to town because my brother died, and then I decided to stick around. Abigail's brother offered me a job. You know Matt, don't you? Well, Matt's my boss, as if it's any of your concern, my friend."

"My concern is Abigail. She's my wife. I'm not very thrilled with you waltzing in here like some hot piece of shit trying to jump all over her right when we're trying to work some things out."

"You can relax on that. I didn't come back here to court and spark Abigail Lane. And I doubt very much either of you are trying to work anything between you out."

"You don't fool me a bit, Lockhart. I know all about you. You're a prick. You're here to do a little sport-fucking in your spare time, the same way you were doing back where you came from. I've been checking up on you."

"Glad I could brighten up your existence. I couldn't be happier."

"I don't give the first shit how you feel. I'm just letting you know your kind of bullshit isn't going to fly around Rhodes. You need to know that up front, otherwise I might have to take steps to make sure you understand. Friend of Matt Lane or not, you'll find your welcome will get worn out pretty fast if you don't watch it. You'll probably in the end decide moving on isn't the worst idea you ever had."

"You're kidding me, of course."

"Do I sound like I'm making anything up? I'll give you a little clue, Lockhart. I'm on the Rhodes City Council. We spend a lot of time keeping this town nice and peaceful and trouble-free. You wouldn't be the first fellow we've persuaded to move on to greener pastures."

"Guess we'll have to see how it all works out."

"Guess so, asshole."

Garland walks off and mingles in with the throng until he's several booths away and then disappears as if he'd never been present. Tom watches him go with a slight sense of wonder at how some towns, like good old Rhodes, get caught in a time warp and never change, while other locations grow up to be real cities and pay no attention to anything much as long as there's not murder in the first degree happening right down on Main Street, but just go along day after day having tax hikes and population booms and allowing ninety-eight percent of its citizens to stay wholly anonymous. He thinks of Abigail and her collection of marriages so far and wonders how many more ex-husbands might be out in the streets this very minute gunning for him without his knowing it. Abigail with her long lean body and lips and raven tresses and how he's been a good boy for six weeks now and kept himself in check and away from her arms for the most part, and now here is some small-town joker standing before him saying how whatever he is up to has to stop or else. Better, Tom thinks, for me to have gone ahead and ravaged old Abigail and left her in the lurch to begin with. He is, after all, taking the blame and being told the consequences for his doing all the things he hasn't done. He looks at his hand on the plastic cup and notices there is no tremble present. He's been in this position before. This is not new. This is nothing to be worried about.

City Council, my ass, he thinks. Park Board, my butt.

Finish this beer and wipe mustard from the lips. So much for airing out the mind among the townsfolk amid the social event of the season. Been better to stay in and watch a ball game or listen to tunes from the classical station, or, god forbid, sit at the keyboard and try once more to write. Which is a hell of a lot more of a scary thought than villagers waving torches and being up in arms over who I'm supposedly bedding. Well, I've got news for them all and I hope they pay attention. I'm not in bed with anyone. I know better. I know what happens when things like that transpire. Regret, despair, guilt. That big realization that comes when you know it's not there again. Love. Gone as it is. Not even the courtesy call to say it is leaving. Goodbye. Sorry it has to end like this.

He hits South Main on the way home, footsteps in rhythm on the walk and crossing the street. At the light he sees a black Audi with the top down, a man with his hands on the wheel looking straight ahead waiting for the light to change, and in the passenger seat is the woman with her hair down her back and her gold hoops glistening beneath the streetlights and a slender braceleted arm reaching up to adjust the visor above her. There is no sun, so possibly she is attempting to keep the moon from getting in her eyes.

Thomas Lockhart knows how it is. He's had the moon in his eyes before too.

FIVE

Summertime in Rhodes is like somebody went from house to house around town unplugging air conditioners, misplacing fans, turning up thermostats and raising windows so wide the cool air escapes and goes somewhere else not the least bit nearby. Perhaps not the white-concrete hot days and nights like the big cities have, Memphis, Nashville, Chattanooga, where the humidity is so high people stay away from doors so they don't have to go out anywhere, but hot in the way there is no breeze and the shade of the trees doesn't help make anything be anywhere close to comfortable, makes it so one does not linger between tasks or look up at the sky and regard God's beautiful sunshine or even want to go somewhere where there is a pool and water, because in the end a person can't stay in the water forever, they have to get out and attend to life, and that is when, in the summertime of Rhodes, they find the heat grinning its cruel smile and waiting for them. People talk about the good old summertime and how welcome it is, but after only a little while they begin looking at the calendar and wishing Fall would step it up some and get here. There is an unspoken prayer for Autumn in the back of everyone's mind.

Five and a half days a week Tom Lockhart makes his way up River Road and turns left on South Main to make it to the dealership in time for work. He works a half day on Saturdays regularly now because it means extra money in his pocket, and if he had to be truthful he would confess how he might as well perform such a task since he has nothing better to do anyway. It is not like he is going to use this time to write and come up with another book and make money off a flood of royalties. It isn't like he has hobbies to pique his interests or finds something absorbing on television he just has to watch. He reads no magazines or bestsellers and is not about to go into town to frequent yard sales and load up the El Camino with other people's castoffs, as if he needs worn furniture or additional glasses for entertaining or stereo equipment from when Cro-Magnon man first began spinning records on a turntable. He considers Saturdays as a way to get him up and moving and a means of making him feel not quite so useless and slothful. He is moving, he is working, he is minding his own business and making extra wages to better his situation, so at least by showing up for four hours he is not at home questioning his right to be present in Rhodes among the living and acting like he is as normal as the next guy.

He has always done his best not to fall prey to being a creature of habit, but on these half-day Saturdays it is hard not to celebrate the end of the work week by stopping off at the Olympia for a cheeseburger and fries and a fizzy cola the waitress draws from an apparatus back by the kitchen. In these days of being past his prime and attempting to stay somewhat healthy, Tom tries to limit himself to one soda a week, forcing water down his throat for the majority of his meals so as not to kill his liver or make his blood sugar soar like an eagle on acid. He avoids beer and alcohol as much as possible because they are chock-full of carbs and calories and he does not wish to grow chunky after spending the majority of his life lean and gaunt and wolf-hungry looking, and he does his best to not subsist on fatty meats and fries dripping with grease like he is certain will be served in Heaven, which bothers him on a continual basis because he knows he is not going to be in that celestial place on high to enjoy such a reward. But on these Saturdays, he cannot find it in him to forsake the Olympia and their cheeseburger special with the fat-dripping greasy order of fries on the side. Since he is not going to surely someday be in Paradise, he is at least going to get some of it here on earth before he goes to eternally burn.

Sitting at a table alone and wolfing down what he knows might in the end kill him, it is a good time to reflect on the past week and all that has happened either good or bad and possibly form some sort of game plan for what might be upcoming.

He hasn't seen or heard from Abigail in two weeks, and he is not sure if that is a good or bad sign. A part of him thinks she is probably on some kind of jaunt that rich folks tend to take and will be returning whenever she wants, at which time the keepaway game will begin all over again. Then there is also the possibility she has tired of fooling with him and his Puritan whims and taboos about her still being married and moved on to somebody else. This is possible and is probably the best solution to the whole situation, but there is a part of him that regrets this if it is true, because it is somewhat damaging to his ego wherein he likes to think he is King of Beasts in whatever jungle he happens into, and it could be that Abigail has spoiled this image by going and choosing somebody else to roll around with. This is a classic case of Approach/ Avoidance, and he knows how the old Thomas Lockhart would have reacted to it. It would have been full speed ahead and no holds barred and let the chips fall where they may, and in the end he would probably win at whatever sexual game was being played out, he would come away knowing he could cash in and be free of it, but there would still be a part of him that would be sorry it was this way, because, he'd told himself, he was not really this bad of a guy. It was the circumstances that had made him this way.

Right.

There have also been no more sightings of Garland Williams (is he husband number three or husband number four?) and Tom is gratified for the lull in the action and the lack of drama he has to deal with. It's not that he's pushed old Garland completely out of his waking thoughts, however, since he's done a little asking around about who exactly Garland is and what standing he happens to hold around Rhodes. Dewey says Garland once worked with Matt in the same office, but he didn't know if it was Financial Counseling or Law or exactly what line of business, since folks like that are into just about every damn thing, money coming in from everywhere. Doug says he's an attorney and been on the Council for a while, even ran for mayor in the primary a few years back, and he and Abigail were married maybe a year before she left him, and he wasn't sure how many marriages it was for either of them. He's like a lot of them, Doug says, wants his own way and raises hell about anybody getting food stamps and being on Welfare and how they all should be run out of town or at least put to work paying taxes like everybody else has to, then on Sunday he's over at First Baptist acting like Jesus likes him better than anyone else. And Matt doesn't like him worth a damn, I can tell you that. They had a big disagreement about something, and then Garland and Abigail started fighting and calling the cops on each other, and Garland broke off from them both, but in the end he and Abigail can't seem to get done with each other. She takes out peace bonds and writs, and she wants everything he owns from the divorce even if she doesn't need it, probably just to piss him off, and it doesn't look like they'll ever stop going at each other. If you ask me, they should have just stayed with each other and avoided all the legal mumbo jumbo. Garland could have at least hopped in the sack with her every once in a while, when they weren't trying to maim each other. She's a hell of a nice-looking woman, Abigail, although I'm sure, Tom, you haven't taken any notice of it. I know how you've always been a stickler for shying away from such things.

Mid-afternoon and Tom arrives home amid a symphony of crocuses and tree frogs and blue jays squawking and crows answering them back in the trees around the house. The idea of a nap is intriguing, but he decides to have a cup of coffee instead, since getting all rested right now will probably mean he will have trouble sleeping tonight, and then it will be him and the moon and the children of the night moving around under the balcony. Nights like this are when the black, dark thoughts come calling, when he is held prisoner to a litany of accusations and admonitions about who he is and what crimes he is responsible for. He thinks one of these days he is going to let some of this baggage go, but he hasn't seen when that arrival time has been posted yet.

He is finishing off the brats he's charred on the grill when he hears the sound of a motor with not much of a muffler silencing it and a door creaking open and then slammed shut. This can only be Dewey riding up in his truck and making such a commotion, so he lays his fork down and goes down to answer the door.

Dewey is already yelling for him by the time he turns the knob.

"Hey, Tom! Tom! Open the door!"

Tom cracks the door first to take a look and make sure this is not some shapeshifter impersonating Dewey wanting to get inside and go for his throat in an effort to amuse himself on a Saturday night. He sees wild eyes and a tie-dyed shirt and opens the door wider to allow entrance, and Dewey shoots by him like there is some big hurry, immediately running up the stairs toward the balcony.

Dewey is carrying a rifle.

"Dewey," he says. "I hate to ask a stupid question, but why are you armed? Are we at war? Have you joined the SWAT team and forgot to tell me?"

"I need to use your balcony a while, man. I'm after a coyote. I've got a score to settle. I know him and his buddies will be coming through here sooner or later. I need an ambush spot."

"You're going to shoot a coyote? Isn't that illegal? Or is this just some weird Rhodes pastime I've been missing out on all this time?"

"Phyllis is dead," Dewey says. "That's what's going on. She got killed by a coyote about an hour ago, right out in the backyard, and I know which son of a bitch did it. I've seen him hanging around the last couple of weeks, like he was waiting on something."

"Phyllis is dead?"

"Hell, yes. The fucker just grabbed her for entertainment, I think. Didn't even try eating her or nothing. Goddamn it, I can't believe she let him get close enough to catch her. She's always been smarter than that." He pulls up one of the lawn chairs to the railing and levels his rifle at the lawn below. "She was eleven years old in March. She's always been careful as hell when she was out in the yard." He sits down and takes the rifle and peers through the scope toward the back trees, squints down the barrel like he's ready to zero in on his target. "I'm going to get that bastard if it's the last thing I ever do."

Tom starts to explain how his balcony is not exactly the Texas Book Depository building, how this is not Dallas, and how he himself is not really keen on hosting an emotionally-crazed man with a rifle ready to fill a portion of the local wildlife full of lead from what was formerly his relaxed dining area, but with the look on Dewey's face he thinks maybe he'll try to change the subject for a minute and go back to trying to reason with him later.

"Maybe Phyllis was getting old and her reflexes weren't what they used to be," he offers.

"Maybe," Dewey says. "I think she was getting a little blind in her right eye here lately. I could tell by the way she cocked her head and looked at me when I said something. She kind of had to turn sideways so she could focus."

He inches the chair closer and sights down the scope again. Tom wonders if Dewey can squeeze off numerous rounds in a matter of seconds like Oswald supposedly did when the targeted coyote arrives, or if there may be a need for another shooter to help out. He looks around to see if there's a grassy knoll anywhere in the vicinity.

"There's got to be some kind of law against this," he tells Dewey. "You're fixing to get both of us arrested."

Dewey doesn't reply, but just gets himself into more of a sniper position. Tom doesn't know whether to keep talking or not, thinking maybe Dewey will accuse him of breaking his concentration, so he goes back over to his plate to finish off his brats before any action ensues. Might as well have a full stomach when the authorities show up to take them to jail.

The moon keeps rising and Dewey remains transfixed in his spot. After about a half hour Tom hears him whisper.

"There you are, you sorry asshole."

Dewey aims and pulls the trigger. There are no loud explosions that might wake the dead or alert the police, but simply whooshing sounds and clicks, and Tom wonders if Dewey has invested in a silencer for his rifle, and if that too is legal these days, and if Dewey, on top of being arrested for firing a deadly weapon inside the city limits, is also going to get booked for possessing illegal firearms paraphernalia.

"I got him!" Dewey whoops, and Tom looks over the rail to see what is left of the coyote that ended Phyllis' time on the planet.

He sees a coyote skittering off toward the woods, ambling off into the thickets at a fast gait, and he watches Dewey aim his rifle again and fire off another round.

"What the hell kind of rifle is that?" he asks.

"It's a pellet gun," Dewey says. "It's the only thing I've got. Varmint Air Gun. Spring-powered cocking, automatic safety. Got it on eBay for a song. Free shipping too."

"A pellet gun? You're trying to kill a full-grown coyote with an air rifle? Why don't you just go buy a Daisy and fill him full of BBs? That'll teach him."

"I want to torture him. Scare the bastard into a slow and miserable death. Intimidate the bejesus out of him and make him always have to think twice about coming out of the woods. Truthfully, I'm not really sure this was the same coyote that got Phyllis. He didn't seem like he was quite big enough."

Dewey goes on to explain how his air rifle really is a dangerous sort of weapon if one is a crack shot like he is and aims for the extremities when wielding it. He sits down and extracts a joint from his shirt pocket and licks it up and down once, then fires it up.

"Here's to Phyllis," he says.

Sunday morning and a day away from everything. Step out on the balcony and the air hits me in the face. Sun coming up behind the trees, broken rays of light seeping through the August trees. Sit down with coffee and think about those Sundays as a boy. In the summer we didn't have to wear a tie to church. Fresh-ironed pants and a crisp short-sleeved shirt. Penny loafers and Oxfords, black socks because nobody who knew anything would ever wear white socks to church. Two dollars in my wallet to tithe to Sunday School. Drop it in the plate at the end of class. And sometimes I'd give only one. Hold on to the other in my pocket so I could buy baseball cards at Sloan's Market. Sit on the curb and cram pink gum in my mouth, sugar flooding my intestines. See if I could come across a Willie Mays.

By mid-morning taking a walk to clear the head. Move some stuff around up in the old think-box so I'm ready to face the world again tomorrow. Life not too bad but nothing much to brag about. Go to work and leave and do my best not to be seen or singled out. By jealous husbands or three-time divorcees wanting most of my body and all of my soul. Don't seem to know how to tell people I don't have a lot more to offer. Out of words and have to keep the feelings unseen, like held breath, never let anything flow out into the air where someone might get the idea they know where it's coming from. Make sure no sound precedes my approach and no one hears me when I go. Because if I've learned one thing coming back to Rhodes, it's this. This is not my home. Nor where I was before and where I've been since, where I am today. A stranger again. Could possibly be one forever.

Eleven in the morning and already the heat of the day makes this stroll almost unbearable. Tom Lockhart with prior plans to walk maybe from his house to the other side of River Grove, take in a little town history reading tombstones, and then double back along the Crockett to view the river and maybe see a boat or two motor by. Get back home and plop a chicken into the crockpot. And take a long blank mind-emptying nap.

When he comes into view of the house, he sees a car pulled up in the drive, the motor running with the faint sound of music seeping out from the closed windows. Strange car he doesn't know, and he wonders if this is another welcoming committee from Garland and his constituents, come to call on him on a Sunday afternoon to suggest he might consider making a move in the future. To anywhere but here.

As he gets closer the driver's side door opens and a man with a beard gets out. The man waves his hand and says, "Hey, Dad."

It is his son, Mitchell. The passenger door opens and a woman gets out. She is smiling at him too. Tom has no earthly idea who she is.

"The next time you move you ought to try and get out in the boonies somewhere, away from human civilization a bit," Mitchell says. "Lord, if I wasn't half Ferdinand Magellan with explorer blood in my veins we'd have never found this place."

"I'm practically downtown. It's a mile away. This is better than having everyone living right on top of you."

"Might as well say dropping off the face of the earth is okay if you can stand the fall."

Mitchell walks over to Tom and they shake hands. No hugs or warm embraces today, just like always. This is the first time they've seen each other since Christmas, and that was the first time in a long time then. They are not close but bear each other no ill will, both of them comfortable in the fact they will always be the best of strangers. It has been this way between them for a long while, maybe not so much for Mitchell as it is Tom, but it is a pleasant gulf with one or the other always somewhere on the other side.

"We're on our way to Gatlinburg for a few days and thought we'd stop by and see you."

We is the collective pronoun for Mitchell and his lady friend standing beside him, who is introduced as Rebecca Warren. Rebecca is beyond attractive, as Thomas Lockhart, he of the all-encompassing eye, notes, and he shakes her hand deciding his son may have inherited his good taste in women from his dear old dad, if, that is, Mitchell actually is truly his son, which, after all these years, is still questionable and yet to be determined. Rebecca, it's explained, is a second-grade teacher at the school where Mitchell is the assistant principal, at some private school in Birmingham Tom has never heard of or seen.

They walk up the front steps onto the postage stamp-sized porch and go inside. Tom wonders how Mitchell and Rebecca are taking in his digs on this first glance, if the fact that he is located here by a cemetery in the middle of nowhere is unsettling to either of them, but neither of them just ups and bemoans the antiquity or the lack of interior decorating or the location of the caretaker's house or anything, but politely follow him into the living room and sit down on a sofa Tom has owned since his first apartment after leaving Covington, so it is older than either of his guests and, he notes, certainly looks the part too.

"Can I get anybody anything? Coffee? Water? Afraid I don't have too much else around. Entertaining is something I don't do a lot of these days."

"No, we're only going to stay a few minutes. We want to check in early this afternoon and get out and do some things." Mitchell shifts in his seat and folds his hands. "I hate just dropping in on you like this. I called earlier to tell you I'd like to come by and see you, but you never answered. I left a message, but I don't know if you got it or not."

"My phone is upstairs. I lay it down and never remember to pick it up when I go out."

"Well, I'll just make it short and sweet and cut to the chase." Mitchell smiles and leans forward and takes Rebecca's hand. "We wanted to let you know in person that we've decided to get married. In October. In Montgomery, which is Rebecca's hometown. You're of course invited. You can even be my Best Man if you want."

"No thanks on that Best Man part. I'd screw it up somehow or another. But congratulations. I had no idea. Last I heard you were a bachelor for life." Tom turns his attention to Rebecca, the future bride who is looking at him like she is so blessed she gets to have him for a father-in-law. "I'm very happy for the both of you."

He studies Rebecca a little more closely. There is something about her, he thinks.

"We haven't set the actual date yet," Mitchell is saying, "until we get the news out to everybody and we make sure we don't have any schedule hangups. We have to check the football schedule to make sure Auburn or the Crimson Tide aren't playing during the time of the wedding, or it could be nobody shows up for the ceremony. But we'll make sure it's on a Saturday, and we'll have a rehearsal and a dinner and the wedding and reception, so it'll be a full deck of cards whichever weekend we choose."

"I'll have to check and see if Covington's homecoming is anytime that month," Tom says. "No, wait. I just remembered we never had a football team, so I guess I'm in the clear."

"You have to show up, Dad, no matter what. No unexcused absences for you this time. I know you're not much for the social scene, but this is required attendance. You don't show up, you have to answer to us."

"Have you ever been to Montgomery, Mr. Lockhart?" Rebecca asks. "I was born there. I went to school at Alabama and got a teaching job in Birmingham when I finished, and that's where I met Mitchell."

"Call me Tom, please, Rebecca. Hearing that Mr. Lockhart stuff makes me think I'm back to teaching school again. And yes. I've been to Montgomery before. It was a while ago."

He thinks about Montgomery. Capitol of the state, hometown of Zelda Sayre. The Confederacy. And other things, Thomas Lockhart, he reminds himself. Other things.

"Mother will be there too," Mitchell laughs, "so you can look forward to that. You'll have to be on your best behavior." He turns to Rebecca with a grin on his face. "My parents don't exactly get along. I had to go through childhood wondering who was going to kill the other one first."

This is not exactly the truth, but Tom says nothing in defense. The reality is he was totally fucked over by his first and only wife, the infamous Lynda, and he'd done nothing but take it and turn the other cheek for about an eternity, figuring it was not a good idea to fight to stay married to someone you never loved or to keep acting like a father to somebody who was likely some other guy's kid.

But, he notes, there are a million stories in the Naked City.

"I'll polish up my manners," he tells Mitchell. "I'll take a pill or something to get me through."

The conversation is polite enough for the next fifteen minutes. Tom learns that Lynda's third marriage since she and he parted is going along fairly un-rocky, and Tom is able to say how glad he is to hear how miracles still occur in the world. There is talk of school and Tom's new occupation as an auto parts supplier, and how weird it must be to live in a house so close to a graveyard, to which Rebecca recounts how such a setting would likely creep her out if she was here on a fulltime basis. She goes on to talk about teaching second-graders and how her real interest had always been in Education and teaching and how she wishes her father was still alive to be involved in her wedding the same way he was in her older sister's wedding five years ago, but he is dead two years now of liver cancer and how she'll be thinking of him when she walks down the aisle, and Tom says how sorry he is to hear about her father, and he does his best to stop wishing that Mitchell and his future daughter-in-law would take a peek at their watches and say how time has flown but they really need to be going.

After a perfunctory half hour more of pleasant chat and catching up, Mitchell and Rebecca load up in the Volvo and resume their trip to the mountains. Tom is informed how they will be in touch to provide more detail on dates and times and such, and Rebecca even volunteers to find him a place to stay for the event. Montgomery gets pretty busy on the weekends, she says, what with all the festivals and concerts going on, so you'll probably need to get a reservation somewhere. I suppose it's like that just about everywhere you go these days. Sometimes there's more people than there are beds.

Something about the way she shakes her head and her hair falls down over her left eye makes Tom look at her more than twice, and he wonders if it's because she is such a pretty girl he is having trouble diverting his eyes from her. He hopes that is not it. He hopes he is not so much of a lech that he would allow himself to fall to the level of ogling his only son's betrothed. But that is not it, he decides. There is just something about her is all it is, something he can't quite put his finger on.

He watches the Volvo make its progress up River Road until it is out of sight. It is mid-afternoon. He could go sit down at the keyboard and make an attempt to be productive in a fictional sort of way, to sit there and balance plots and conjure situations and create characters to tell the story the world has long been waiting for, but instead he opts for a nap. There are the problems of existence to try and relate to, and then there is oblivion, and he knows which of these he excels at.

SIX

It surprises him on Wednesday afternoon when the Parts Department door pushes open and Matt walks in. This is maybe the third time he has seen Matt in person at the dealership since he started working back in April, and this is August now, so Tom immediately begins thinking there must be a fly in the ointment somewhere. Matt Lane does not take time from his private life to visit any of his business endeavors. He has people he pays good money to who do that sort of thing for him.

"I know, I'm fired," Tom says. "I'll go clean out my desk."

"No," Matt says. "This is a prison sentence you're serving, and you got Life. The only way you get to leave is in a casket."

"Plenty of them around where I live already."

"You have any decent coffee?" Matt walks around the counter and picks up the cannister and gives it a sniff. He decides he's whiffed worse in his time and pours a Styrofoam cup full, looks at the bag of sugar and decides black coffee is the ticket for right now. "I've been missing you, Tom. You've been extremely quiet lately. I keep expecting you to give me a call and the two of us go play a round of golf or something, but I just sit by the phone like an ugly girl on Saturday night waiting for it to ring. I used to get all my updates and info on your current behavior from Abigail, but it seems like you've gone and pissed her off to the point that she's damned if she's going to have anything to do with you again, or at least until she thinks she's got you in a position where it's impossible for you to tell her no."

"I haven't talked to her. To tell you the truth, Matt, your sister's a little too much for me these days. For one thing, she didn't tell me there at first that she was still married. That's one of those things that needs to be common knowledge. The way I see it is one of us is a head case and is chockful of problems, and I'm of the opinion it isn't me."

"Ha, you make it sound like you're another one of her victims, but I know better than that. Abigail's a piece of work, all right, but the two of us know who's always had her number. My little sister has been nuts for you since junior high."

"Maybe, but she's had a lot of guys on her dance card in between all that time. I'm just this fellow who turns up every couple of decades like a summer rerun."

Matt laughs again and takes a sip of coffee, makes a face and sets it down like it's used motor oil from the Service Department next door.

"Speaking of Abigail, I thought it might be a good idea if maybe you and I had a little chat about her. Maybe not about Abigail so much, but just about a few items she seems to stir up now and then."

"I think I know where this is going."

"I had a call from my former business partner," Matt says. "Garland Williams. You and Garland have met, haven't you? I was told you'd had the pleasure of his acquaintance."

"Yeah. We're pals."

"Well, to let you know, Tom, Garland is kind of a big man around Rhodes these days, or at least he thinks he is. It kind of shows you what a Podunk town this place has become. He's got his law office and his place on the Park Board and his seat on the Council and he's pretty much convinced himself that he's the bee's knees, which if folks don't know it for a fact he is more than glad to educate them about. He's also Abigail's third husband. Still her husband," he adds.

"He mentioned that. I guess he thought it would impress me. At the time I didn't know what his status was in the grand scheme of things."

"He's another in a long line of poor choices my sister has made through the years, construed and acted upon by the aid of liquor and recreational drugs of the highest ilk." Matt shakes his head and considers his coffee cup once more. "I'm here to tell you, Tom, Abigail can be bad news when she puts her mind to it, and she for damn sure does it often enough. I can't begin to tell you how many times I've had to bail her out of some bad situations she gets herself and a lot of other folks involved in."

"Sounds like not a lot has changed around here, buddy. Abigail's been that way all the time I've known her, even when she was a little girl."

"High-strung is the term. But I thought I better give you some heads-up about old Garland. He's a smart dude, but he's got a temper. He's a real hothead sometimes. He'll go off on you in a second if you don't keep an eye on him. That's why I cut ties with him. Between his moodiness and him and Abigail going at it and divorcing I was always wondering what he was going to do next. As it was, I probably complicated matters even worse, telling him he and I couldn't work together anymore. I think he despises me as much as he does Abigail, which is really saying something. And since you're working for me and Abigail likes you, you're automatically going to be at the top of his list. You're at the head of the class."

"First time I've been number one at anything in quite a while."

"You need to come out to the house sometime. We'll shoot some pool and have a few brews. Right now, you wouldn't have to worry about Abigail being around, since she's away for a while."

"Away?"

Matt grins again.

"She's on one of her rehab stints. Seems like every year she has to go in for a couple of weeks to get good and straight for the new school year. Good thing I know everybody on the Board of Directors. Makes it easy getting around all the terms of employment rigmarole."

Matt hangs around a few more minutes just to visit and make sure he's got his message across, has a second cup of deepest darkest coffee and asks Tom if he's satisfied with his job, tells him how much he appreciates the work he's done since he got here, bullshit like that, and then he's out the door and back to his financial world. Save for Gordon Lightfoot singing about the Edmund Fitzgerald from the celestial Sirrus above his head, the shop is quiet and tranquil, as if everyone in the entire principality of Rhodes owned automobiles with absolutely nothing wrong with them. Over on the muted television, "Family Feud" is in high gear, brothers and sisters and in-laws and feisty grandmas hugging and dancing because they are on the verge of winning the jackpot, and Tom studies them immersed in their joy for a minute before he reaches for the remote and turns the set off.

In these days of Daylight Savings Time, the sun doesn't start going down until mid-evening, then it lingers for almost an hour with widening shadows spreading before the darkness actually takes over. After a meat and three at the Olympia, Tom is home in plenty of time before any of this starts to happen. It is about as pleasant an early summer afternoon as is possible in Tennessee, so rather than waste the time watching the depressing evening news with wars and shootings and political corruption, he takes off for another of his walks to stretch his legs and clear his mind of the bothersome tedium he's been partaking of for what feels like long stretches of time. It is like whatever he might be guilty of, he has paid for it by navigating the days and nights of this endless summer.

He is fifteen minutes into his trek into River Grove when he sees a flash of red ahead of him on the road, and he comes up on a Camry parked by a section of tombstones and trees and a sign that says Sanctuary Meadow. A woman kneels beside the rear driver's side tire, her hands folded in front of her as if she is in the middle of a prayer. She hears him approach, and stands up and turns around to see who it is.

Good God, Tom thinks. Merciful Creator.

It is the woman he saw at the Memorial Day picnic in town, the vision of beauty he first saw at Thompson's. He remembers how in both of those instances she was singled out in his sight from all the others, first standing at the bar in Thompson's relating some animated story to a crowd of her friends, then walking by him like a dream at the side of some guy who was probably the age of his son Mitchell (if Mitchell is his son), and he thinks how whether it was in the bar or out in the sunshine of May the fact is still the same, that this woman is maybe also only old enough to be his daughter, for he is old, he is ancient, but she is young, he thinks, young and beautiful, and here she is, and here he is too.

"Having trouble?" he asks.

"Yes. I think I have a flat tire."

He looks at the tire, flat only on the bottom like they always are.

"No thinking to it," he tells her. "That is definitely your classic flat tire. In my personal experience I haven't seen too many tires flatter than this one."

He walks closer and looks the tire over again, careful not to direct his gaze on this woman for fear he will fall to the ground and weep over such a face.

"Would you like me to change it for you?"

He sincerely hates the idea of such an ordeal of labor, but he will do it for her. At this moment he will do absolutely anything. Smitten, he thinks. I have it right between the eyes.

"There's a small problem with that," she says, a bemused smile on her face, cheekbones that rise a few more inches upward toward the summer sky. "It seems my spare tire is deflated too. I'm not sure how that happened. It's certainly not supposed to be that way."

"Sounds like you're borrowing a chapter from my life," Tom says.

He roots around in her trunk and presses the spare, making some sort of show like he knows what he's doing. Yes, the tire is flat. No, there's not much he can do about it. Might as well, he thinks, not try hiding how mechanically inadequate I am.

"Well, I'm on foot, but I was on my way home. I've got a car there. We can get it and I can go get a friend of mine to fix the flat. He's got a garage and tools and all that sort of necessary stuff. If you want to go with me, we can see about getting you back on the road."

"That would be wonderful," she says.

What big eyes you have, he thinks, although she is for damn sure nobody's grandmother.

"How far away do you live?" she asks.

"Not far at all. Just up here around the curve. It's the stone house by the cemetery gate."

"Is that you who lives there? I've been wondering who it was that moved in. Every time I go by I try to figure out who's living there."

"That would be me. Been there a couple of months now. Not to be nosy or anything, but why would you be driving by my house so much? Seems to me you'd have better places to hang out in than a cemetery."

"I do some part-time work here. Plant a little and tend some of the gardens and stuff. I come a couple of days a week and spruce the place up a little. Keeps me busy and off the streets. I really enjoy it."

She laughs and her eyes flash and dance again, like heat lightning in the late afternoon. Something in her voice is familiar to him. He's heard it somewhere, maybe in his dreams. A lot seems to come to him when he's sleeping.

"So you plant flowers around River Grove. What else do you do?"

"I'm on the radio. WRTN, 90.5 on your dial. The Public Library station. I play classical music and tell the temperature every half hour."

"Hey, I listen to you all the time. I thought I knew your voice."

"I'm Martha Jane DeMars," she says, stopping in the middle of the road and extending her hand. "I'm very pleased to meet you and extremely happy you came along today."

He allows himself to finally look at her, and it is just like he thought it would be. He is a damn goner.

"I'm Thomas Lockhart," he says. "I don't have that many friends, but if I did they'd call me Tom."

"Hello, Tom."

They are at the house now and he opens the El Camino's passenger door for her to get in. She is wearing shorts and the sight of her legs is as disconcerting to him as the rest of her. Probably, he thinks, he has seen women more attractive than her in separate aspects, but none that he can remember all in one complete pleasing package as this Martha Jane DeMars. He is trying desperately to tell himself that he is twice her age but is having trouble staying aware of such trivial facts at this time. Anyway, he is fairly sure his brain and his ancient body will remind him of these hard truths later on, but at least for the moment he gives himself a pass. It's not like he is in the presence of a heavenly apparition as this too damn often in the continuing disappointments of his real life, so why waste it?

He wonders if she notices the complete and total disarray of the Camino's interior as they drive to Dewey's, deciding she would have to be Rayette Charles if she didn't, but that's the way it goes. First your money, then your clothes.

Dewey is sitting in his chair, certainly by this time of the day full of a goodly torrent of Mateus and nicely buzzed, regarding the summer day while he tosses peanuts to a small squirrel. The squirrel has a white tail and not much meat on its bones, and seems to be spending a lot of time studying Dewey before taking the next offered peanut.

"Got a new pal?" Tom asks.

"Apprentice," Dewey says. "In training."

Tom explains the flat tire problem to Dewey, and Dewey folds up his chair and carries it to the garage. In a minute he is following Tom and Martha Jane in his truck. When they arrive at the Camry he gets out and surveys the situation, then quickly goes to work jacking up the car and changing the tire.

The good thing about Dewey, Tom thinks, and the way his friend has always been, is that Dewey consistently accepts whatever the situation is and goes right ahead and deals with it without having to write a book about it. Take, for instance, what is happening today. Tom shows up with a beautiful young woman right out of the blue and Dewey says nothing about it, just picks out a tire that will fit and gets his keys and is ready to go. Tom remembers the days of his youth when he was crazed beyond recognition, when his every activity was studied by everyone in town and discussed until the cows came home, but he never had to worry about what Dewey was going to say or think about it. Let it be, Dewey would always say. In the end it all comes out in the wash.

Dewey finishes getting the tire changed and lets the car down from the jack. He declines any payment from Martha Jane DeMars, her being a first-time customer and all, and tells her not to worry, that Mr. Lockhart here will square everything when he comes by the garage to pick up the patched tire tomorrow. He starts the truck and drives off, a cloud of white smoke left in his wake, and Tom and Martha Jane are left alone.

"Well, that was easy," she says. "I'm not used to things being that uncomplicated. Here I was all prepared for the world to end and everything."

"Life should be simple all the time," he tells her, "but it always amazes me when it is." He is so brilliant and wise he can hardly stand it.

"Thank you so much for helping me."

He thinks this is probably going to be the end of it—and it should be, he reminds himself, because she is spring and he is getting to be the dead of winter—but he is surprised when she follows him home and instead of continuing up River Road turns into his driveway behind him.

"I have always wanted to see inside this house," she tells him. "I am not going to miss out on this opportunity. You have to invite me in, whether you like it or not."

He takes her on a tour, shows her the dowdy kitchen and the spartan living room with his possessions still in boxes and no pictures hanging on the walls, lets her peek into his makeshift study where there are no open books or piled-up manuscripts or a work-in-progress anywhere to be seen. He motions at the bedroom upstairs and tells her that's where he sleeps sometimes when he's not roaming around in the wee hours or out on the balcony counting shooting stars and wondering just exactly what it is that's out there in the shadows going bumpety-bump in the night. She climbs the stairs and takes a look around at the yard and the woods and the lines of tombstones scattered up the hill on the other side of the gate to River Grove.

"Wow," she says. "This is cool."

"Sometimes I sleep out here. I turn the radio on your station and it's nice and peaceful here under the stars."

"You're listening to Otto, then. Nobody works the overnight shift anymore."

"Who is Otto?"

"Otto is the automatic pilot. We plug him in on a feed from corporate, then we all go home for the night. Somebody comes in at five in the morn-ing and turns him off."

"Damn, and I thought I was out here among friends."

"Otto doesn't have much of a personality. He seldom says a word."

"I noticed that. But you do. I hear you doing the weather and describ-ing the lives of the composers."

"That's me."

She tells him how she's from Jonesborough, just this side of the end of the world, and how she went to UNC-Wilmington and got a degree in Education, but she started working on the college radio station there and went on to a Country station to read the news and a Classic Rock station as a morning co-host, but how what she really wanted to do was write children's and young adult books, and then she started having some problems back home in Jonesborough—I won't go into them, she said, I won't bore you with the sorry details—and so she'd come here to work at the NPR affili-ate and live with her aunt and try and write a manuscript or two. Nothing published yet, she says, but it's not for lack of trying.

When he tells her he's a writer too (he doesn't tell her how he's not truly a current writer but more of a has-been who in actuality probably ranks as a never was if one really gets down to it), she is impressed enough to ask what he has written and to look at his two forlorn works of ancient history and request to borrow them, and of course he says yes, even if it is not for artistic purposes he is lending them to her.

Are these love stories, she asks? And he tells her, in a sense, yes they are, but neither one ends happily. The characters are more screwed up in the end than when they started out.

He keeps expecting her to say she has to go, that she has to be somewhere in only a while, to meet someone, perhaps the man he saw her with before, but she continues to stay, to sit in the living room and thumb through his books or walk from room to room and upstairs to downstairs examining the layout of the house and what could be construed as his lifestyle. After a while he is not so paranoid about the way he keeps house or how he tends to store things away by simply dropping them on the first available surface, but he begins to talk to her and tell her stories of his time in Chattanooga as a teacher and his early days here in Rhodes before it became such a hotspot for Southern charm. He describes his curriculum back in the lost days of Covington, how he had become convinced he would stay there four years and then leave to write several Great American Novels and change the course of the world doing so. And get rich. How he had arrived all starry-eyed with lofty ideas and high-flying notions, and somehow, what with the Viet Nam war and the way the world seemed to frown on anybody like he was who spouted off about the government and the Conflict that was really a War and the way he'd had to sweat when the Draft Lottery got held on TV and wonder all the way through if his number was going to get drawn so that it and his life would have a heck of a good chance of being up. He talked some more about how he'd begun to change in almost every way from who he'd arrived on campus being, how it seemed he was a good guy up to a point for a while but how the time came when he would find himself doing all sorts of stuff he couldn't explain or comprehend how he could ever have done such awful things to begin with. I mean, he told her, who in the hell was I anyway?

I fell in love with this girl, he finds himself telling Martha Jane DeMars, and when she left me for some guy with money, well, that was when I got mean. That was when something turned in me and all at once I was at war with the universe. Everybody in the world on both sides. I didn't know who or what to drop my bombs on first.

And Martha Jane DeMars sat on his balcony with a bottle of water in her hand, watching him and listening while the sun went down over her shoulder. Her light brown hair glistening in the last-ditch rays, falling on her at such an angle it was to Thomas Lockhart like she was receiving the sole spotlight from the fading setting sun. An other-worldly light appearing in her eyes. Her voice singing like a melody from a place of enticing dreams. Something in her smile calling to him. Saying I am here before you, this is no dream. All he can do to not go to her now and take her to himself. Could be the wrong way to behave. Not what a man my age in my position should even be thinking about at a time like this.

Someone like her, he thinks. Looking for someone like this since forever. Maybe there had been one. Hard to remember, been so long. And here on this perhaps evening, maybe there is now.

Then it was like a dream when Martha Jane DeMars rose from her chair in the budding moonlight saying she had better be going now, that it was getting late and she had to be up early tomorrow for work, and taken a step and came into my arms, just like that. Kissing like I never thought we would. Feel her heart beating against me, hold on to her for the longest while because I don't want it to end, because all this magic had been so long ago and far away. Wondering about her, if she felt the same way too. And when I let her go it is like there is something in me that goes with her and never wants to be away from her again. Because who knows how long before this sort of something ever comes back? Who knows for sure if once something wonderful is gone if it ever does return?

He walks her to her car with the inflated borrowed tire and kisses her. She opens the door and sits fumbling with the seatbelt, and he can't stop from bending down and kissing her again. Lips sweet and hungry and why do they have to go? The door closes and the car starts. Moves backwards and she waves through the glass. Good night, she is saying. Read those lips he's just finished tasting. Silent in the night but the sweetest sound he's ever heard. Beats, he thinks, all those prior threats and name-calling.

All too soon she disappears from view, and were it not for the lingering remnant of her on his lips and the scent of her skin he could easily say he had been in a dream and all this magic had been nothing but his imagination. But he knows this is no conjured visitation from some fantasy, that what has transpired is as real as the darkness of the night around him, but it is still difficult for him to accept something so wonderful after growing accustomed to and living within the hard edges of the world for so long. He knows what to compare these feelings to in his own experience, but he dares not think of it now. He is afraid to let the memory come back. He is afraid to say the words out loud.

I should not have let a thing like this happen, he thinks. Nothing good will come of this.

And Guilt begins to speak to him, telling him how he has traveled roads such as this one before, and how he needs to think this through completely before he ups and does something stupid and dire, jumps in and ruins someone's existence for the sole reason he is looking for an answer somewhere. He thinks of Martha Jane DeMars and her kiss and knows what an addictive thing she could become to him, envisions what it would be like to be with such a woman in this his time of need, his fleeting self reaching out to her for peace and solace one last time before he departs the earth. The voice reminds him how a moment like this always seems to end with him, the way he always wants too much, the way he goes to any length to get it, the cruel person he has been since a November night in Covington thirty years ago. He sees Peterson in flames, hiding whatever prints he had perhaps left behind on the soul of Faith Mercer—Faith Mercer falling, jumping, who knows, descending towards the earth with maybe the thought of him being the last thing on her mind, or possibly she was thinking of someone else, some other faceless man who may or may not have been the father of the baby she may or may not have been carrying to her death—but in the end he is the one who must wonder if because of his actions Faith Mercer chose to be on the balcony of Peterson on a Thanksgiving Eve and jumped or fell, if it may have been his child inside her and it is his fault she hit the sidewalk and lived no more. It is all conjecture and surmise, theories and possibilities he or no one else will ever know. But there is always a reason for everything, and the reason for all this might just be him. He can never walk away from the thought thinking he is innocent, because whichever way it went down, he played a part in it. His fingerprints are always going to be there.

He is guilty of one huge sin that can't be turned around.

He took advantage of a human life because he knew he could, because he told himself to go on and do it to pay back heartless Fate for what It had done to him before.

For giving him the taste of Maribeth McAllister and then taking her away. For making him live with the fact he would never be with her for the longest part of forever. He had decided someone, somebody, everyone, would have to pay for the life he'd had to forfeit. And Faith Mercer was perhaps dead because of him, and maybe another life inside her too. He'd told himself then how enough was enough, was too much and never should have been allowed the chance to start, and how he'd have to spend the rest of his life atoning for his great sin some way, if only by staying distant and far and away from the smiles and laughter and sunshine of the real world around him, because he was the one with the curse, he was the one God would always find guilty. He is all the bad news in one volume. Maybe it was only hard luck and cruel fate and rotten circumstances that caused it all to happen, to come down around him and shower those who never deserved it to suffer because of him, by being around him, by coming into his arms in the black poison of the night wherein he spoke and breathed and drew prey in to himself.

It was his fault and he knew it. He had spent years now doing his best to not allow it to happen once more.

But now, here was Martha Jane DeMars, and it was as if he could see the sign upon her. Here she was. He would have to be careful or it would happen again.

SEVEN

Four days of stealth. Driving to work in the mornings not daring to turn on the radio. For fear of hearing her voice on the air. Giving the temperature or introducing a symphony. Because he knew if he heard her speak he would surely be lost.

On Friday afternoon closing the shop, the phone ringing. There is the first inclination to not answer, to lock the door and leave for the day. If it's that important whoever it is can call back tomorrow. Saturday being emergency day. Where somebody has to be desperate for a part to come in. But Tom answers anyway out of some sympathy for his fellow man. Who could be marooned somewhere with no chance of rescue, alone out in the windy-mean elements in the world dying despairingly-alone. Because he knows how it is. He's been there.

Martha Jane DeMars says his name. He knows her voice immediately, since she has been whispering in his brain in dreams at night.

"You haven't called. You said that you would."

"I thought perhaps I shouldn't. I thought you might just have been polite that night and I'd best leave you alone."

"Why would you think a thing like that? I don't kiss anyone just to be polite."

"I figured you could have been just humoring an old man because you're a nice person. There's in case you didn't notice something of an age difference between us, and I didn't want to come across as some old creeper putting a kind young lady on the spot. I'd rather not be thought of that way."

"I'm not that way, Tom Lockhart. I don't know where you got the idea I was."

"I sensed it. It's the way of the world. I was trying to give you plenty of backout room so you wouldn't think ill of me down the road."

"Lord, you really are a weirdo, aren't you? I don't know if I've ever run across anybody like you before. Most guys are too busy beating their own personal drum and trying to get their hands on you to waste any time worrying about how you're feeling about things."

He takes the Fifth and says nothing. Could throttle everything with an errant word.

"Well, now that I've shown my hand by calling you—since you've already admitted you weren't ever going to call me back—we're at least on speaking terms again, so the next question is are you busy this evening and would you like to meet me down at Thompson's for dinner and something to drink? We can talk and watch all the people watch us while they wonder why an old geezer like you is out with a spring chicken like me and if one or both of us is crazy or if you're rich and I'm a gold-digger or what exactly is going on between us."

Tom, despite sensing he is in a whole different ballgame with a bunch of unexplained rules and regulations he hasn't been versed on yet, this sort of transparency coming from the mouth of one so wondrous as Martha Jane DeMars is enough to get him to agree to about anything, especially sitting in soft light with music playing and blessed spirits trickling down his throat while gazing into the soft brown eyes of a woman the likes of whom he has given up hope of ever being near again. To talk. To gaze upon the female form while angels sing. To flirt. After so many years of being alone. How does he possibly say no?

Inside Thompson's with its dark-wood walls and music from another age coming forth from the speakers above his head. Tom often wonders why it is that what was popular thirty years past is what is being played these days, that people who weren't born when a tune was in its heyday would go about their lives having such an unfamiliar song being their soundtrack? He tries to think if this was so when he was young those ages ago, and doesn't think so. But it is hard to remember precisely the way things were from so many years back. One's memory tends to play tricks and sugarcoat.

Martha Jane DeMars with a glass of dark beer, makes a face when she takes the first sip. It always takes me a minute to get accustomed to the taste, she says, but always after that it's Katy bar the door. Tom a trifle surprised at the way the beer disappears from her glass; if he'd been asked beforehand, he would have pegged her as a tee-totaler. Perhaps a glass of wine here and there. Young and tender, good chance the ways of the wicked world haven't overtaken her yet. But never judge a book by its cover, he reminds himself as she tanks it down. She looks like she's been in taverns before.

Two Thompson Burgers quaffed. A basket of fries shared. Music from overhead falling like rain around the booth—Ronstadt, Doors, Beatles, Dylan reminding the room how everybody must get stoned. Eyes and ears lean forward and secrets are told, Martha Jane with the tale of leaving her boyfriend behind after four years of being together, really for no reason much at all, she says, only because I came to the conclusion he loved himself a lot more than he ever would me. A girl can tell such things sometimes. Tom careful divulging any more of his secrets, avoiding additional mentions of personal heartbreak and regret and dreams that got smashed. Avoiding Death altogether. To go unmentioned at all costs. Because one never really wants someone to know that maybe there's a killer sitting across the booth from them.

He does speak of Covington and how it was in those days when he still had ideas about how the future held great things in store, how there possibly was love around every corner and certainly out in the moonlight, and how hard it had been to learn that sometimes one is not allowed to see those visions all the way through to the end, that sometimes, despite all efforts and through no fault of one's own, the big bad world comes tumbling down.

And one has to run at full-speed to get out of the way. He supposes it is that way, he tells her, in just about everybody's life. Baby, the rain must fall, and all that jazz.

Over Martha Jane's shoulder he sees two women enter and take a table by the bar. He is sorry to see one of the women is good old Abigail, home, he guesses, from rehab, and footloose upon Rhodes once more. The question arises in his mind how it is that someone just returned from a period within a program to help one cope and solve an existing problem should choose on her return to frequent a place where a goodly portion of her problems have possibly been generated? But he decides this is none of his affair and it is best he stick to the business at hand, which is the all-revealing and fascinating conversation going on with Martha Jane DeMars across from him. He will let Abigail turn and twist in whatever winds she chooses to get blown by. She is, after all, a big girl who needs no guidance from him.

Abigail, of course, as he feared she would, sees him, which he chalks up as cruel fate and just his luck. She walks over with a sort of smile on her face, her red lips slightly parted and her black hair frizzed in a new style that makes her come across as close to wild, which is not a bad visual effect at all if one is a red-blooded male. She is wearing a royal blue dress that disguises none of her physical charms and leaves little to the imagination. This is not what he needs this moment. He has been down this sort of road too many times before. He knows how the avenue curves and gets bumpy when you don't expect it. One must endeavor to watch out.

"I thought I saw you hiding over here. For a minute I thought you were with one of my students, but it's dark in here and I was mistaken."

"Hello, Abigail. I see you're back from your banishment."

One eye blinks the slightest bit at this greeting, and he can tell she is momentarily searching for something clever to say back to him, but she is on the ropes from the remark and it takes a second to regain her footing, so she settles for a smile instead.

"Oh, did you miss me? I wasn't sure you knew I was out of town."

"Your brother told me. He came to visit me at work to see if I was running the company into bankruptcy or anything. Your whereabouts came up in the conversation."

Abigail is checking out Martha Jane all this time, who sits with her hands folded in her lap with a faintly puzzled look on her face, like she is perhaps wondering who this woman is who has interjected herself at their booth. Tom starts to explain to her what is going on, but since this is Abigail in their midst he is pretty certain he is not going to have much time for discussion on how far he and Abigail go back and express his own personal belief that she is bad news and big trouble no matter how enticing her personal package appears, and the best thing to do is be patient and maybe she will go away.

"You haven't introduced me to your friend," Abigail says.

"You're right. I haven't."

"I'm Abigail Lane," she says to Martha Jane. "I'm Tom's boss's sister. Tom and I are old friends. We've known each other since practically forever. Certainly," she adds, "since before you were born."

"Gee," Martha Jane smiles. "That's a long while."

"It is," Abigail says. "It means the two of us know each other up and down by now, which is why I'm surprised I've not heard tale of you before. Tom must have been hiding you from everybody all this time since he came back to town."

"Actually, we just met," Martha Jane says. "We've only known each other for about a week." She looks up at Abigail and smiles sweetly. "I hope that helps clarify things," she says.

Tom is expecting any moment for there to be a challenge issued and some version of a frontier catfight to ensue, but he is saved when a fellow from behind the bar arrives wanting to know if Tom and Martha Jane would like another pitcher of beer.

"You might want to check her identification before you bring anything alcoholic in content out," Abigail says. "There's a chance you might get busted for selling to a minor."

She turns and walks back to her table by the bar, as if she has just delivered a stunning riposte in a devastating fashion. She sits down with the woman she came in with, presumably to chat about careers and men and how sorry a town this truly is and how they should both consider pulling up stakes and getting out while they're still young.

"You don't have to worry," Tom says to the wait-dude. "Spiritually and morally she's at the head of the class. I'm the immature one around here."

Maybe the moon is full or there is something in the air, but within a minute a confrontation begins over by the bar. Voices get raised and Tom and Martha Jane turn to see Abigail fling a perfectly good frozen margarita in the face of a guy who in the dim light of the room looks a lot like Garland. The fact of the matter is this is indeed Garland with tequila dripping down his nose and cheeks and settling on his shirtfront, and Tom is almost entertained in a cruel sort of way to see him wiping his face before advancing toward Abigail in a menacing gait. This sort of scene is not exactly the way Tom wants to derive pleasure on a Friday night, and before he checks himself and comes to his senses he is on the way across the room to get between Garland and his doubled-up fist and Abigail with another tumbler of hooch preparing to toss the second of her Friday night Happy Hour Buy One Margarita, Get the Second One Free into Garland's face. He stands in the middle of this pairing with the two of them looking at him, and he gets the feeling both are presently trying to decide if it might be him instead of each other they would like to maim, bludgeon, or murder next.

"Whether you believe it or not," Abigail says, "I don't need your help right now."

"This is none of your goddamn business," Garland tells him. "Nobody rang your fucking bell for anything."

"That may be so," Tom says, "but somebody needs to play grownup around here. I'm a hell of a choice to be the one to do it, but here I am." He turns to Garland and holds up a hand, like he is a traffic cop and he's ordering a line of cars to stop. "Why don't you just back off and go home?" he suggests. "You can probably save yourself a lot of trouble if you choose to do so."

"Good luck trying to talk sense to him," Abigail says. "You can't tell this stupid bastard anything. I've already got a peace bond against him, and he still won't leave me alone."

"You," Garland says, "ought to be sitting in jail now. Tell everybody how you took a hammer and busted up my den with it, the television and a home entertainment system I paid a goddamn mint for."

He inches Abigail's way again and Tom sticks his palm into Garland's chest, stopping him in his tracks. He is not a big guy, but he is bigger than Garland, who is sort of sawed-off in a hulking and meaty way, like some bull in Madrid before they lead it into the ring to get taunted and teased and speared and stabbed. Tom keeps his hand stuck in Garland's chest until Garland finally swipes it away and takes a step back, and then the two stare at each other, Garland wondering just how far Tom is going to go with this knight in shining armor bullshit, and Tom wondering if at the ancient age of fifty-three he is going to have to battle some other guy over some woman, which is something he never did in high school and is something he wonders why he should have to engage in at this late date.

"Fuck this," Garland says. "And fuck you. None of this shit is worth it." He gives Tom another hard glare and turns for the door, takes a couple of steps and then stops and turns around again like he's having second thoughts, that maybe it might be worth it after all.

"You're right," Tom says. "It's not worth it."

They stare at each other another ten seconds, then Garland pushes out the door. Music is still playing and the Eagles are having peaceful easy feelings despite the uproar, while thirty customers in Thompson's watch the door close behind Garland, everybody looking at the door first and then at Tom and then over to Abigail to see what is going to happen next. The bartender and his staff lean on the bar as if fascinated by this presentation, and Tom is tempted to take a bow and raise his hands to acknowledge the applause soon to come his way.

"Thanks for nothing," Abigail tells him, gathering up her bag from the table. "I don't know how I would have ever made it without you."

"You're very welcome."

He watches her as she and her friend leave, halfway wanting to warn her how Garland might be outside waiting on her, but he doesn't. Screw this hero stuff for one night, he thinks.

He heads back to the booth and Martha Jane is standing beside it, her purse slung over her shoulder.

"Leaving so soon?" he asks.

"I think I may have gotten myself in the middle of something that's absolutely none of my business," she says. "I feel like a fifth wheel on a Ferrari."

"I apologize, Martha Jane. I'm not really a part of any of what was going on. I just happened to be here when it started."

"It kind of looked to me like you had one of the leading roles in the play. You certainly weren't a supporting actor."

"Sometimes things happen that are beyond one's control."

"I guess," she says. "Whatever."

She does not sit down again, but tells Tom how she has to be at work early in the morning (even though tomorrow is Saturday and she has told him that Otto works the weekend shifts) and how she has to go home. She doesn't stay out too late at night because her aunt stays up and worries about her until she comes in. It's been a nice evening, she tells him. I guess I'll be talking to you. Bye now.

When she's gone, he notices how there is still a fresh pitcher of beer remaining on the table. There is also a twenty-dollar bill face-up beside it, meaning that Martha Jane has paid her portion of tonight's bill along with the tip and then some. This halfway pisses him off, dominant proud male that he is, and he starts to go after her and stuff the bill into her hand, but right now, what with his adrenaline flowing strong from his standoff with Garland, and his anger at Abigail for showing her ass in front of Martha Jane, and Martha Jane herself for becoming snooty and unwilling to listen or make any attempt to understand what has gone on here, so he is simply all around hacked off at everything this minute, which includes the staff behind the bar and the populace of Rhodes and the masculine segment of town who all jointly need fat lips and kicked asses, and the women too, just because they are women and make him feel guilty about never living up to their expectations or him always doing something to ruin their lives, and he always comes back to being ticked at them in the end because they all have this way of stretching him out and making him wish he'd never come close to them or wasted his time dreaming how someday he might.

He is not, he decides firmly, going to waste a perfectly fine pitcher of draft. He sits down. He can drink beer and listen to music with the best of them.

He is a goddamn pro.

The audience's collective nerves traveling back from being on end. Barroom settling into conversation, laughter, and music again. Staff behind the bar eying Tom in a wary way, wondering if he is the next to cause trouble.

Don't have to worry about me, he thinks. Blessed am I the peacemaker, for I shall not suffer contusions.

I was a happy boy during Freshman Orientation Week. Felt I was on the right road at last. After a few missteps, dalliances, and errors. Left Rhodes with some ill will my way, male and female alike. None of them, it seemed, able to take a joke. Ha Ha. But I never wanted to hurt anyone's feelings or raise any ire. Misunderstood, I suppose. Thought it most natural to find dark roads and park. Sometimes it didn't even matter if I liked the girl or not. Nor whose girlfriend was whose. Not wanting anytime to be alone and I had so much to say and give. I remember a girl saying I only thought of myself. Which was an untruth and unfair. I was a kind and loving fellow. I saw no gain in keeping it all to myself.

Study this cellphone sitting on the tabletop. I could call her. Maybe she's home by now. Try and make her understand.

I gave up team sports early. Didn't want to block for anyone or pass a basketball to somebody else, because I knew I could run and score myself with no help required. Ran long distance instead. The longer the better. Mile, five miles, ten. And I always knew I could go further. Wasn't even interested in finishing first, because that way I was racing other people. Didn't want anything to do with them. Wanted it to be just me. A coach said I didn't seem interested in improving my time or learning proper techniques, and I said all I wanted to do was run. For as long as I could until I was far away and nobody was in sight. You've got this way, Lockhart, he said, of not trying to be a good teammate. Down the road you're going to find out that no one has things their way all the time. You'll never get anywhere until you learn to compromise. And I nodded my head in agreement so he'd think I was listening. All the while forgetting every word he said. Because no one could see I was off somewhere else and didn't mean anything bad about it. It was just the place I was going was where I needed to be and no one else could be there.

Pour another glass. Starting in on Martha Jane's portion now. Left her sad twenty on the table. Guess this is all on her. And if these bar people were worth the first damn somebody would be over here now with a frosty fresh mug.

I turned eighteen the first week at Covington and had all my clothes in one big suitcase and everything else in a trunk. My folks driving me there on a Saturday because Freshmen couldn't have cars on campus. A baseball game on the radio and a stopover at Krystal on the way. I had an assigned dorm room where I stashed my stuff and said goodbye. Couldn't get them to leave and get back to Rhodes without me fast enough. Which I've always regretted, because that day was the last time we were all together. But I had nothing to say even then. Anything we needed to talk about had already been said. As I had been in that long period of leaving for some time by then.

That first Saturday night alone, no roommate or much of anyone on campus yet. Dorms and halls and houses and buildings, gymnasium and an ancient rotting library. I walked up and down the grounds, trying to see where I fit, knowing there had to be some place for me. Studied doorways and windows and memorized them and waited while all of Covington wrapped around me in some form of welcome and recognition. To say hello. This is me. I have come looking and trying to find it. And on that night to walk down Rainbow Hills into the Saturday night town. McClellan. A movie house and two restaurants. Strip with a hardware store and a pet shop. Bookstore and a bank. Jewelry store with watches and rings. A pizza parlor. And I went into a bar. The Dixie Pub. Underage but I knew how to get around it. Acted like I was old. Miller High Life on the first try. Jukebox playing Ray Price. A football game on a TV above the bar. Heads raised watching. Roll Tide. I sat at the bar and watched for a while, drained my glass and pushed out into the street. Nobody my age anywhere. And looking in the closed bookstore window stood a woman. Green loose dress with sandals, hair in a ponytail, purse slung over her shoulder. Window full of bestsellers, none with my name on them yet. And I saw how it would be, some years from now, later, when this same woman would stand in that same spot and look in the window and see my name on a book. Author. And she would see me and know I was the guy. And say it's you. I've been wanting someday to meet you. Because what you write speaks to me. It's no wonder nobody reads anymore, she said to me, sudden-like, because when you want to buy a book you go to the store and they're always closed. It's like if you have a job and are working that by the time you get off the rest of the world is already at home eating dinner and you're out of luck. She was speaking to me and I stopped and listened because she was at a bookstore window and she was pretty like someone I'd seen in a movie. She was older than I was—everybody was older than me—and she smiled and said I don't generally just start talking to strangers on the street but it's been that kind of day. It's been that kind of week. Her eyes behind wire glasses I thought looked red from crying. But she kept smiling my way. I kicked my boyfriend out of my apartment because he was going to bed with my sister. Can you believe such a thing? She's seven years younger than me and in high school and he's my age and going behind my back. And I don't know how long it's been going on. And so I'm out just walking around because I didn't want to stay in all alone and let my mind run away with me. I didn't know what to do with myself tonight. I thought I'd buy a book or do something and get my mind off of it, but it isn't doing any good. I didn't know what to do and then here you came along and I just spoke to you out of the blue. That's probably a stupid thing to do, but I've done it and I can't take it back now. I was thinking about walking down to that place you just came out of and letting myself get picked up by somebody, but I chickened out. I don't like men that much. Some of them scare me. And I asked her if she wanted to take a walk with me. And she smiled and said yes. I guess you're a perfect stranger but you seem nice. Are you a student? I've been out of school three years now. I went to school in Louisville. I'm a teacher now. I teach Spanish. And we walked for a while. I told her how I'd taken Spanish two years back in Rhodes. And how I couldn't seem to get it. Had to butter up my teacher to get a passing grade. Asking about bullfights and carrying boxes of books out to her car. Sang "South of the Border" and smiled at her all the time and got a B. And she said how all the time she had students trying so hard to butter her up. Most of them boys and I don't know if it's a grade they're after or something else. You never know what somebody's thinking. And really I'm just out here not because I'm sad or anything but because I didn't want to think about any of it anymore, the mess I've made of my life. Living and sleeping with somebody I don't love just so I won't wake up alone or have to cook for myself. Which is stupid, don't you think? Because I'm happier sometimes when I'm by myself, away from everyone. Do you know what I mean? I said I did. I did it all the time. People get to me. And she said it's not that it's people, it's just some of them. Sometimes it's good to meet new people who aren't the same and think they know who you are and everything about you. Like you, she said. You don't act that way. If I was younger I'd love to be around you. And came near me on the sidewalk and hooked her arm through mine. Hello. I'll make a deal with you. You don't tell me your name and I won't tell you mine.

Lockhart on his feet and over to the bar. Pitcher empty. Like Sinatra says, one more for the road.

Sit down again. Look around and see how the room is thinning out, those folks still here engaging in words to woo and make promises. Made many of those in my time. Could make quite an extensive list of how many I've broken.

She had a car parked around the corner in a lot. Light blue Mustang, convertible top up. Somewhat battered and starting to rot. Rust here and there. We got in and she pulled out a joint. We smoked and kissed. You're so nice, she said, why do you have to be so young? Because I'm getting older every day and I can't stop thinking about it. And someday I'm going to blink and I'll be an old woman and I'll maybe still be looking for someone like you. Do you have a girlfriend? Because if you do, she's lucky. And I said no. And she said oh but you will. I can tell. I'm just so sorry I came along before you. Because in another world you and I could love each other like nobody's business. She told me how it hadn't been but a month since her father died and how she'd had to not be honest with him for a long time and not tell him about the man living with her because it would have upset him to know such a thing, to think that she would be sleeping with somebody who didn't deserve her or love her and was only there like all men are to have that part of her in the dark and not worry about what happened later when she wanted something else because they wouldn't be around by then to hear it. They'd be gone. And so my father died thinking all I did was teach school and come home late and was sacrificing my life for a bunch of wild teenagers. Hoping someday somebody nice and decent would come along and take me away from it, like I was some innocent little girl who the big bad world was trying to harm. And I sat there listening, the taste of her on my lips, and knew she would never be the girl her dead father had wanted her to be, and I wondered if anybody ever really became what people thought they ought to be, what they envisioned being themselves for the longest time of their lives.

Scoot this chair back and stand, pick up keys and phone and make my exit. One foot after another down the walk, across the street. Back to the Camino in the Piggly Wiggly lot. Closed now too. Maybe had too much to drink but I'm all right. Sometimes it brings me back from the dead. Pull down the tailgate and sit for a minute. Dial her number. Answer me, damn it. You can't just tell me what is in your heart and then leave me out here all alone. Because I may be old and on the brink but I am still a little boy. Who's sometimes lost with nowhere to go.

No answer.

All right, be like that. Don't answer. Hate to resort to drastic measures, but it appears a personal appearance is in the cards tonight. I'm a man who enters on cue.

Thomas Lockhart on his lonesome way up the road. The Camino growing smaller behind him, left parked for safety's sake. Hops and alcohol dancing in the old brain. He doesn't need the police chasing him down. Just simply hopes he is headed the right way. Martha Jane in residence with her aunt down some street on this north side of Rhodes. Grew up through here but a lot has changed since those days. Think to be somewhere but really be somewhere else. Hear a church bell tolling. Losing track if it's eleven or twelve chimes. Have to look at the phone to know if it's still today or tomorrow already.

Time goes so fast one can't keep track.

While one feels one has always been on some sort of journey looking somewhere for a woman.

On a December night, in the middle of finals, I walked Maribeth McAllister back to her dorm. It was late and supposedly the doors had been locked for an hour, but it was the end of the semester too, and the rules seemed not to apply anymore. Everyone leaving for the holidays the next day, if they hadn't gone already. The campus deserted with no cars much to be seen and no one in sight, so maybe the world had gone away or ended while we'd wandered off.

We had been at my place, making love the way we'd been doing all week long.

That was the first time she told me she was leaving. She wasn't going to come back. We were on the porch and I was asking what time she was leaving to go home the next day and how we'd have to call each other and make plans for after the holidays and next semester when she got back.

I won't be back, Tom, she told me. I can't. There's something that I haven't told you. I wanted to but I couldn't.

She was going home for the holidays to Montgomery, and she wasn't going to return for the spring semester because she was going to enroll somewhere closer to where she'd be living. Because I'm getting married, Tom. There's a man I never told you about. He's graduating next week from Auburn. We've been together three years and it's been bad between us for a while—he wanted me to quit school and come home, and I wanted to finish here, and we'd halfway broken everything off—and then you came along and I couldn't tell you no. I couldn't stay away from you. You charmed me off my feet and before I knew it I wasn't thinking straight. And when I did, when I knew I needed to not go flying out on a star with you, that was when I decided I had to go back and let you go. Because it's true. We could never make it together, Tom, you and I. You'd always be out there with your big dreams and plans and all those books you're going to write, and I'd be back here on Planet Earth with my feet on the ground watching you up in the sky with your wishes and starry notions, and we'd just keep getting farther and farther apart and I'd be so sad because I couldn't hold you and you'd be sad too because you couldn't take me with you, because we're both smart enough to know how things like they are with us together never last and never work out for the best.

How you have to do what's going to work in the end and not gamble your life away wishing on the moon.

Walking back to my apartment that cruel night. Unable to understand how a smile becomes something poisonous in one's heart. Deep cut that maybe never heals. And how you feel that abiding ache that won't depart and tell yourself how you have to do something to make it not hurt so much. Forget tears and heartache, because they won't help. When the blows come and one is going down. Only one thing to do. Call it an act of war and fight back. Make somebody pay the price you've paid. Only way to stay alive. Because once you're down sometimes you don't get up. Have to do something to let the damn universe know you're still alive and not expired for good. Get it fixed inside your soul how two can play in a game like this.

Maribeth McAllister, Faith Mercer, Covington College, McClellan. Abigail. Lots of lessons he needs not to forget.

But for this night, though, Martha Jane DeMars.

The old red blood flows through him.

Take a left off South Main and follow this avenue called Cut Rock. A little out of the old stomping grounds now. Two more rights to be near Auntie Em's house, or whatever name Martha Jane's aunt goes by. This street named Ruth and over there is one called Cathy. Whole sub-division of women's names. Barbara, Nicole, and Emily. Litany of some sub-contractor's former girlfriends. Turn right once more and this is Sherry. Can you come out tonight? Frankie Valli woman.

And one is so hopelessly lost, hooty and turned around, adrift in an unfamiliar hometown. Pull out the phone and dial for assistance.

"I should be sleeping right now," she says.

"First let me explain this strange night to you. Which I would love to do in person if I could find your damn house. It doesn't seem to be where I thought it was. It could be I'm lost. Down some dark street and dogs are barking. Do you hear? Afraid any minute they'll be after me."

"What do you mean you're lost? Where are you?"

"Somewhere in your neighborhood. Sherry Lane. Not to be confused with Penny. Walked all this way to make it right with you. Also to bring you back your damn twenty dollar bill. I agree I'm on the cusp of helplessness but I'm not yet destitute. Perhaps spiritually, but that's another story. Monetary issues not overwhelming yet."

"You walked here? At this time of night. You must be nuts, you know that? I can tell too you're under the influence. You've been drinking, haven't you?"

"That's why I'm hoofing it. Don't want any trouble tonight. But couldn't go home with you feeling ill toward me. Because I like you. And I want you to like me too."

"Now you're trying to butter me up. Guess what? It's working. Did you say you were on Sherry?"

"Yes."

He starts to sing a Four Seasons medley but doesn't. Screeching falsetto out here under the streetlights could draw attention.

"Start walking north and take the first right. That's Betsy. I'm the corner house. There's a porch with my car parked on the curb in front. I'll be the woman on the porch. Call me if you get lost again."

One foot in front of the other. Life peachy again. Pulse beating and blood racing and it feels like ages past when runner's high would set in. Where everything is working in sync and there is no pain around. Drift by these houses of porchlights and sleeping people. Hope they're all asleep. Would so hate some military-type to think I am the invading enemy and begin firing rounds my way. Too damn old to dive for cover or go darting and gallivanting down the road for safety. Anybody listening and watching out there. I come in peace.

Tom can see the top of Martha Jane's head above the railing of the porch, the light shimmering out his way in the moonlight. He ambles up the sidewalk, taking care to walk in a straight line and not go toppling over into the shrubbery. He tries to tell himself this is serious business he is getting ready to be engaged in, but in his mind he is now the Great Wallenda walking a wire across a canyon or between two skyscrapers. Must keep the feet balanced at all costs, else its oops and over the side and plummeting down toward death with the arrival time from the long fall tomorrow afternoon sometime. He orders himself to straighten up and engage in this important business of the heart, for this is the sort of thing one does not need to allow the attention span to stray or meander or arrive at unprepared, for romance and love will eat one alive if one is not alert and ready and prepared for just about anything.

"You don't look as bad as I thought you would," she says.

"I'm faking it."

He walks over to the porch swing where she is sitting, stands for a moment with arms raised in surrender, showing his hands to her so she will know he is not armed to the teeth and here to do her harm.

"I can't believe you walked all the way here," she says. "It must be three miles at least. I'm beginning to think you might not be quite right in the head."

"My feet are my friends. Anytime I'm confused or in grave peril I can always count on them for deliverance. Exits and entrances I'm pretty good at. Not so hot at standing still. Become too much of a target."

"Okay. Go ahead and tell me what that ruckus back at Thompson's was all about."

"My boss is Matt Lane, whom I've known since elementary school. Matt gave me a job when I came back for my brother's funeral, after I'd been in Chattanooga teaching for thirty years, where things over a matter of time managed to go completely to shit. You'll have to believe me when I say not all of it was my fault. Had a share in some of it, but wasn't totally guilty of anything worth getting exiled for. Been guilty of plenty in my life before, so I take complete blame for those moments of shame, but I had evil forces working against me in Chattanooga. Had to choo-choo right out of there."

"Go on," she says. She is smiling.

"Abigail—the woman with the foul mouth and the oh so bad manners—is Matt's little sister. For a long while Abigail has had some sort of strange design on me, wants to add my head to the wall in her trophy room, I guess, so that's all started up again with me back in town. It's not like there's any kind of commitment or covenant between us, since she's been married three times at last count. Heck, Martha Jane, she's just this rich woman who's had her way her entire life, and I guess I represent one of those few things she hasn't been able to trap, extinguish, and take to the taxidermist."

"Well, she's certainly enthusiastic," Martha Jane says. "I'll give her that."

"The guy starting all the trouble is the latest of her husbands. His name is Garland Williams, and from what I'm learning he's a big mover and shaker here in Rhodes. Got a law business and is on the city council. Has a big say in running the parks. Anyway, it seems Garland is not the least bit enthused about being the latest of Abigail's ex-husbands and is trying every trick in the book to get his licks in while the battle is going on in earnest. He's even taken it to the point where he wants to get me involved in all the drama, like he needs to challenge me to a duel for the hand of the fair maiden or some such crap as that. All I want is for the two of them to go off somewhere and give each other fat lips and black eyes until they're both completely satisfied and leave me out. I gave up junior high jazz like this forty years ago."

"Poor Thomas Lockhart. Such a burden he has to bear."

"Now that's not fair. I'm telling you the truth."

"I'm just kidding. God, where is your sense of humor? You have to admit this was a pretty strange scene I had to sit through tonight. I thought for a minute there I was going to end up on the evening news, like I had something to do with a deadly triangle gone wrong down at a smoky bar. I have to admit I was almost ready to start laughing right in the middle of it. You were so ferocious. See, I'm not totally innocent. I've been in the middle of stuff like this before too. You should have got a load of my former boyfriend back in Jonesborough. Talk about craziness and drama. Shoot, I could write a book about things like that."

"Somebody already has. Thousands upon thousands, editions of discord and strife and marital woes. Millions of copies sold."

"Why don't you sit down? I do forgive you, you know. I wouldn't be out here losing sleep talking to you if I didn't."

"I haven't done anything to be forgiven for. Not tonight, at least. Maybe some other time, but not tonight."

"Keep telling me how innocent you are. Maybe someday I'll believe it."

He finds himself dangerously close to her in the shadows of the porch and the night, and so he goes ahead and kisses her because he knows it's a crime if he doesn't. Martha Jane is a good kisser and he is glad he has surrendered and done such a thing he's told himself he shouldn't do a million times before. Her arms wrap around his neck and he pulls her as close as he can without going through her and they rock back and forth in the swing and kiss and he tells himself to remember every instant of this for later because he may need it at some point in the future when he is dying. He attempts to hear the katydids singing and the tree frogs croaking and the traffic going by on South Main miles away, but dares not open his eyes because he may discover he is not really here in this place with this magical woman at his advanced age and state of mind where he has convinced himself a night and a woman like this would never come his way again, what with youth and life being behind him by now, and what with men his age not being allowed to have times like this at this stage of their time on the planet, and he is afraid he will find all this is a dream and not really happening, that a moment like this is nothing but a fantasy and will fade as fast as it came and leave nothing of itself behind to behold later, when it is dark and cold and one is absolutely and completely alone.

Even in his clockwork mind, where he has always been aware of the passage of time and the dissolvement of dreams, he does not know how much time has gone by since he has taken Martha Jane DeMars into his arms. He does not want to know, either, nor does he want this to end anytime. But soon she leans away from him and smiles, says boy oh boy oh boy to him, and sits back against the swing and exhales a sigh out into the night air. "Whoa," she says, "we've got to slow down a little here. You're getting me all worked up. I'm not used to feelings like this coming at me from out of the blue. Maybe I can handle you and maybe I can handle the moonlight on a summer night, but I don't think I can do so good a job when the two get mixed together."

"So you're telling me that when the sun comes up tomorrow you're not going to feel so affectionate anymore?"

"I may be worse. I think you may be too much just all by your lonesome." She kisses him quickly, then pushes herself away. "I've got to get to bed. I have to be at the station tomorrow morning. It's my turn to check on Otto and make sure he's still on the job."

"Otto can wait."

They kiss again, this time not a snippet but a symphony of duration. They're both breathing heavily when they come up for air, and Tom knows he needs to hit the road before he arrives at that place where he can't come back. Seems like a stupid idea, but there is this need to be a gentleman. To say goodbye and go home.

"You need to go to bed. We can see each other tomorrow."

"Let me go inside and get my keys," she says. "I'll give you a ride home."

"No, go to bed. I'll walk. Believe me, I need the air."

"Are you sure? I'll worry about you. It's so far and it's late."

"I'll be fine."

He leaves her behind to watch him go, then he's back in step and deep into the dark of the night again.

EIGHT

Indian Summer comes quickly, stunning and gorgeous in its golds and greens and reds and wondrous shades, so much that it seems it will never end, that this time there will be no dull-brown colorless fall trooping in from the bleak beyond taking away the blue skies of the day and the sharp stars of night, the moon that rises in the heavens by late afternoon and watches over Thomas Lockhart during the darkness and the festivals and parks and downtown Rhodes, where he walks with Martha Jane DeMars wondering if this is indeed that thing called love he is seeing so close to him these days.

Not only seeing, but touching too. And tasting.

It has been six weeks, and it is all he can do not to say the thing out loud. But it is always on his mind and on the tip of his tongue and he doesn't know how long he can let it stay silent, even with the fear of jinxing himself and messing everything up. Because he knows how the world is. He knows how it can be. He is nobody's fool when it comes to things like that.

But it was true and he knew it. He might not broadcast it shouting it out from the highest hill, telling the goddamn daffodils, but he knows it for a fact anyway.

Martha Jane DeMars was in love with him. It was true. There isn't any doubt in his mind, and he, Tom Lockhart, is a lucky so-and-so.

He'd known it from the night he'd walked home from her aunt's house, miles of pavement in the midnight hour, under the moon and stars, wondering if the old monster was about to emerge from within him and if he was going to turn around and go back to where Martha Jane was sleeping and screw everything up somehow, do something to destroy the wonder the night had brought his way. Because it was his way to do such things. He'd learned it a long while back. All he had to do was examine the descent of Faith Mercer on a Thanksgiving Eve, and he could be assured that he was the cause of not only that event but others too. All for revenge. All to close a wound that would not heal by trying to transfer it to some other person, to get it away for good, because that was the way it was, that was the way it came to you and that was the way you gave it back.

But this time it was different. He could see it and read it. He wasn't entirely blind and stupid. Martha Jane DeMars was in love with him, and god have mercy and don't tell anyone, but he was in love with her too.

And for these six weeks it had been just that way. He had gone to work and waited for the hour when he could lock the door, and then he would drive to pick her up and go somewhere for dinner, sometimes downtown in Rhodes or perhaps up or down different highways to neighboring towns to out-of-the-way restaurants, or maybe to a movie or a store or an outdoor concert, but mainly to places where they could talk and be alone together, where Martha Jane could tell him of her day at the station or what she'd planted at River Grove or if she'd managed to make any progress on her children's book, her manuscript, and wonder of him also if he had perhaps managed to write even a single word (he hadn't) on his forthcoming novel or what he'd done all day before he came to her, and laugh as she did at his stories of high school days there in Rhodes and how he ran long distance back then, and his teaching days in Chattanooga and all the fun he'd had for so many years until he retired (cough, cough), and how, she sometimes wondered of him, it was that he never spoke of his college days at Covington but only smiled and said it was a time where he learned a lot about life but truly didn't like thinking about too often now, because those were not his best days back then, and he didn't like to dwell on the negative side of his life too much, because it made him think of things he'd done and said that he never should have allowed himself to do, and this was now and that was then, and no matter how he thought about it or regretted a large part of it there was no way to ever take it back, so the less said or meditated upon it the better it would be in his own heart, even if he could never completely let the bad parts go. They stopped off at Dewey's house one particular starry Friday night to find Dewey's lawn chair vacant. There were boxes piled up and items scattered about, and Dewey and his squirrel Leopold saw them come in and asked if they wanted to take a look around and see if there was something sitting in the floor or stored in any of the stacked boxes they believed they could not live without.

"Having me a yard sale, folks," he told them. "I'm selling out and getting rid of all this junk. Putting a sign in the yard and leaving town—on a jet plane like Mary Travers sang of if the fare is decent—and getting out of Dodge. To put it in layman's terms, everything must go."

"You're moving? When did this come about? First I heard of it."

"I've been thinking about it a while, Tom. I've been sitting up here like the fool on the hill for a quarter of a century with a bunch of junked and soon-to-be obsolete cars surrounding me, drinking wine and reading James Joyce, and I've finally arrived at the conviction that this is not where it's at. This is not where I want to wake up dead one morning. I guess the final straw came when poor Phyllis threw a seven with the coyotes. I haven't been the same since. It's like that incident tore out any resolve I had to keep making my stand here. I tried sucking it up and training Leopold here, but, man, it's just not the same. Something's missing. It even came to me that I didn't even shoot the right coyote that night on your balcony, and that the real coyote responsible for Phyllis' mauling is still running around out there and will one night make his way back here again, and who's to say the same fate may await Leopold? It's like life is one mean and vicious cycle, and if I don't get out now I'm going to experience the same bad bullshit all over again. So tomorrow I'm transporting Leopold off to the park, and next I'm putting the house up for sale, and then I'm leaving. I've had enough of Rhodes for one lifetime. Hopefully, there's no such thing as reincarnation and I end up back here again."

"Where in the name of god are you planning to go?"

Dewey smiles and his eyes narrow in a conspiratorial way.

"I'm thinking Ireland, buddy boy. Home of James Joyce. Already have my visa and passport. Once I get there, they'll never get me back on the plane. My grandmother came from Belfast, so I'm entitled to take up residency. Find me a cottage with a thatched roof and a woman that looks like Maureen O'Hara and I'll be set. Can you dig such a scene?"

Tom smiles and shakes his head because he knows there's something else behind all this. You don't leave the country over the death of a squirrel. He holds Martha Jane's hand because this is so weird to him.

"I can dig it if you can, Dewey."

"Do you still have a turntable?" Dewey wonders. "I'll donate all my LPs to you as a parting gift."

Coming to the house of stone and perhaps the appearance of the odd ghost, the stars above twinkling diamond-bright. His first time to be alone here with Martha Jane like this. Tom keeping his distance so the sad sorrowful poison he carries has no chance to ruin things. But Martha Jane is not to be told no this night. Into his arms almost instantly amid the moon and the heavens and the wild beasts looking on from the woods and thickets. Her eyes saying stop hiding from me. Keeping away. And Thomas Lockhart at last gives up. To think maybe this is meant to be after all. To think maybe after all this is love. That he's been telling himself for so very long was gone from him forever.

If, truly, it was ever there in the first place.

Martha Jane with her brown eyes so tender asking why it is, Tom Lockhart, you always try to run away? Has love scarred you so badly before? Because you can't just let the bad things win. Love comes at you all scatter-shot, from every direction and angle, and you have to do your best to not let it blindside you. Because even if it does hurt so bad that first time it doesn't mean it will be that way forever. And Tom smiling saying that it wasn't so much a case of him not being able to take a punch, it was just having his soul stomped on while it was trying to get back up that bothered him the most. And she said I can never tell if you are joking or not. Because it appears to me that you would always be the one doing the stomping. Cautious and careful as you are. Nobody could ever sneak up on you and hang you out to dry. And Tom says, ha. Look what you've done. Taking an old man like me for quite a spin. Round and round and down and out, falling and falling and wondering when I'll ever hit the ground.

I don't think you're very old at all, she said. I think you're just the right age for me.

"I don't know what I'm going to tell my aunt," she said. It was the next morning, and she had to go home. "She's going to know I never came in last night. She's going to know I spent the night with you."

"Tell her you had another flat tire."

"I could tell her I'm a big girl now."

"I noticed that."

A Saturday morning. Tom at work by eight, right on time. Hard to concentrate on this job after such a night before. He is supposed to walk around in the storeroom with a hand-held wand and scan the tags that are empty or low so that new product will arrive in the coming week, but his mind drifts so he sometimes scans spaces two or three times without remembering what he's already done. Sometimes he forgets to scan at all and has to try and remember what he has missed. The bottom line is he is basically worthless this morning. His mind does not care for manifolds or radiators, tail pipes or wiper blades. All he wants to concentrate on is the memory of wondrous Martha Jane and their blessed night together. All the rest can go blast off to another planet.

He has been going through the motions when the phone rings.

"I was wondering about you."

It is Matt calling early on a Saturday morning, which sounds a dull alarm in the back of Tom's head, because Matt never calls, and especially on a Saturday morning. The air raid sirens begin firing up in his mind, making that starting-up moaning sound like somebody has just broken the glass and pulled the lever.

"I wanted to let you know," Matt says, "there's been some trouble. Abigail and Garland got into a bad fight last night. Garland came all the way out here and drove his truck right up to Abigail's front door. Both of them had been drinking and shit just escalated. They started arguing and a lot of it was about you. Garland told her to stay away from you or he'd fix it where she wished she had. He had a gun and was waving it around, saying he was going to shoot you the first chance he got, then come back and put a hole in her too. There he was, peace bond and all that crap. I don't know what he was thinking—if the son of a bitch was thinking at all. He kept threatening her and you and finally Abigail just pulled out her own gun and shot him right there on the spot."

"Good god," Tom says.

"I don't know if he's going to make it or not. He's in intensive care over in Athens right now. He's still alive, but it's touch and go. The police have been here all night and this morning too. They may want to talk to you before this is all through."

"What about Abigail?"

"She's sleeping right now. Sedated. Gave her statement to the police and they haven't decided if there will be any charges yet. They know about the peace bond and how he was out here on private property, so I don't think it will go any further. But I thought you ought to know what happened. I'm afraid you might get involved in this. It's none of your fault, I know that, but you're still kind of in the middle of it."

Matt hangs up and Tom gets busy powering down the computer and turning off the lights. Fuck this, he thinks.

Damned if I'm going to be here finding somebody a hose to fit their Bronco while the cops are on their way over to grill me about my part in this week's domestic strife headline story. I already know this plot. I'm a writer, whether I act like it or not. Local lawyer/councilman and estranged wife drawn into conflict because of stranger in town driving wedges between them while they're trying to reconcile. Outsider in town behind all of this since everything was peaceful until he showed up. Troublemaker from way back. Shake the head back and forth. Oh no, no, no. Find another boy, folks. Been working and guarding the cemetery and getting astounded by the appearance of romance in this desultory world. Do not need this version of crap getting flung my way through no fault of my own.

He drives home and takes a seat on the porch to see what happens. After a while his stomach begins growling, so he grabs his keys and heads to Dewey's to see how the yard sale is coming along. He thinks he might go inside and raid Dewey's refrigerator for leftovers. Dewey has always been one hell of a cook with a good spread on the table most nights, and the old saying is you can't take it with you. Perhaps he can do Dewey a favor and eat up what is in the icebox so Dewey won't have to worry about it. Anyway, he'll at least be in a strange place hiding out, where he can see the SWAT team go by on their way to his residence to either beat him senseless and take him in for questioning or tote him away in a body bag because he resisted arrest.

There's a good-sized crowd at Dewey's, cars parked along River Road and in the drive and pulled in on the grass on the hill. Most of the throng seem to be of the WASP male variety, come in their Silverados and Rangers and Rams to see what loose auto parts they might haul away, what restorable hunks of metal they can hook up to their trailers and take home to stow in their yards and garages. Bubbaettes congregate inside the garage tables laden with glassware and cooking utensils, ancient stereo equipment and aged boomboxes. Tom even spies Leopold the apprentice squirrel dashing and darting around feet and ankles, trained already in the art of knowing how to procure comfort and food scraps from upright beings. He is a fast learner and Dewey is a good teacher.

Dewey is fascinated by Tom's tale of gunfire and violence overnight at the Lane Manor. Maybe, he tells Tom, I should re-consider leaving town. I didn't think the people around here had enough passion to kill each other.

"Not everybody is as vibrant and full of life as you are," Tom tells him.

He sticks around a couple of hours, watching Dewey sell off his possessions while polishing off a plate of grilled chicken tenders from the far recesses of the refrigerator. He has no idea how long the chicken has been pushed back behind the eggs and the two family-size bottles of Mateus, but it tastes so good he believes it will be worth a case of botulism later. While he eats he keeps his eye on River Road down the hill, watching to see when the authorities might be making their way to his house to carry him off to Golgotha.

He checks his phone for more information, but other than a small mention on one of the local news sites there is no further mention of Garland and Abigail and the life and death situation Matt has described to him this morning. With no police on River Road and no more messages from Matt he is prone to believe he might be safe for the night.

He calls Martha Jane to fill her in on the situation, but she already knows. She knows, it turns out, much more about it than he does.

"This is one scary story," she says, "and there you were that night right in the middle of those two. You could have been killed, Tom, just like that. Murdered. You have to think about these things. This may be the small town you grew up in a long time ago, but the world has slipped in and brought a lot of what's bad out there with it. People kill each other all the time these days and never think the first thing about it."

"Maybe it's not as bad as what's been reported," he ventures. "Maybe Matt was exaggerating a little."

"The man died, Tom. That makes it pretty bad."

"God, really? I didn't know that."

"He died about an hour ago."

"I'd better try and get in touch with Matt. I'll call you back."

He doesn't want to get any closer to this situation than he already is, but he calls Matt anyway. When there is no answer, he leaves a message asking Matt to call him back, that he needs to know which way to go on all this. Does he play dumb, or what?

It is sunset and Dewey's yard sale is winding up. The backyard looks almost naked in the setting sun, no rusted cars with their metal glinting in the dying rays, the tables in the garage stripped and empty save for a coffee cup here and a saucer there. Dewey extracts a wad of bills from his overalls pocket and begins sorting them out on the table in stacks, hundreds and fifties and twenties, tens, fives, and ones, a few folded checks—only from people I know, he tells Tom, I wouldn't trust most of these folks as far as I could throw them—and the pile grows high to where Tom hopes an unexpected gusty storm doesn't come up any time soon and blow it away, because it would be quite a loss of funds if that was to happen.

"Garland is dead, huh? Man, that's weird to think about. That son of a bitch has been around Rhodes almost as long as I have. It's hard to imagine this town without that asshole being in the middle of everything doing his best to make it more of a shithole than it is already." He looks at Tom and grins. "Boy, you come back to town and all sorts of shit starts hitting the fan."

"It's a talent I have," Tom says.

They share a joint and sit among the wreckage and debris of the sale, listening to the classical music coming from the console that nobody bought during the sale. Dewey talks about putting the house on the market on Monday and how much he is going to ask for it, and mentions he might ask Linda to be his real estate agent, even if it may cause some discord and make Doug jealous as hell all over again.

"What the hell," Dewey says. "I'm leaving for far-off lands anyway. I don't have to worry about keeping the damn peace anymore."

After another hour of seeing no police cars travel down River Road and listening to classical music that reminds him of Martha Jane DeMars and more specifically Martha Jane DeMars' body as it was against him not so very long ago, Tom says good night and drives home. By the time he arrives his phone lights up and it is Matt calling him back. He is almost sick of thinking about Abigail and Garland and how he is involved in anything awful like this is, but he thinks of how Garland is dead and it might be smart to garner as much information as he can about it before the vice squad pounds on his door and starts asking a bunch of questions he doesn't know how to answer.

"I haven't heard from anybody," Tom says. "I'm not real sure what to expect."

"Don't worry. It's all under control now."

"Let me get on board with you. Garland is deader than Abraham, Martin, and John, and you're saying everything is jake. A while ago you were giving me the heads-up that the cops were on their way to either bust me or run me out of town on a rail, so I don't get it. How does the fact that Garland's dead make everything better?"

"The police have been here talking to Abigail and have pretty much cleared her of any kind of crime. Self-defense, Tom, is what they've settled on. Garland was on private property with a firearm making threats, and they've decided Abigail was justified in protecting herself. They're closing the investigation except for all the paperwork. I'd be surprised if they even talk to you. I think you're in the clear, so you can rest easy."

"Yeah, that's what they told Custer at Little Big Horn."

"Well, that was Little Big Horn, and this is Rhodes. There's a difference."

Something in Matt's tone and choice of words reminds Tom of a long-ago event, an incident back in high school where there was a cheating ring going on in a Latin class. There were rumors of people getting caught and suspended from school, thrown off the football teams and cheerleading squads, but Matt told everyone all was cool then too, and there was something in the way he said it that inferred that somebody who was larger and more in power than the teacher making the accusations would turn this tumult into nothing but a pleasant little zephyr, which is exactly what happened. Nobody left the football team. The cheerleading squad remained intact. The teacher resigned her position.

"What about Abigail?"

"She's a little shook up," Matt says, "as you can well imagine, but she'll be all right. I think she might leave town for a while and get herself collected again, maybe let all this blow over. You might consider keeping a low profile for a bit too."

"A mole sticks his head out more than I do. I get any lower profile-wise and I'll be in China."

When he hangs up he wants to immediately call Martha Jane and tell her the latest, but he decides to let it ride and wait and call her in the morning. For some strange reason he does not want to go to his beloved balcony this night, not to meditate, not to listen to music, not to stargaze or listen to the barking of foxes or the howling of coyotes. He walks into the room where the desktop sits in its dormant state. He studies the pile of handwritten notes strewn on the table beside it, possible plots and would-be settings and evolving characters, and a gloom settles over him because of his emptiness and lack of anything to say. He has been waiting how many years—fifteen? twenty? —for the words to come to him the right way, but he is more void now than ever. He would have thought that with the arrival of Martha Jane DeMars and her promise of a long-awaited spring he might be bursting forth with verbiage and inspiration now, but that is not the case. He recognizes his ancient defenses in play again, that armor that has told him through his lifetime that some dark day he will have to pay the price for the terrible wrong he has done to the world. Proven or not, he thinks of the death of Faith Mercer and the perhaps-child inside her, that it may have never been said or a finger pointed his way, but the cause of that fall was always on his head, whether he was the only one in the world thinking that way or not. He knew what he and Faith had done in his bedroom. He didn't know if he was the only one she had done such a thing with, but he knew he was there and what had been in his heart when he did it. He was guilty of something; he just couldn't say exactly what or how much. He also wasn't stupid. He knew how things worked, how the forces and fates got together and collaborated and made sure no stones were ever left unturned. He knew the judgment was that he had not paid his total debt to the world yet. There was more sadness and loss waiting for him, and it would reveal itself to him in its own time. He thought of how Martha Jane had come to him as if out of a dream, and he wondered if her appearance and presence was a preamble to the penalty headed his way. He had spent a long time wondering when his payment would come due, and maybe this was it. He did, it was true, have a hard time believing that something this good was only a disguised comeuppance beckoning him in for a closer look.

And it wasn't just Faith Mercer he owed payment for. There were others, faces and names he'd thrown away and forgotten, but he knew they were out there and he knew what he'd done to them in their lives and their hearts, and he knew he would have to answer for all that too. He had known all these things for years. Perhaps that is why he has been brought back to Rhodes at this point, under all these circumstances that have enveloped his nights and days. It could be that the gods have chosen this town from his past as a reckoning point for his just rewards, for him to see the totality of his existence from start to finish before it is taken from him. He has carried his curse with him in strange lands and different places over the years, and now he is on familiar ground to have it set down before him again, the charges completely leveled, the verdict brought forth in his home where it all began.

There comes over him in a sort of flash moment how the life he'd wanted had never accompanied him on his journeys. He had attempted to summon the music and the magic of his being when he came to Covington in that summer before his freshman year, and he remembers seeing something of it there at first, from time to time, but knowing almost from the start that a part of him was gone already, and knowing too in his self that it would never be back or return in its entirety. There were parts of him, sure, something here, something there of who he was, but the whole of it would not come his way again. He had been so young then, and innocent, that he had not thought to mourn such a passing. He took it as a belief that this parting with who he wanted to be and this meeting of who he would become was one of those things that everyone goes through, he was not any different from all who had come and gone before him, and so he would just have to learn to adjust to his new environment, his new beliefs, the new person he was soon to become. It was only a metamorphosis he was undergoing. He was not the first guy to go through such a thing, and he would certainly not be the last. This was the way the world was, and it was time for him to get down to learning it.

What he did not know was how things came along and it was like they were happening to someone else, but it was you who ended up being in the middle of it, and it would take quite a long time before you realized you had been the one to do what you had done.

It was the way life came and went all in the blinking of an eye, and it had taken him a long time to learn such a thing.

NINE

Colors of the day sharp. Night skies breathtakingly clear. The time to travel to Montgomery for Mitchell's wedding simply pops up all at once on the calendar. Thomas Lockhart begins thinking about the trip on the first day of October, and by the time a week has passed he has developed a full-blown case in his head to use as an excuse for not attending. One, he sees not much of a reason to begin acting like he is some engaged and loving father, which he isn't, or put on any kind of show to a bunch of strangers he will never see again that he has done his best to bring his son up in a wholesome and godly manner, which he hasn't done that either. He is not in the least interested in being present at any function like a rehearsal or a dinner or a ceremony or a reception where he is in the same city as ex-wife Lynda, much less at close quarters. He even has to consider renting an automobile for the trip, since he has his doubts on the El Camino's ability to withstand a lengthy road trip, three hundred miles as it is to Montgomery. He can come up with all kinds of reasons to cancel the trip, not to mention the underlying question of whether he is or is not the father of the groom. So, he could argue, exactly what is the point?

But the real reason is he doesn't want to leave Martha Jane. He finds himself strangely dependent on her these days and has not the inclination he has always had in his life before to take off for parts unknown and leave without a word of goodbye. This sort of behavior is not in the works this go-around, and he knows there is a lot more in play here than at any previous point in his life. He does not want to go anywhere without her. He has even done the unthinkable and asked her to go with him, to face his ex-wife and possible son with her by his side, but Martha Jane will have none of it. I haven't figured out what kind of journey you and I are on together just yet, much less add in an ex-wife to go with a son I don't know and a whole entire crowd of absolute strangers to the equation, she says. I'm still coming to grips with a murderous woman with a gun and a dead husband with a big funeral to show for it. I may need some time to catch my breath and do some thinking, Tom. You go ahead and do what you have to do with this wedding, and while you're gone I'll go home and visit my father. He's not in the greatest of shape, so this seems like the perfect time. I'll go home for a few days, and when this is over we can meet back here and exchange notes. It might do us good to get off the whirligig for a while. I don't know about you, but I'm really dizzy. You make me light in the head, Mister. Too much more and I'm going to fall over.

Early Friday with the sun not yet making an appearance, still an hour away as Tom throws a bag on the front seat of the Camino and winds up River Road toward the interstate. If he has no major problems along the way he will arrive in Montgomery by lunch, in time to find a motel room and take a shower before hunting down the church where the rehearsal is to be held. After that is the reception, and he has a sport coat for tonight and a suit for tomorrow, a couple of new dress shirts, two ties, and black dress shoes he hopes won't bite his toes too much. He has done his best not to dwell on this weekend, since he has not for a while or even ever been much of a family man, but he is determined to fulfill some form of position as a father, if only for the image it might present to Mitchell's future in-laws. Might as well, he concedes, give the kid a fighting chance against what appears to be a stacked deck he's heading into, because from every indication Tom has seen Rebecca's family is loaded.

As in filthy.

As he leaves the city limits, he searches his innards to see if he is experiencing any sentiment for leaving the old hometown on this early morning, for departing from home sweet home for a few days, but he is not surprised to find anything of the sort dwelling within him. Perhaps it is all the Abigail business and Garland in his plot out at River Grove, a lot of things happening in the blink of an eye that keep him detached. From his porch he watched the hearse and a long procession of vehicles go by with Garland to his gravesite. He was there to see it, but Abigail was nowhere to be seen. Spirited away to a nice antiseptic location where the rich always seem to land. This is all as he has believed it is and is always going to be. He feels not much because this is not his town anymore. It is the place of his birth and he resides here again, but there is a difference. Rhodes is another city on the map, and he has come back to it as a stranger, and a stranger is what he will always be, a stranger that Rhodes and some of its citizens are beginning to have second thoughts about.

By nine he is well into his trip. The Camino, surprisingly, is running like a champ, and he is sorry he has doubted it, because, he thinks, I have no faith anymore, not in people, not with any mechanical object, not anything new or old or yet to come. I am always going to regard what is behind me and what is ahead as something possibly dangerous, something unreliable and untrustworthy that could slip into deceit and treachery in the blink of an eye. He can trace backwards to why he has come to feel this way, but what he doesn't know is if he will ever be free of it, even with this new life he's living, even with Martha Jane DeMars, this woman he regards as one who can't possibly be real and must be an illusion he has lately embraced, all this because it is ingrained in him that once one is cursed, once a man has allowed himself to slip into the darkness of his black soul and made no plans for an escape, that man will remain in a world without light for eternity. That is the law as he has always known it, and it is hard to tell himself anything different these days, no matter how dream-like and magical new images before him appear.

He stops at a drive-thru for a sausage and biscuit and a cup of coffee, unwilling to go inside even to use the restroom because he fears the Camino, after running so smoothly the first leg of the trip, will not start again when he comes out and will leave him in one hell of a state. He motors on, watching the temperature gauge and the oil pressure for omens of disaster, wondering if he can make it all the way to Montgomery on one tank of gas.

Soon, when he is at last convinced the Camino is not going to rise up against him and the interstate is not going to send a convocation of evil motorists, potholes, bumps or mad truckers to destroy him, when he is assured finally that he is as inconsequential as every other driver on the road in their metal compartments heading god knows where for god knows what, he relaxes some and listens to the muffled wind outside his window, reads the signs advertising restaurants and hotels and food, computes the distances from Montgomery on the mile markers and formulates an estimated time of arrival, and when his phone rings in the seat beside him he does not answer. Nor does he turn on the radio for the sound of a familiar tune. Whoever it is on the phone he can talk to after he arrives. Whatever song is playing he already knows he doesn't want to hear, for voices and music harbor thoughts and memories, both of which he is going to get a snoot full of starting tonight. Everything can wait until then. There is no need to rush anything.

All goes precisely as he has planned, and he is safely stowed in his motel room at three in the afternoon. The two phone calls he has received are from Mitchell, wondering if he was indeed on his way and coming to the bevy of ceremonies, and Martha Jane, who is on her way to Jonesborough this afternoon after she finishes her Friday morning show. He calls Mitchell back and tells him he is in town and where he is staying and finds out where

he is supposed to be for the rehearsal at six, and then calls Martha Jane and
gets no answer. Her phone is probably silenced from being in the studio at
work, and he thinks how sometimes she goes a day or two before she remembers to turn the ringer back on. I'm so absent-minded, she says, but he
wonders if she is like him and enjoys taking a welcome break from talking
to the world from time to time.

After a short nap that threatens to evolve into a coma, he showers and
begins fitting himself inside formal clothing. He opts for a shirt with no tie,
slacks and shoes that don't pinch, bite, or cause him to make contorted faces
while walking. He is not much of a fan of dressing up, and it has been some
time since he has been what is classified as presentable. He guesses he will
have to go the full route tomorrow for the wedding and the reception, but
for tonight, as an ornamental bystander, this garb will do. It's not like he has
to report to someone or impress Rebecca's clan with his nattiness.

At five-thirty he is in the car and braving the evening rush of the
capital city of the Confederacy. He sees Jim Crowe monuments and statues
from time to time, but really, if he did not know where he was, he would
not be aware of such reminders and mementos of the Civil War. To him,
Montgomery is about like all the other Southern towns he's ever been in.
There are generals on horses and cannons and memorials to the dead gallant
forces, stone soldiers holding muskets along the road, and in traffic ever so
often a pickup truck rumbles by with a Rebel flag decal pasted on the back
window, and a car at a red light has a license plate that says *Forget? Hell No!*
or another that says *Heritage, Not Hate,* or any of those maxims folks still
fighting the War tend to attach, paste, or display on their possessions for
others to see. If he didn't know where he was right this minute he could
easily be in a thousand towns south of the Mason Dixon Line. Rock-A-Bye-
Your-Baby, Bubba.

He finds the church with no difficulty, not because he has explorer
genes in his makeup but mainly because Rebecca's church is so large it is
hard to miss, sort of like passing Buckingham Palace and not noticing it
sitting there. The church stands out with a massive steeple and acres of
asphalt for every Moral Majority Evangelical Christian in Montgomery to
park their Audis and Mercedes and battle-ready SUVs in, the immense sign
at the entrance welcoming the community to the church and posting all
the different Saturday and Sunday services any of the privileged can choose
from to attend, just so this entire section of Heaven won't be blocked and
jammed and at a standstill when the members are ready to depart out into
the secular world and resume telling everyone how to live. Tom circles the
mass of buildings to find the auditorium entrance and sees softball fields
and a golf course and a rolling cemetery that makes River Grove look like

somebody's backyard, stately markers and stones and mausoleums, all at the ready for anyone who might drop dead while worshipping here.

There are clusters of balloons and signs taped along a walkway, and Tom parks the Camino between a Land Rover and a Jaguar sedan, feeling the urge to leave a note on their windshields telling the owners to please be careful and not scratch his car. There are lots of vehicles parked in the lot, maybe close to a hundred, and he thinks this is a hell of a turnout for a Friday night rehearsal. If there are this many people in this wedding, he shudders to think how many are going to show up for the ceremony tomorrow. And the reception that follows. There is no doubt in his mind the whiff of money is in the air.

He follows a group of perhaps fifteen people inside some doors and down a hallway decorated with more signs and balloons. Everyone seems to know each other, talking and laughing in that way the affluent and comfortable tend to do since they're already assured they'll be blessed in this life and ascending to the clouds immediately afterward when all this earthly business is said and done. He remembers his own religious upbringing in Rhodes' one Baptist congregation, how the church had been there forever and nobody seemed satisfied with anything but just wanted to add more buildings and get bigger than the Methodists and the Catholics and the Church of Christs. Years later now, he figures all of them are still at it, Matt and Doug and Sherry and Linda and everybody else who thinks they have to go sit in a pew and get seen. It's not really this way and he knows it, though. Some people—unlike him—are actually genuine in their acts and beliefs and not always looking for a way to escape situations. Like he does. He wonders when it was he and God had their big falling out? Was it him who'd started the fight? Or was it God who had brought something unwelcome upon him, and he, Fighting Thomas Lockhart, had decided he wasn't going to take such guff off the Old Creator anymore? It was hard to say.

The auditorium where the wedding is going to be held is not the main meeting area for the church, but a supplemental gathering place that is fundamentally to Tom totally un-supplemental and is, in fact, large enough to seat most of Montgomery if Jefferson Davis was still around and decided to make a speech. There are balconies with double sections all the way around and a three-sided floor seating arrangement stretching to the raised podium, and Tom is certain the choir loft could hold enough singers to bust out the stained-glass windows if they tried. The place is pretty impressive considering it is not even first-string for this congregation, and Tom wonders how much is actually needed to be considered more than not enough.

He takes a seat in a distant pew and waits to see what goes on from here. Groups of people are filing in and stopping to speak to each other, and

Tom gets the familiar feeling he always seems to get within a crowd—everyone knows each other but him. He is a stranger and on the outside of every social interaction, and so he must be careful not to overstep his bounds, because nobody likes a stranger telling them how to live, because he is not a part of them and never will be, so why would he stick his nose into matters and try to have things his way? This is nonsense and he knows it, but he's felt this way since he was a child on the playground and there's no changing it now.

He sees Mitchell walking toward the front of the auditorium, stopping by the piano to speak to several men who look to be his age, so perhaps these are some of his friends and are a part of the wedding party. Tom wonders if he should go approach his son and let him know he is here, but for the moment he prefers to remain afar and aloof and watch Mitchell in his natural element. Mitchell seems composed and not the least bit ill at ease, so maybe Tom's concerns about Mitchell's marrying into money might be unfounded. Probably it is just the fact that Tom is biased against the wealthy and well-to-do, and no one else in the world seems to have problems with them. That, he thinks, is what happens when you read *The Great Gatsby* at too young an age; he has spent a goodly portion of his life thinking the rich were all out to get him. In his old age he now realizes it has not been that way at all. The truth is he's hardly ever been noticed by them whatsoever. They have a hard-enough time believing he actually exists, much less wasting time worrying about him.

"God, Mitchell assured me you would be here, but I said I'd believe it when I see you in the flesh. Here you are and I'm still having trouble. For a couple of years now I've been telling anyone who asked about you that you'd fallen off the face of the earth."

Tom doesn't have to turn to find out who is speaking to him, for he knows the voice all too well. It is ex-wife Lynda, present here as Mitchell said she would be, and he looks upon her and wonders what he'd ever been thinking when he first asked her to marry him, and then he remembers it was because Mitchell was on the way and he thought he was the father. He is still unconvinced, but what else is new? He looks at her and it appears she has aged at least ten years since he saw her last. Her hair is a brighter hue of blonde than before, heavy on the bleach, like the bottle slipped some while being measured out and added a few extra milligrams to the concoction and brightened the blonde already present a few lighter shades toward bright and dazzling and something better viewed through sunglasses. Lynda's lips are redder and glossier than Tom recalls, but she is still recognizable by the skin-tight yellow dress she wears with a neckline that exhibits her chest and neck which are not, he can see, what they used to be, and the sound of her voice, as it always has, rises and carries and makes itself heard above any others, or, for the matter, heavy construction involving jackhammers and dynamite explosions anywhere near.

Lynda stands beside his pew with a man in a blue Hawaiian shirt wearing a choker composed of seashells around his neck and sporting a gold earring in his right lobe. His shirt is untucked, probably because his stomach would have a hard time breathing if it was constricted in any way. The man looks at Tom with a smile on his face, like he is the winner of the Fair Lynda and Tom is the loser, like he is happy being precisely the manner of dumbass he appears to be.

"This is Terry," Lynda says cheerily. "Terry's my hubby for four months now." She lets the happy news settle. "And this is Tom," she says to her grinning spouse. "Tom is Mitchell's father and who I was once married to. I didn't think the two of you would ever get the chance to make each other's acquaintance," she says.

There's a malicious twinkle in her eyes. Tom can make it out beneath the eye shadow.

"Good to meet you," Tom says. He stands and offers his hand. He knows what Lynda is up to already, which would make him pretty damn stupid if he didn't. Some things never change.

"I wasn't sure you'd make it to the wedding," Lynda continues. She turns to Terry to explain. "Tom and Mitchell were never that close, you know."

"Mitchell and his mother were inseparable, so that evens it out," Tom says. "It was hard for me to get a word in edgewise."

"Thomas and I weren't together too long after Mitchell came along," Lynda explains. "We were almost immediately in the process of going our separate ways even then."

Tom decides to let it go and smile and not bring up the actual facts of how he'd spent a lot of time with Mitchell while Lynda was "out" places at night, he and Mitchell in a two-bedroom apartment with Mitchell crying and sleeping and Tom making bottles and changing diapers while wondering at the same time if Mitchell was actually his kid and who exactly Lynda might be screwing at what certain point of each particular evening she was absent. It was a memory he didn't much like re-visiting, especially not now. He smiles again and lifts a hand in farewell and moves toward the front of the auditorium to have a word with Mitchell. The further away he gets from Lynda the better he feels. Again, some things never change.

Mitchell is pleased to see him and breaks from his conversation with his friends to give him a hug. This form of affection has always felt rather contrived to Tom, but he goes ahead and endures it so Mitchell can hold on to the illusion that he actually does have a father and is not alone in the world with Lynda as his mother and a walrus of a stepdad like Terry representing him on the family side, for as far as Tom can tell that is all Mitchell seems to have going for him tonight, since there are no aunts or uncles or grandparents or siblings in his existence from either his or Lynda's side to bolster him in this procession of ceremonies. Mitchell, Tom believes, is almost as solitary in his existence as he is. Maybe he might be his son after all, since they seem to share the state of isolation in common between them. Perhaps it is DNA.

"You made it!" Mitchell exclaims. He turns to a group filing in and finds Rebecca among them. "Here's Rebecca," he says to Tom, leading her his way so they can greet each other. Another young woman and a man come near, Rebecca's brother and sister-in-law. They shake hands and smile, then the couple steps aside so a lady can come forward and meet Tom.

"This is Mrs. Warren, Rebecca's mother," Mitchell is saying, although Tom does not hear him. It is difficult listening when his eyes are taking in who is before him holding out her hand, when his mind is changing gears at high-speed and racing along like Steve McQueen is at the wheel and a heart-throbbing ride is fixing to ensue. "Mrs. Warren, this is my father, Tom Lockhart."

"I don't really think I have to call you Mr. Lockhart," Rebecca's mother smiles, her brown eyes wide, taking him in. "I believe it's safe to call you Thomas." She pauses a moment and searches his face, looks into his eyes like she's making certain of something. "That's what I called you before," she says. "A long time ago."

"That's the name I still go by," he says. "And I'll just call you Maribeth."

"Thomas and I know each other from many years past," Maribeth tells Rebecca and Mitchell. She is smiling and mysterious in that way of hers Tom remembers. "We went to school at Covington."

"For a while," Tom says. "Only a while."

"I left early," she says, "to get married."

"I remember," he says. "You never came back."

"Wow," Rebecca says. "It's a small world sometimes."

"I had no earthly idea you were Mitchell's father," Maribeth says. "It never occurred to me. I guess it should have with your last name and all, but he never talked about you much. He just said you were a schoolteacher. Of course," she amends, "Mitchell and I have actually never really sat down and talked that much. We always seem to be busy with somewhere else to go."

"Mother is constantly out of town," Rebecca explains. "It's hard to discuss anything much when she's off in another country somewhere."

"Oh, I'm not gone that much," Maribeth says. "Only once in a while, really. The two of you stay so busy with school you never come and visit."

Tom standing dumbstruck in his tracks, doing his best to look pleasant and calm even with an ex-wife a section behind him and a possible son beside him and a future daughter-in-law nearby and Maribeth McAllister of the distant tragic past materializing like atmospheric smoke from a magic incantation, a spell bringing forth what was gone and lost back to being seen and alive and in the present tense, perhaps even to be found once more, thirty years absence standing here before him. It is a trip. It is, he thinks, almost much too much to take in at one time. Must come up for air and breathe very soon. Or asphyxiation is sure to come.

A bearded man in a rugby shirt claps his hands and asks everyone for their attention. He is here to get this show on the road, he says, to get everybody in their places and go over what happens tomorrow. He introduces a man in a sweatshirt wearing an Alabama Crimson Tide cap beside him, the Reverend John Tillman, he says. Soon he is pointing and instructing and describing the sequence of events for Saturday's ceremony, explaining and informing and waving his arms at a man at the piano and a woman at the organ to begin playing random excerpts of *The Wedding March.* Groomsmen and bridesmaids walk down the aisle to where the preacher in the Alabama cap and Mitchell stand, and a pre-school flower girl strews imaginary rose petals on the carpet before Rebecca and some man who is not her father—her father, John Warren, is dead four years of cancer—but who is her uncle and her father's brother, walk down the aisle while everybody spreads out and makes a circle at the front.

No vows are spoken, but the preacher tells a story about how he once tried to marry a couple who seemed to get confused about every little detail they got told and instructed about at the rehearsal, and when the next day came for the wedding they were both late because they didn't remember it was four in the afternoon but thought instead it was six, and everyone laughs when the preacher checks with Mitchell and Rebecca to confirm the time so such a thing won't happen again tomorrow.

In thirty minutes the rehearsal is over, and the announcement is made that all present here need to proceed to the dinner, which is being held a few miles down the road at a restaurant called Henri's, which Tom deduces is probably fairly high-scale and a place where he doubts he can get a decent cheeseburger. He's been casually moving away from the crowd to a place along the wall where he can stand with his back pressed against the stone beneath a stained-glass window of Christ Himself holding out his hand while a figure in graveclothes walks toward Him and Mary Magdalene and a few other assorted biblical personalities, thinking perhaps he can blend in here and be unrecognizable. He decides the representative of the walking dead in the window is Lazarus, which is certainly appropriate for what has gone down before him just recently, since it's not too goddamn often a Maribeth McAllister long-considered dead and gone from his life comes back and greets somebody like himself right before one's very eyes. Tom doesn't know whether to go to his own grave this minute because, well, he's now seen it all, or stand against this wall and wait for the next unexpected volcano to blow its top. Studying Maribeth and her strawberry-blonde perfectly coiffured hair atop her head and down her pale smooth neck. Watching as she turns around to look his way and smile when she sees him looking back. Taking a deep breath now as he sees her speak to her son and daughter-in-law and then move away from them.

And she is coming his way. Watch her approach and see how different it is, how strange it feels for Maribeth McAllister to be walking his way rather than fading away and disappearing from sight, and until these last few moments, being gone forever.

"You are coming to the dinner, aren't you?" she says. "Don't bother telling me no, because that's just not going to fly. I want to talk to you. We have some catching up to do, so make sure you come. I'm saving a seat for you beside me." She looks at him imploringly. "You absolutely have to come, Thomas. I'll make everyone else go sit at another table. It will be just you and me."

In the Camino he turns the key halfway hoping the battery will be mysteriously dead and the car won't move, but the engine fires and he follows the line of automobiles down the road like he is a part of some mind-boggling parade. He sees Lynda and Terry ahead of him in a massive pickup truck raised off the pavement by enlarged tires that make the truck look like it is perched on a mountain. He doesn't turn on the radio, but sits instead for a moment of silence waiting for God to suddenly scream out, "April Fools!," but the silence continues and the Almighty does not manifest, so he keeps his foot on the accelerator and follows along, assured beyond doubt that this dinner coming up is going to be one to remember if he manages to live through it.

Henri's is a darkly-lit building where shrubs and manicured bushes adorn the front walk and one has to adjust one's pupils to small solar lighting along the ground to keep from sauntering off the walkway and busting one's ass while plummeting into the darkness of the lawn. Tom makes his way through the vegetation and the obscured path to a heavy oaken door with a long handle, pulls it open and sees a smiling gentleman in a tuxedo in the vestibule. There is a lady at an upright desk busy writing names and filling reservations. Wait persons take turns leading groups down a hallway to murky rooms, wherein promises of quality food, drink, and top-notch service await them.

True to her word, Maribeth is waiting for him, standing off behind the desk. She walks over to meet him before he has the chance to tell anyone whose party he is in, hooking her arm through his and smiling.

"Gotcha," she says. "Now you have to sit beside me, because I'm not letting you go the rest of the night."

There are two long tables set up in the middle of the room, each one seating maybe thirty people. Maribeth bypasses them all and leads him to a small booth off in a corner. They sit and she sets her jacket on one side of the seat and her purse on the other, sending out a subliminal message that there is no room for anyone else to join them.

"I really want to talk to you," she says, "and I don't want to be interrupted."

Soft, unobtrusive music plays in the background, no bands of minstrels or Maurice Chevalier show tunes to set the atmosphere, and no one—not even the future bridal couple—wander over their way to speak to Maribeth or perhaps try to find out who this strange man she has suddenly latched upon is. She orders white wine for herself and Tom sticks with trusty water for the moment, unsure as he is where this evening is heading.

Maribeth fiddles with her napkin a moment, then gets right to the point.

"I'm doing my absolute best to not freak out seeing you tonight. I wish I could describe what I went through the moment I saw you. I had things go through my mind like you wouldn't believe, especially since right up to that split second before you appeared I was a hundred percent certain I'd never see or hear from you again. Thirty years of forgetting about you, and then all of a sudden it goes up in smoke."

"Life can get spooky at times."

"No, it's not like I'm saying you scared me or anything like that. It's just I had you penciled in somewhere on the other side of the rainbow or something, you know, married and happy and having a wonderful life. I never thought I'd see you again. It's like all the times I ever thought of you—and it's at least a million times through the years—I told myself I shouldn't have ever left you the way I did. But there was my engagement and a lot of other things happening. But I always wondered what would have happened if I'd come back to Covington—what would have happened between us? Who knows, huh? But I was back home and engaged and life was marching on. I didn't know what was the right thing to do."

"Yeah. You always said that. I tried to tell you different."

"You did more than try. Because of you I almost changed my mind. I looked for you at Faith's funeral, but you never showed up. I think I would have come back with you if you had."

She takes a sip of wine and continues to study him across the table, her brown eyes clear and shining, and he knows she has seen her share of exquisite nights and fancy restaurants and glittering cities since those days, those faraway nights at Covington, that final week she'd spent with him.

"So you're Mitchell's father," she muses. "You were that guy who was married to his mother. I've met his mother, been around her a couple of times now. She's a real piece of work. She doesn't hardly seem like your type, Tom, if you ask me."

"She wasn't. She never was. Of course, when you look at it, I guess you weren't either. Maybe there's just no such thing as my type."

He doesn't say anything more, decides to just settle back in his side of the booth with his ice water and looks at Maribeth McAllister-Warren seated across from him. This is close to being more than he can imagine. She looks not that much different from Covington days, older, sure, but age seems to fit her fine. Maybe even better. She doesn't have the young and innocent look she had then, that face he'd memorized, but she has evolved somehow into a mature version of that past vision, one whose eyes know a great many things than before but are still not certain they believe all they have seen, one whose speech is not so fast and excitedly hopeful as it once was, but capable still of poetry and musical language and evoking some air of magic a guy doesn't get a whiff of every day, probably, if the truth was to be acknowledged, a voice that may make one think enchantment is on the way and fixing to happen, even if it isn't, even if, yes, maybe it was only there for a flash in the way back when and then was gone forever. Her hair is a darker shade of the straw color it once was, but the cut is expensive, the cheekbones still lofty and high, her lips fuller and moist, more so even than he can remember. Time has been good to her, as he always knew it would be. She is simply Maribeth McAllister, then and now.

She begins talking of their time in the past and how much it has meant to her, then and now, and how it always will, and Tom sips his water and waits for his baked chicken dish to arrive and thinks how, when he has been asked the question over the years on just why he is who he is, why exactly he tends to act the way he does when all the rest of the world is so different, and who he is really, after you get by the flinty exterior and the way he laughs at everything and how there is always this feeling he is heading somewhere opposite than one would necessarily think he should be going, he could possibly be different.

(Mostly because I never had anybody tell me no before, because I guess I never asked anyone for anything and I suppose that's why. Maybe the way it worked out was I'd learned early on never to request anything in grandeur from my parents or Sam because they were all the time busy as hell giving and *taking from each other and it was all such a big deal that didn't involve me. All the interaction and obligation and requirements made it seem like it was easier and less cumbersome to simply take what I had and give away what I wanted to and lay low and wait until what I really wanted came along. Saw a bolt-action toy military rifle and settled for a cap gun. Smiled as I did at girls and held their hands and took them to movies on Friday nights, but somehow never got around to taking them anywhere in particular again. Figured I'd seen the best of them already and none of what they offered would ever be my cup of tea, so I let somebody else take them to dances and concerts and make out with them at parties. Had a better time of it working my jobs at the car wash and the Piggly Wiggly. Saving my money to get the Pontiac Dewey's dad sold me cheap, the shit-brown Tempest with the three on the column and the six cylinder you could run all day and hardly use gas, those plain tan bench seats and the staticky radio that went in and out no matter how strong the station signal was. Drove that car two years until somebody stole it off the school lot one afternoon while I was running my five miles, running the way I did most afternoons then when I wasn't working somewhere trying to make money, not really running against anybody but simply trying to get my time down every time I got out there, like it was something personal between me and the stopwatch and God and none of us needed anybody poking their nose into what we were doing. Trying, like they always did, to figure out what I was up to out there on the track by myself running for no reason anyone could see in particular. There were girls, sure, now and then, who'd write in my annual how much they liked knowing me and hoped to see me in the future too, and sometimes during that summer before I left I'd pick them up in my Fairlane I'd bought from the insurance money on the stolen Tempest with a cooler of Miller High Life and we'd scream down the two-lane highway roads off to lanes that led to ponds and pastures and nowhere in particular, which was always my favorite place to go, and we'd drink and take walks and kiss beneath the moon and get in the car with the radio on Accessory. The music playing and most of the time I got to do with them what I wanted. Did my best to make sure they wanted it too. Always only one time, then never again, because once for me, in those days where there were no expectations for the present, I was content to wait and see what was out there still to come.*

Covington full of people not like me, but already I was used to that. It didn't bother me and in truth I liked it just that way. Since we were different but there together, they went their way and I went mine. For two years it worked out fine. There were girls I could see my one time and I got a job bussing tables and washing dishes at a diner downtown,and running the register at the bookstore, and I could go to class and study what I wanted. Had my scholarship to buy me books and help pay for tuition, and after freshman year

I had an apartment in a big deteriorating house off campus behind Dixie's Pub, where I could go sit in the evenings and fill up on illegal beer and walk back home in five minutes to fall dead asleep before morning came and I got up to do it again. And I was all well and good with my education and my sometimes-sex with women who would always be strangers and my dinky two rooms and the fact that I wasn't with my good grades and my academic scholarship going to have to report for active duty in Viet Nam anytime soon, and I could have gone on a couple more years before I had to worry about what exactly I might do in my still-to-come life. Happened one afternoon to come across Maribeth McAllister in her shorts with her legs winking at me walking toward the student center to get herself something to snack on while she studied for an American Lit test coming up the next day. The same test I had to take because I was in the same class. Maribeth whom I'd taken lingering peeks at for months. Who'd just finished up being Guinevere in the Drama Department's production of "Camelot." I'd toked up and gone to see the play the Saturday night before. Maribeth had a nice way of delivering her lines and singing her tunes with her fine-spun strawberry hair cascading down her back. Maribeth, who had all at once become an obsession with me. Found myself thinking and pondering while washing dishes, studying, and getting blitzed at Dixie's until closing. Of Maribeth McAllister. Watching the lights of the jukebox blink and glow. And on the way home singing songs out into the night. Dogs barking and I'd have to pipe down. Looking up to see if the moon was coming with me. See on those nights how it always did.

Rebecca coming to our table, Mitchell trailing behind. The two of them wanting to know why we are sitting so far from everyone else, and what, exactly, is going on. This is the rehearsal dinner for our wedding, Rebecca says with a smile. You two might want to be a little more sociable.

Maribeth saying we'll only be a minute longer, and then we'll come join everyone. We've got a lot to catch up on.

"You're not very talkative," she says.

"Just taking it all in," I tell her. "There's a lot to think about."

That day I couldn't stand it any longer. Walked over to her table where she sat reading and asked if she minded me sitting down. Because I so want to talk to you. I was so bold and brave. While shaking like a leaf in a gale. I wanted to tell you what a good Guinevere you were. Made me want to be Lancelot very badly. And if I'd been old Lancelot, you'd have never seen Arthur again. She blushed and smiled and said you're so nice but I'm not very sure how to take you.

Sat with her two hours until I absolutely had to leave to go to work. Asked her what she did around Covington besides study. I go to the cafeteria and the library, she said. Sometimes we go out and eat. We? I asked. My friends and me, she said. Some of the girls who live in my dorm. But I guess I better tell you right now. I'm sort of engaged. Sort of? I said. You're either engaged or you aren't. We haven't set a date just yet, she said. But he's back home and I'm here. But I don't just stay in my room, if that's what you're asking. I go places. I play tennis over at the courts. The lights stay on until ten at night. And I said I could come and play with you sometime. But I don't have my own racket. Besides, I'm pretty lousy at tennis. You'd beat me every game. And she said smiling. That sounds like fun.

Most of the time we walked over to the courts but didn't play. Sat on a bench and talked and I did all I could to make her laugh. Told her about Rhodes and all the girls I couldn't get interested in. Run away by myself to keep from having to talk to them. Long runs on country roads while I plotted all my future novels. Thomas Wolfe and F. Scott Fitzgerald, move over. Because here I come. Swapped out my evening shifts for the lunch and afternoons, skipped classes so I could work and then be off at night. To spend with Maribeth. Spring semester coming to an end and one night on our bench I kissed her. Her lips coming close and I didn't have to ask. And I knew right then I had her. And also knew she had me.

Three weeks and we stopped any pretense of tennis or American Literature discussions. To hell with Hemingway and if the lights go out at ten o'clock. Because we preferred the dark by then, shadows of the night. Soon on the way to my two rooms and my bed. Oh god, she said, I don't think I can ever go home again. Because there may not be a way to leave you. You don't have to, I told her. You can stay. Summer classes starting and blending into Fall. That first week past Labor Day. Told me she was leaving school and going home and not coming back. Because you and I can't go on like this. I'm still engaged, you know. I must have been crazy to let this happen.

And never believed she would do it until the Saturday she left three months later. Drove her Monte Carlo out of the lot with suitcases and boxes packed in the trunk, a promise made the night before how she was going home and thinking everything through. I'll call you, she said, But I have to make some kind of sense out of my life. I have to do the right thing. I never planned on someone like you coming along. I didn't think this would happen. I never thought it possible I'd fall in love with somebody like you.

Tom listening now while Maribeth talks of years gone by and a husband and children and life in Montgomery. How through it all she's never stopped thinking, Thomas Lockhart, of you. I suppose it's true I'm as in love with you today and right this minute as I was back at Covington all those years back. Swept away like I was by you and the stars and the moonlight.

He does, yes, hear what she is saying, and then he watches as she gets up and goes over to the tables full of family and friends to get back to the business of Rebecca's wedding. Tom touches a napkin to his lips, stands and takes in Maribeth going from person to person and table to table, the familiar smile on her face and her voice coming across the room to him like a song. He realizes all he has to do is take a few steps from this room and he can be on his way to being gone from all this, vanished like he was never here in the first place. Tempting. He wonders if there has ever been in the history of the world anyone who knew how to disappear better than him. And if there will ever come a time when he considers remaining where he is and living the life that is there before him, rather than wanting to be away and afar and done for eternity with what the world is trying to pass his way.

A restless night in the cheapest motel in the capital of the South. Runaway dream with scenes and glimpses from the past. Tom finds himself wandering Covington's campus once again. Showing up for Moratorium Day. Hell no, we won't go. Sees himself and six other students standing by a flagpole by the administration building looking foolish. Signs and placards. Rest of the campus not giving the first shit. All insulated from bullets and wars and civil rights. At Covington all of it means nothing. White people walking around getting watched over by God. And in the vision he finds himself following Maribeth down shaded lanes and inside buildings, not knowing whether to let her see him or not. And into Peterson Library to see Faith sitting at a table by herself. Don't go upstairs, he wants to tell her.

Tom watches Saturday morning TV and eats snacks from the vending machine out on the walk. Football games with players giving their all for the alma mater. At last to dress in the charcoal suit and drive to the church to see if Mitchell goes through with this formality. Twice this morning Mitchell has called to check on him. Didn't sound nervous whatsoever. While Tom wants to take a flying leap out of his own skin.

When he gets to the church he enters the auditorium and goes and takes a seat along the far wall. He has already seen Lynda and Terry sitting ringside on the groom's side, and so he moves to the bride's area and sits as anonymously as possible looking at the handout the usher has handed him. It is not that elaborate a ceremony, he is happy to see, a couple of songs and a prayer or two to go with the exchanging of vows and rings. Tom sits and sizes up the audience trying to determine who will attend the reception and who won't, thinking if he plays his cards right, he can maybe make a quick appearance and mouth his congratulations and be gone before anyone has time to notice he was present to begin with.

He watches an usher escort Maribeth down the aisle. She is dressed in a blue dress with black high heels and a white orchid blossoms from her breast, and if anyone didn't know better, Tom thinks most of the men present would never take their eyes off this mother of the bride for the daughter. Rebecca is due to make her entrance any moment, but Maribeth is the real show-stopper here in her fiftieth or so year, and Tom has to at least give himself some credit for recognizing such steadfast beauty right from the beginning, for Maribeth McAllister-Warren is these years later a vision for even the sorest eyes. What kills him—and there is much here in the last day gathered in force attempting to do him in for good—is he is not surprised at Maribeth and her eternal beauty. He spotted it long ago in ages past. He knew it from the start.

It is as if a fog has entered through the doors and the stained-glass windows and enveloped the auditorium with a spell to hide all but one thing for him. Tom forgets about his maybe-son and the future life Mitchell will have with Rebecca, and all he can see and think about is some form of grainy film depicting him, Thomas Lockhart, late of Covington College and Chattanooga, Tennessee, and currently a citizen of the city of Rhodes, walking down this aisle with all these gathered around him and entering the pew where Maribeth sits, inching down to sit beside her, to take her hand and be with her through this ritual as if they were a couple, as if it has always been the plan for them to be this way. There is something in him now that makes him want to blink his eyes and banish this thought forever, for a voice tells him if such a thing like this was ever meant to be it would have already happened back in those days when all the world was young and every day a surprise. He knows it has been too long for any of this business now, that the dance was over and the band has stopped playing and put their instruments away in their cases and loaded everything back on the bus for the long journey home. He knows, yes, this is finished already and it is nothing but a waste of another day in a fleeting life to try and make it into anything approaching wonderful again. All those dreams have been put away, stashed and secreted even if no words were pronounced over them, and there is no use digging them up and hoping to see them perhaps breathe once more. He wants to go back to Rhodes and Martha Jane DeMars and look for new love with her, but that cannot happen this moment. Martha Jane is on the way to her own home to visit her father. Tom wonders what in the name of god she will say about him and her to her father, if she tells him anything at all.

The ceremony is short and over almost too quickly to be considered legal. The minister motions for everyone to stand while Mitchell and Rebecca exit down the aisle. An usher comes and escorts Maribeth out, who is smiling the smile she will wear for all the pictures that will be taken, the smile that goes along with the rest of her that will steal the show the rest of this night. Tom can only look at her and shake his head at the wonder of everything about her. He watches another usher escort Lynda down the aisle from her seat on the opposite side, Terry following after with a goofy smile of his own on his face, like maybe he might have had something to do with all this. Tom takes this all in from his seat in the thirteenth row, glad he did not go up and claim any kind of credit for anything that caused this affair to happen. Lynda passes by and Tom feels more unlike Mitchell's father than ever before; there is no way, he knows now, he could have ever had anything good come from the time he has spent with Lynda. He is convinced Mitchell's existence is someone else's doing.

The reception is at a country club three miles away. Tempted as he is to forego it, he still drives down the highway and enters a shadowy lane that leads to the party site, a sign instructing which turn to take to find the clubhouse. He pokes along through the dark winding trail, afraid any minute a deer will leap out and total his car, listening as he drives to Eric Burden tell him how we all have to get out of this place. First things first, he tells Eric, then I'll be more than glad to heed your advice. But first I have to finalize this piece of business. I've come this far and have to at least make a showing of myself before disappearing again. And thinking how easy all might have been had not God had to say oh by the way and thrown Maribeth McAllister in his path once more. Something, God tells Tom, for you to contemplate as you begin another one of your journeys down the rocky road of love. Here she is, and here's a Lynda for you too, just as a little reminder, and back in Rhodes there's an Abigail with a smoking pistol, and all that other debris you've left scattered from Covington to Chattanooga and back to the old hometown of Rhodes. This is what will be traveling with you when you take the road back home tomorrow. This is your dowry to bring to Martha Jane DeMars when you return. Good luck explaining everything, painting your nice vivid picture for her of how everything in your life has simply had a funny way of happening.

He supposes, if he had any modicum of pride within him, he ought to be somewhat cowed and ashamed at the appearance of his car when compared to the vehicles he sees parked in the club lot. Land Rovers and Beamers and other extravagant slabs of glistening expensive metal surround him, bright and lustrous paint contrasting with the Camino and its flecks of rust, shining hubcaps of silver and brilliant gleaming spokes, convertibles and fancy emblems and hood ornaments that look like somebody raided a bowling alley trophy case. He walks up a pathway where men in suits and evening dress linger to chat and have a smoke before entering into the music and conversation, the dancing and the drinking, the catered food and the towering wedding cake off to the side, the hired orchestra against a far wall opposite the tables of food and drink, a wet bar, where one, if one is of the mind to, can get good and soused for the price of contributing to the tip jar while watching women glide by in their dresses, thinking of who perhaps one could talk to or even touch, and at some point examining the passing smiling figure of the blue-clad Maribeth McAllister-Warren, and then to take a breath knowing how this woman is a vision rarely seen in real life, a viewing of dreams of beauty and otherworldness, one of those things that can never be imagined, something once dreamed that never truly had the chance of actually happening in this lesser not so dazzling life.

Pictures are still in the process of being taken, so the bridal party and the families have not arrived yet. Tom locates an unused stretch of wall and takes residence there. The food and the orchestra and the dance floor are removed from him, so he thinks if he remains motionless he can blend in with the background fairly easily. He sees Lynda and Terry coming in the doorway, finished with the pictures Lynda undoubtedly pushed and shoved herself into, and he is glad he didn't allow himself to be set up for such a fake rendering, for he has no penchant for seeing himself in a photograph. Whatever pose he takes always looks acted out, whatever expression is on his face is some sort of disguised mask he has conjured up for the occasion so his true self won't be revealed later on.

The orchestra is playing, alternating between Glenn Miller and REO Speedwagon, and some of the more eager hoofers take to the floor to dance. The family begins to filter in, and it is not hard for Tom to spot the shade of royal blue adorning Maribeth. He watches her make her way into the crowd, being stopped and hugged and chatted with by everyone she passes. Everybody seems to want to have something to do with her, and he wonders why it is he is here watching from afar Maribeth come and go, where she lingers and which direction she takes next. He wonders if he is unconsciously moving along the wall away from her, taking one step from her each time she draws closer. This, he thinks, is one damn funny way to act when a long-lost dream has appeared and offered to take him back to the magical days of sunsets and stars again.

I get funnier all the time, he thinks.

After ten minutes of playing this game of Keepaway, he comes to the conclusion that he is accomplishing nothing by skirting the issue this way, so he walks across the room through the dancing couples to the center table where Mitchell and Rebecca sit surrounded by who he guesses are friends and other strangers who might be family.

"I've been looking for you," Mitchell says. "We wanted to get you in the wedding pictures."

"I disappeared. You know me, I've never been much for getting my mug shot taken."

He offers his congratulations and well-wishes and gives Rebecca an embrace, simultaneously remembering that he has forgotten to purchase a wedding present for the occasion, and he wonders what kind of father can forget such an important thing like that. Probably, a voice tells him, because you are not really Mitchell's dad. And this Rebecca is not your daughter-in-law, despite the bylaws that have it ascribed that way.

And this woman in blue, approaching him now with her glittering necklace and dangling gold earrings and her face that maybe didn't launch him out to sea but certainly kept him out on the tributaries for a while, makes her way to his side like she belongs there, or, as is quite possible, he belongs to her, and lays her fingers on his sleeve and looks into his eyes.

"I think we should dance," she says.

He thinks how, despite the fact he has loved her all these long years and been in her thrall for months of Sundays and endless cycles of the moon, he has not yet danced with this woman before, and he hardly knows how to tell her he is not much of a hoofer or that he has not had time to imagine a moment such as this occurring any time soon or within his lifetime. He follows her out to the floor, her hand in his leading him on, and the orchestra is playing *Moonlight Serenade* while heads turn and eyes watch the two of them as he takes her in his arms and they touch at long last and she is close enough to him for him to know this is no dream, that this is real, that he should pay attention starting now, because this is really happening.

"I'm driving my friends and family crazy," she says, "paying so much attention to a total stranger this way. It's a little more than they can handle, and that includes Rebecca. I think she's so worried about what her mother is up to with her new husband's father that she hasn't paid a whole lot of attention to her own wedding day."

"I hope Mitchell hasn't spilled the beans about any of the events of my sordid past to anybody, else they'll all be lighting torches and getting lathered up to run me out of town before the night is through."

"No, you're still a mystery. I get the feeling everyone's waiting for me to tell them about you, but so far I haven't. Of course, there's a reason for that. I don't know myself."

"I'm the same person. Just thirty years older."

When the song ends they walk to the bar, where Maribeth orders champagne and Tom thinks why the hell not, and says make it two.

"I did all the talking last night. I think it's your turn now to tell me about you." Maribeth stands close to him sipping her champagne. It is like she is daring him to look into her eyes, to travel deep within them and be under her spell and tell her all. It is almost like before with her now, like he could easily get that way again despite the circumstances and years and the fact he has told himself this is the reason he has not been the fellow he always thought he'd be, but instead just may be the one who caused Faith Mercer to end it all and possibly take another life with her. And even if it truly didn't happen that way, the truth is it could have, because that was the path he had taken, that was the road he'd led her down, and whether that was what did it for her or not, he was the one who had made it possible, whether it happened or not, it was still the truth. He looks in Maribeth's eyes and sees her face and imagines her skin, the jewelry and the earrings and the necklace and her bracelet, the oh-so-blue lace dress and the perfect fulfillment of all he has dreamed so long ago, and he has to blink and catch his breath.

"Let's go outside," she says. "There's a table on the terrace and it's such a beautiful night. We can catch up. You can tell me all about you, all those things I never got the chance to know."

Christ, Tom thinks, she's good. She's even better than I remember. He has to give himself a break for all of it that has gone down. Because he was then and now. Human. No wondering why anymore. He knows.

There is a clamor and someone announces it is time for the couple's first dance, and so the band goes into *At Last* and Mitchell and Rebecca glide around for a couple of verses and refrains while pictures get taken and guests smile and drink. Then it is time to cut the cake, and bites are taken and portions are smashed into each of the couple's faces while the room applauds. The music starts back up again and people crowd the floor, and Maribeth takes Tom's hand and leads him through a portal to a small porch bedecked in flowers and moonlight. When they arrive at the railing she slips into his arms and he looks at her and he is twenty-one again, and the idea of it frightens him, for he is so much older now and it looks like he has learned nothing along the way.

"Kiss me like you did on that last night. We can talk later. God, we can talk any old time."

"We need to slow down. Maybe you don't think so, but this is happening too fast."

"Do I scare you, Tom? All this time I thought of you as being big and brave and all grownup. I don't want you to have bad dreams or anything, dearest." She smiles at him again. "Damn you, kiss me. Don't make me have to tell you again."

He does as he is told, knowing as he tastes her lips that he is doing what he has told himself he would never do again, but this is Maribeth and she is back from the grave of his memory, and how could he walk away now without thinking of this moment for the rest of his life? And how can he do this now, after all his lectures and admonitions and vows to himself, after

Martha Jane DeMars and the moonlight and her kiss and the appearance—
yes, he had seen it for himself this time—of love once again before him
here in his arms, despite their ages, despite their separate pasts, they were
together and finally it was as something meant to be, and yet here he is, wary
of what had been his present and enchanted by Martha Jane DeMars who
was his possible future, and now this Maribeth, this past, is in his arms and
he is with her, and he sees it all swirl in a mist around him, Maribeth's lips,
her touch, that empty wretched feeling he's taken with him from her, that
poison in his heart that said he would never be the one left behind again,
that he would always be the one walking away and leaving, and he saw how
it brought him from the Lyndas and the Abigails and others, and he saw
Faith Mercer falling and the world going up in flames before him, sadness
and bleakness and despair, and then there was Martha Jane come to him at
last, but she was going away now, she was disappearing like all dreams do,
and he was back where he started, he was with Maribeth in the storied past,
and it was like the world was turning in circles and he was so accustomed to
the ups and downs and round and rounds he was not even dizzy anymore.
It is like all of this is normal.

He is somewhere above, looking down on it all, and when it comes
into focus it does not matter, because he still cannot see it clearly enough to
know what it is.

The party continues after Mitchell and Rebecca leave the reception
amid rice and confetti inside a soaped Volvo with tin cans clattering from
the bumper. The orchestra keeps playing and people dance and cast glances
at Maribeth, wondering what she is up to this night, and most of all they
look at Tom and try to decipher exactly who this man is that Maribeth-
McAllister-Warren can suddenly not do without. Tom can see the questions
in the eyes of the revelers, these members of the family and friends, who are
doing their best to put this all together, and he sees the gaze of Lynda studying him with this mother-of-the bride beside him with her arms locked in
his like she is not even considering ever letting him go.

When they leave the reception, Tom walks down a dim hallway toward
the parking lot, where Maribeth comes close to him and announces she's
had too much to drink, and would he drive her home? She points at a silver
Mercedes and tells him it is her car, dangles keys in front of him, but Tom
is not so much of a fool to take them from her, tells her instead no, that he
will drive her home in his car. She makes no mention of the El Camino's
obvious vehicular limitations, but simply plops down in the passenger seat.
She wraps a shawl around her shoulders and begins directing Tom on how
to get to her house. It doesn't take but a few wrong turns for Tom to deduce

Maribeth is lost due to her alcoholic intake, and so he meanders down roads and streets and intersections and through four-way stops, until finally the boulevard opens up and he is on his way toward what is definitely not the poor side of town.

If he didn't know better, he would think he had entered into a medieval world of moats and castles and ivory towers behind high walls, but this, he decides, is simply the common architectural concept around these parts, people living in immense structures with long circular drives and gates that state you can't come in without the magic words. Coming from his background where the wealthiest person he's ever run across is Matt and his brood, sister Abigail, and all the other heirs to the fortune, Tom has to admit Maribeth's place is higher and haughtier than what the Lanes have produced through the years. The thing of it is it's not even close, that whoever the guy Maribeth was married to and whatever his family was into to get to this state far dwarfs the incidents and expressions of affluency Matt and Company have, that he, Tom Lockhart, pauper from way back, has never been up close to to experience, to grasp what money is all about until this moment before him now.

Maribeth's residence is something else.

She tells him to park in front of the garden, which is at the side of the house surrounded by a white wooden fence. Reds and greens and purples abound under the floodlights and the stars, and the abundance of floral reminds Tom of Martha Jane and her plots and greenery at River Grove. Maribeth unlocks a door and he follows her inside, down a hall with pictures of birds and family and more flowers, hutches and cabinets with dishes and silverware behind glass fronts. Off to the right is a kitchen with shiny pots hanging from the walls, a couple of ovens and refrigerators and coffee urns at the ready for a banquet or club gathering. They pass into a dining room with a long table with seating for all the knights, Lancelot and Arthur and Guinevere on the side, and then they arrive at the living room with oak and marble mantles and porcelain. Maribeth takes off her shawl and there she is, all blue lace and soft skin, lips and eyes and hair, most everything he remembers about her and more he has forgotten. She comes into his arms again and they kiss, and she is pulling him with her toward a stairway, and Tom comes to the conclusion that all this is heading down a road called Serious, and that now is the time when he needs to decide how many miles down this freeway he really wants to go.

She is unzipping the back of her dress, baring her shoulders, taking his hands and placing them against her, leading him into a bedroom where she shuts the door.

"You're the one I've been waiting for," she says.

"Really?" he asks. He goes ahead and kisses her because, well, he is human the last time he looked, he is still a male, and this is what God or someone celestially in charge has set in front of him, but it is not like he has had something like this lodged in his mind all this time, this is different, and he needs to step back a moment before going forward, because the footing could get treacherous from here on out, and he could slip and fall forever, and no one has to tell him how it is certainly a hell of a long way down from where he is.

He thinks of the last time he has seen Maribeth before this weekend, before the rehearsal and the dinner and the wedding and the reception, this moment with her skin against him. He sees her closing the door of Frazier Hall that last night at Covington, just after she'd told him she was leaving and going home to get married, how she couldn't stay and she would never be back. To forgive her, she'd said, but it was too late now. I hope one day you'll come to understand how it is. Her eyes moist. How sometimes things that seem meant to be simply can't happen.

But it's not that I don't love you, she said.

Thomas Lockhart remembers her saying that all too well.

He tastes her lips in the dim light of the room and her arms go around him and pull him to her, and this, he guesses, is when the music swells and the scene goes dark and everything that goes on from here is left to the imagination, and he supposes he is to float off in this fantasy cloud and receive some sort of reimbursement for all that was not his all these years and everything that engulfed his heart and wrapped it in thorns and bile and venom and bared teeth, he thinks he should be happy with this now, for this is his reward for suffering and he can let go of the idea of Faith Mercer falling through the air, on purpose or not, still falling to her end, with maybe his child—perhaps she was pregnant, perhaps it was his, he will never know—inside her, and the young teachers at school he bedded and left behind, and his lost job because God finally paid him back for his actions and misdeeds and made him a victim at last, and the failed marriage with Lynda, someone he didn't even like and became a cuckold for, Abigail with her flaunts and teases and unawareness of anything to do with something called love, and Martha Jane—tender, tender girl, a blossom for his blind eyes, somewhere now maybe thinking of him—while here he is in this bedroom with Maribeth, someone he hardly knows, has never really known, yes, here he is.

He makes himself pull back.

"This isn't right," he says. "I think maybe you've had a little too much to drink."

"I know what I'm doing."

"Maybe you do, but maybe I don't."

"Hold me closer."

"No, not tonight. Not like this. This is crazy. I've had enough crazy nights to last the rest of my life, Maribeth. I don't need another one, especially with you."

He steps away and her arms fall to her sides. Her face clouds with disappointment.

"Don't be like this," she says.

"I have to go, Maribeth. We'll talk tomorrow before I leave to go back."

"We can talk later," she says, "but not now." She reaches for him. "I don't want you to go," she tells him. Maybe she will cry.

"Most of me doesn't want to go either," he says, "if that helps any. But I'm going anyway." He opens the bedroom door. "I'll find my way out."

When he is halfway down the stairs he looks up and sees Maribeth standing at the top railing watching him. She is something from a dream. She is all he has ever wanted for the longest time. He keeps taking the steps down, being careful not to trip, making sure he keeps moving toward the front door and not turning on his heels and going back up to where she is. Maribeth unclothed, waiting for him after all this time, ready for it to be him and her.

He can't find the damn doorknob fast enough.

TEN

When he gets back to Rhodes on Sunday the afternoon sun is beating down like it's never going to stop or set and its everlasting light will last forever.

He silences his phone so he won't have to deal with Maribeth calling him over and over again, and has a peaceful ride back with the music playing from the dashboard radio, his cell in the empty ashtray staying nice and quiet. After a mostly-sleepless night, he'd forced himself from the bed and pushed himself out on the road before anything or anyone had the chance to pursue him, telephone calls or knocks on the motel room door or even perhaps Cupid with his bow aiming to send an arrow through his heart and bid him come back to the massive estate where Maribeth lay naked in bed waiting for him.

It's just all much too much.

He has not allowed himself to think everything all the way through yet, this Maribeth ghost from the past throwing her wealthy self at him after all the time of being apart, the coincidences of Mitchell and Rebecca, the aloof nature of having an ex-wife who is hard to imagine as even being real, if he had ever done such a thing as marry her. And this is just in Montgomery on a wedding weekend. He is not even adding in Abigail with a gun in her hand and a dead Garland and brother Matt who somehow has managed to smooth everything over so Abigail is free to walk the streets of Rhodes without any interference from a now-removed husband. There is the job he must go to on Monday, there is Dewey packing up and selling out before disappearing without a trace, and there is Martha Jane DeMars, out somewhere this very day making her mind up about him and her, wondering if he is the person for her to be in love with to the very end, and Tom Lockhart wonders if the time is near when there is any kind of answer to all these questions.

A pickup truck pulls out of Dewey's driveway, towing behind it an aged Saab, which Lockhart recognizes from it sitting at the side of Dewey's house since he first returned to Rhodes. Seeing it roll away, Tom figures the moving process is in full swing, so he pulls in and drives up the hill to the garage. Dewey sits in his chair, but there is no *Ulysses* in his hand to peruse, no Mateus beside him on the cantaloupe crate. Even Leopold the apprentice squirrel is not present.

"You look a little bereft out here, sitting all alone with nothing around you."

"I'm making myself get used to being devoid of possessions," Dewey says. "I never knew I had so much crap just sitting around. Wait until you get your own house. You'll be surprised. Now, if I make any kind of noise whatsoever there's an echo reverberating off the walls."

"Did you sell Leopold too? I don't see him around anywhere."

Dewey's face clouds, and he gazes off at the expanse of River Road.

"Leopold has disappeared. I'm not sure if the damn coyotes got him or if he knew I was in the process of moving and decided to move on to greener pastures. I guess it's just as well. I'd have had a hard time smuggling him aboard Aer Lingus, much less getting him through Customs."

"Aer Lingus? Ireland? That's where you're going, huh?"

"That's the plan, amigo. I'm making a clean break with everything. I need a new country. No drugs or contraband to screw this up. The only relaxant I'll be indulging in will be coming from a tap down at the pub. Have my couple of drinks and sit on my stool and sing a few verses of *Too-Ra-Loo-Ra-Loo-Ra*, then it's off for home I go. No damn cars, either, Thomas. Shoe leather or a bicycle for me from now on out."

"Sounds like quite a plan. Maybe I should go with you."

"Maybe you can join me later, but not at the moment, old buddy. No offense, but your lifestyle's too damn colorful for me right now. I'm leaving to get my head together and find some serenity and peace. You, my friend, have a way of showing up and bringing with you gun-wielding women and the off corpse here and there. You get over there and they'd drive the both of us out of the country like we were St. Patrick's snakes or something."

"God," Tom asks, "how many cars have you gotten rid of this weekend? It's desolated out here. You'll have to move now or you'll be spending next summer mowing the yard all the time. With the cars gone there's a good chance grass will grow out here again."

"How did the wedding go?" Dewey asks. "Did Mitchell take his punishment like a man?"

"He was fine. I was not. I'll have to tell you about it."

Inside the house Dewey begins rummaging through the refrigerator and the cabinets to find whatever ingredients he can for dinner. Tom was on the verge of leaving for home for his own hot dog banquet, but he knows Dewey's culinary expertise, so he sticks around. Dewey is a great cook, and Tom wonders why his old friend never pursued a career as a chef. Probably because he would have to adhere to somebody's schedule, and Dewey has never been one for that.

Spaghetti with Polish sausage meatballs turns out to be the fare, a sauce concocted from what remnants are left in the refrigerator, garlic bread fashioned from hamburger buns, and Tom polishes off a plateful and leans back in his chair.

"It's too damn bad you weren't born a woman, Dewey. I'd marry you just for your cooking."

"I don't have to be a woman anymore for us to get married, but it would still never work out. You say either and I say eye-ther."

Tom tells Dewey of the Maribeth sighting at the wedding, how she is now his perhaps-son's mother-in-law and who appears to be not only a voluptuous phantom but loaded to the gills too. He doesn't mention any of the touching or embracing or outright passionate coupling, but his description of Maribeth alone causes Dewey's interest to rise.

"Hell, Tom, if you don't want her then give her to me. Looks and money have always been at the top of my list. I can postpone and even cancel this expatriate shit for good if I've got something like that to fall back on."

Three hours later Tom glides out to the car, stomach full and in a pleasant whirl from Dewey's pot and several shots of whiskey, just, as Dewey says, to kill off the contents so the bottles can be thrown away. Jack Daniels is what Frank Sinatra used to drink, Dewey demonstrated. An ice cube and a couple of fingers in a glass. Maybe four. Glub glub. Son of a bitch could drink all night and never go to sleep until the next day. Not me, says Tom. Call me Baby.

By the time he gets home and gets the car unloaded it is pushing nine and the weekend is getting the best of him. He remembers his cell is still silenced from this morning, so it is no wonder he has not had any calls from Maribeth or Martha Jane or anyone else on the face of the earth. He looks and sees there have been a few calls, three of them, all from Doug, a text or two. He wonders what that is all about. Maybe some criminal activity in the cemetery while he's been away. But plenty of time to find out about that in the morning when he is supposedly in his right mind. Time now to tuck it in and examine the inside of the eyelids. Say so long to all the wonders this weekend has wrought.

The last vision he has before sliding off into oblivion is of Maribeth McAllister. There are two Maribeths standing naked before him, one young, one old, and he does not know which one to choose. Probably, something tells him, the best choice is neither one. It is a real dilemma, he thinks, he is going to have to give some serious thought to. He is not so certain what he wants or what he doesn't or what in fact he actually should be desiring right now.

The phone unsilenced. Coming to life early this Monday morning. He is awake already when the rings begin, but hesitant to answer something so shrill and demanding at such a wee hour, deducing that if someone wants him this early it cannot be anything he really wants to hear right from the morning get-go. He tells himself to be an adult, silences Otto in the middle of some obscure rhapsody, and answers.

"Man, I've been trying to get in touch with you for a day now."

It is Doug, his fourth call since yesterday afternoon, so Tom knows there's something of import here. Doug is not one of those people who call repeatedly to discuss the weather.

"You may have already heard, but I'm going to tell you anyway. This is something you need to know about."

"What's going on?"

"It's Martha Jane, Tom. She's in the hospital. She's been in a wreck. I knew you two were seeing each other, and I knew you were gone for the weekend, and I didn't know if you'd heard or not."

Tom waits to hear more.

"Like I say, she's been in a pretty bad wreck. Her aunt called me to let me know. She knew your name but didn't know how to get in touch with you. I told her I'd let you know, but I didn't want to leave a message for you to find out that way."

"When did this happen? Where is she?"

"Saturday night. She was coming back from a storytelling festival or something. It was a one-car accident. She supposedly just went off the road and hit a tree. She's in a hospital in Johnson City right now in critical condition."

Doug knows nothing else to tell him. Tom clicks off his cell and stands transfixed on the porch looking at his coffee cup, black and smoking and offering him nothing but further awareness and caffeine to keep him awake. There will be no going back to sleep and having sweet dreams. Which he had been experiencing earlier. Escaping from the strange possessiveness of Maribeth and the urges of Abigail back into the tender arms of Martha Jane DeMars. Now being told that all that had given him ease and made him smile, upon this brutal awakening, now he cannot have. Not fair, he thinks, but tells himself to snap out of it, for this is not about him. Martha Jane, he thinks. How can this be happening? Is it because once again I have come too close and cursed who I've come near?

He calls Matt and gets the answering service, so he leaves a message and says he is not going to be in today and maybe not for a while. Sorry. He does not explain why, and he doesn't know why he doesn't.

Back into the Camino and up the street to Dewey's house. To tell him what has happened and where he is going, just so somebody will know if he never comes back.

Dewey offers to let Tom take his truck for the trip to East Tennessee, since it runs like a top and is not ancient and not on its possible deathbed like the El Camino. Tom takes the keys and thanks him, grateful to have something he can speed in and not have to worry about disintegrating along the way. In a few minutes he is outside of Rhodes and the school zones and what rush there is and on the interstate. He leaves the radio off and keeps the cab silent so he can think. He inches the speedometer to eighty and watches the lines and the trees go by in a rush of yellows and greens. Anytime now the leaves will begin falling and the world will be gray and barren again.

The way he is down inside right now.

He hits Knoxville at just the right time and isn't delayed by traffic. Once he passes by the entrance to Gatlinburg the traffic thins and he makes good time. The big problem is he doesn't actually know where he is going, since Doug only told him a hospital in Johnson City and that is the extent of his knowledge. He doesn't have Martha Jane's family's number and knows no one else to call and has to stop and study his phone to locate possible medical facilities. He will find the right one, though. He will find Martha Jane DeMars somewhere.

He gets lucky and manages to find the right hospital just off the first interstate exit. He parks the truck and calls to see if Martha Jane is there, and she is. Is this luck? He does not know. He parks and goes inside at a trot.

Don't do this, God, he thinks. Don't let what I'm thinking happen.

A lady at a reception desk tells him where Critical Care is but says he is not allowed to go in unless he is family and it is a designated visitation time. He thanks her and finds an elevator, looking for the fifth floor. He will get in some way. Or at least he will be close. To be with her when she wakes. Because he has something to tell her.

God, don't let her die.

No one is in the vestibule when he gets off the elevator. Searching until he sees a fellow in scrubs sitting at a computer behind the nurses' station.

"Can I help you?" the man says, and Tom is thankful that at least for a moment there is someone in this world who recognizes that he is present and existent.

"I'm looking for a friend who's here. Martha Jane DeMars."

The man punches his keyboard and studies it a moment.

"Yes, she's here. Looks like she's in surgery right now. She was in CCU for a while, but now they've taken her back in.

"Any idea what her condition is?"

"Not good. They have her listed as Grave."

"Where is Surgery?"

"Down that hallway." He points over his shoulder. "You can't go any further than right here, though. No one but medical personnel is allowed past this point. But I'll let you know when something changes."

Back over to a waiting area, two small couches and four chairs scattered around the walls. Television on the wall muted and tuned to *Animal Planet*. Zookeeper rubbing a tiger's tummy. Expect any minute for a giant paw to gash her throat and send her pith hat flying across the cage. Sit down and there's a *Good Housekeeping* and *People* and *Sports Illustrated* in a pile on a table. Everything six months old. Only time in my life I've known how things are going to turn out. Sit here alone and hope no one disturbs me. Because I have to think. Don't need the sound of human voices keeping me from getting this straight.

Learned a long time ago not to ever ask for too much, because I knew all too well I for damn sure wasn't going to get it. Bicycles and baseball gloves and such, always the wrong color or the wrong size. Got to where I was content with nothing, since I never got disappointed when it was like that. Nothing has no great expectations.

Haven't quite known what to think for six months now. As if I ever did before. Strange enough to think you are settled in and life is not going to go haywire anymore, how you have learned to be a grownup and have a grip on all things troublesome that are hiding out there. Perhaps I got overconfident. Figured I'd made so many mistakes in the past that maybe I was wiser now and wasn't going to resort to doing something dumb. Like marrying Lynda. Whoops. Like jumping all over my principal with no thought of what might come from it. Thought I was immune because she was the one who'd started it, and what was I supposed to do? Would have been fired if I didn't, and her husband made sure I was canned because I did. Should have stayed away like I did after Faith Mercer and Covington. Swore then I'd never make a mistake because of a woman again, love or lust or whatever. Because it always ended up with somebody sad. Hurt or deserted and possibly dead. Hell, I could be dead right now. Garland had a pistol. Unfortunately for him, so did Abigail. Probably still has it, wherever she is right now. May just have a bullet with my name on it, who can say? And I wanted none of it this time. Wanted to go to work and come home and sort it all out for once. Write another book and let that be what was important. Didn't ever think I'd run into someone who'd throw me for a loop.

Like Maribeth had way back when. Like she attempted to do again this weekend. But I surprised myself for once. This time I didn't let the moon get all the way full.

Martha Jane on that first night I saw her. Me in my world and she there in hers. Talk and laughter going on all around, music and spilt beer making rungs on tabletops. Gossip from years past. Wrinkles and graying hair. Doug almost bald. Charlie still at the Piggly Wiggly playing lecher. Sitting listening to Linda talk about death and reunions and who went to jail and who got married three times in one decade. Knowing full well that once upon a time Linda had been in love with Dewey and Dewey in love with her. But Big Bad Love had scared her and made her take up with Doug instead, because Dewey was scary. Dewey who didn't care for much of anything like real people did. Mostly, money. And Linda just couldn't live without money. Join the crowd, I say. Everybody move over a seat. Make room on the bus. And Martha Jane standing by the bar talking to two people, a man and a woman. And me of course honing in on how she seemed so deliciously alone. While all the talk going on around me on varieties of subjects present and past that should be holding import was tuned out and silenced. As I studied this dreamboat. Who was just my style. But so young. And me so old. And the sign of the pentagram on her, telling me not to draw too close.

And later at the Fourth of July picnic. She came sauntering by with some fellow. And before I knew it I wanted him dead. But had to sit and watch her go. Because I was old and had a past no one should see. Content myself with the Abigails of the world or even the pleasure of my own company. Because all that stuff was down the road behind me, back in the annals of the murky past. Died with Maribeth driving away on a Saturday. To enter into her chosen world of safety and money, privilege and security, knowing it would never up and leave her. As perhaps someone like me might.

But on that day of Martha Jane's flat tire. Blessed puncture I thanked the Almighty for. There she was on that narrow lane. Knew somehow she'd been placed there. To give me one last chance. Redemption in love, magic, and romance. What at one time I thought Life was all about. Until the days of hate and anger and revenge took me over. Made me believe a price had to be extracted for what the world had done to me. Which was just the way it goes. But never could learn anything easily. And so had to find out the hard way how sometimes what you do can bring someone else to their knees. Or off a balcony to a grave. Maybe all because of me. And I thought I had to pay for it the rest of my life.

Martha Jane's kiss that night. And me with the inconceivable notion that maybe I'd been forgiven and the Heavens spoke my name once more. And during those first weeks to believe things would once again. Be peachy. And then this unpredictable unthinkable weekend with Maribeth. And now this. This hospital. This room where I sit to be close to Martha Jane. She can't die. I refuse to let her die.

Tom out of his chair and back to the desk to see if there is any news. Nothing has changed. He wonders if somewhere in this maze of hallways and rooms Martha Jane's father and family are in vigil too. He thinks of trying to locate them, then wonders what he would say. What could he say about being an old man who is suddenly in love with their Martha Jane? How to say it is not anything that has just instantly happened, but the truth being that he has been in love with her forever. Before she was born. He'd been out in the world searching for her. Would they understand?

He feels lacking in any real information, so he steps back to the nurses' desk to ask a question or two. Has she been conscious through this? What kind of physical damage has she suffered? Will there be permanent effects? What are her chances of getting through this?

Is she going to die?

No one knows anything and no one tells him anything. It is like he is in orbit and looking for a place to land and is on the far side of his destination and no one can communicate with him now. The woman he has come to find may as well be in another country this moment, another world, for he feels unconnected to any of her being. Perhaps they have stood in an embrace beneath the stars and the heavens in the not-so-distant past and whispered vows to each other, but that does not matter here today, that does not apply. He is as far away from her now as he has been from Maribeth McAllister for thirty years, and he wonders if the time arrives when he and Martha Jane are face-to-face once more if there will still be what they had between them, or will it be gone like the coming day had chased it off? He does not want it to be this way. He wants he and Martha Jane to keep what they had found in each other. He remembers the sudden nearness of Maribeth Saturday night, her voice, her breath upon his neck, the taste of her that was something different than what he'd recalled before, and he'd somehow known in that instant that the woman in his arms was not what had caused him to sway or charmed him or carried him off to a place of wonder where the searching world could never find him again. This was not the same Maribeth as before, and never would be again.

After another hour in his appointed chair, dozing off sometimes to dream of better moments and waking to see a new program on the overhead television, a snake handler, a dog trainer, a veterinarian who saves all sorts of exotic animals from extinction, he finds himself ravenous and knows he must eat something. He studies a sign by the elevators and takes one down to a first-floor cafeteria.

He picks out a cellophaned ham and cheese sandwich from a cooler, adds some chips and a bottle of water and sits down at an isolated table by a window out at a courtyard. The sun is slanting its rays on a hospital garden planted by the entrance, and Tom sees the greens of oak-leaf hydrangeas growing in gigantic postures, the deep reds of pansies, pink morning glory in full bloom thriving in the daylight of October even with summer gone for weeks. This is the most beautiful time of the year, he thinks, everything bursting forth in each and every particular blaze of glory with a victorious and defiant show of eternal life and a death so unwelcome it dares not arrive. It is hard to imagine, sitting and looking at pageantry like this, that in a few weeks' time it will all be gone, spirited away almost overnight. Six weeks from today he could sit at this very place and, if he didn't know any better, never be able to imagine the beauty that had once been here.

When he gets back in the elevator, he sees an elderly black gentleman with silver in his whiskers and a sport coat from better days standing in front of the floor buttons. Tom presses the number five and steps back, and the man looks at the panel and waits. After a moment the doors close and the elevator starts upward. The man turns to Tom and smiles. He has gold in his teeth.

"I keep forgetting what floor I'm going to," he says. "My wife is in a room up there somewhere, and every time I come downstairs I forget where I'm going back to. I have to get off at about every stop and go and take a look around." He shakes his head and smiles again. "I don't think I'm losing my mind or nothing," he says. "I just think my wife's in such terrible shape I don't want to go back and see her anymore. Cause it seems like every time I do she just gets worse."

"It sounds bad," Tom says. "I'm sorry for you and her. I hope everything works out okay."

The door opens and he looks at the man for a second and steps out.

"Much obliged," the old man says.

When he comes out of the elevator lobby and approaches the nurses' station, he sees there are more people inside the enclosure than before. There is a bustle and a sense of purpose that he does not like at all, and he doesn't go back to the waiting room to sit and wait for someone to come and tell him something. He is not a family member. He is just this nobody who showed up off the street. Perhaps he is not going to be informed of anything, but he can inch closer and see if he can find out for himself what is going on.

Let this be about somebody else, he thinks. Don't let this have anything to do with Martha Jane.

There are murmurs and whispering. Confabs and protocol. The nurse who was there before looks up and sees Tom standing by. He comes out from behind the desk and touches Tom on the elbow. Go away, Tom thinks.

"It's bad news," he tells Tom. "I'm afraid your friend didn't make it."

Tom is silent, decides saying nothing may be all there is inside him.

"We're not supposed to announce anything until the family is informed. There's an aunt in town, but she's with the deceased's father, who isn't well enough to be here. The mother is deceased, so that's all there is. Like I say, we're not supposed to release any information except to the immediate family, but I thought you ought to know."

"Thank you."

"There's not much more I can tell you. She died on the operating table from injuries sustained in the automobile accident. She never regained consciousness."

"Can I check back with you later?"

"I'll be here until seven."

Turn and walk toward the elevators. Get the hell out of here fast. Stop and look back and want to rush past all the doctors and nurses and surgeons down that hall where Martha Jane rests on a table. Do they cover her face with a sheet? Like they do in the movies. Turn grim-faced to those at bedside and say there's nothing more we can do. Think of all those bedside death scenes. Beth in "Little Women" and Garbo in "Camille" and Melanie in "Gone With the Wind." Ali McGraw in "Love Story." God, gets pukier as it goes along. Think of imaginary stuff so there's no time to examine what's real, what is gone now and won't ever be back.

Martha Jane is no more. Martha Jane is gone. Our time of being in love is done.

Going down. Mercifully, the elevator not stopping until it gets to the main floor. Door slides open. Step out into the lobby. Crowd filing past to take my place. Going up. And I am on my way past potted plants and coffee kiosks. Helpful volunteers giving directions, greeting arrivals and allowing the sorrowful to depart in peace. Through electric doors that open wide. And lead out into a parking garage that goes on forever. Find Dewey's truck and follow the arrows and signs to exit into the first of a billion anonymous streets. Click off the radio. Silence all there is now. Drive forever and still be nowhere. And forevermore have nowhere to go. Because wherever the road goes. She is not there. Martha Jane.

Gone from me forever.

ELEVEN

It was a small funeral. Martha Jane, Tom learned, didn't have that many friends she still kept in contact with. Anyone she'd ever had much to do with when she was younger had married and moved away, and for a while she had kept up with them via Christmas cards with newsy letters enclosed within, maybe sometimes by email or a phone call, but after a while that had dried up as she'd had her own life struggles to contend with. There'd been her one close friend, Ruth Fulkerson, whom she'd always made it a point to go and see when she came back home, but Ruth had died of ovarian cancer four years ago, and Martha Jane was just not very close to anybody else. It almost depressed her trying to make do with others, like they were a poor substitute or something.

The visitation was two hours before the ceremony. Martha Jane's aunt brought her father to the funeral home, but her father didn't completely understand what was happening. There were maybe thirty people who came to sign the book and fifteen who stayed behind for the service. Besides Tom in Dewey's truck and the hearse carrying Martha Jane's dad and aunt to the burial, there were two other cars in the procession, comprised of four women Martha Jane's age and a solitary man, who was probably somebody's husband. Tom figured the women were old classmates of Martha Jane's from high school, but they all looked vanilla and plain standing around the small tent like they were in no way linked to the beauty of Martha Jane DeMars whatsoever and couldn't be of her generation or ilk, all finally sitting down in the chairs that no one else was present to sit in. Tom was the only person standing. None of the women were as pretty as Martha Jane, and he knew for certain it had always been like that.

The preacher not only prayed and delivered a short eulogy but also sang *In the Garden* a Capella too, and Tom thought how the guy wasn't so accomplished at any of the three but was at least versatile. When the service ended Tom walked off alone and got inside Dewey's truck and drove it to the other side of the cemetery to where there was nothing much but trees and squirrels and graves with flags and balloons and inscriptions etched on the stones. There were Halloween decorations and leftover Christmas trees and Santa and his reindeer from last year, which was depressing how they were still there and no one had come back to get them. He got out and sat on the bed of the truck and looked at the sky and watched birds fly back and forth. A congregation of Canadian Honkers passed by above him, checking the road and the grass for food, taking a respite, he guessed, from the long journey south for the winter. They foraged and hooted and honked and paid him no mind there in the back of Dewey's pickup.

When he thought it had been long enough for the people to leave and the diggers to finish with their job, he got back in the truck and wound his way back to Martha Jane's gravesite.

There were only a few flowers left by the grave, barely covering the fresh dirt the diggers had sculpted. Tom spotted the flowers he had sent and walked over and picked them up. He looked them over and laid them on the dirt approximately where he thought Martha Jane's heart was. He thought of her body inside the casket, a silver stainless job that had given off light in the sun when the pallbearers (employees from the funeral home) brought it up from the hearse and placed it on the slabs. He had stood at the back of the tent imagining how the world was going to be without Martha Jane DeMars in it. He was trying not to be selfish and think only of himself and the effects it would have, but he couldn't get the picture out of his head of his own stone house and how she had been there with him, the flowers she had tended in River Grove, the lane where she'd had the flat tire that had brought them together, the night at Thompson's when she'd smiled down into her beer glass, looked up at him with a happy tear in the corner of her eye, and said oh god, Thomas Lockhart, I think I'm in love with you.

Hear the distant sound of mowing from the grounds crew. Bluest sky with no clouds. Prettiest Indian Summer day any eye has ever seen. Tom thinking how he never wants to see anything this beautiful again.

Her casket was closed and I couldn't see her.

Because he will always know. Martha Jane has gone.

He takes his time and lets it sink in. May as well get it straight right now. Get this goodbye to Martha Jane done the right way because he knows he won't be back again. Because she is not here and there won't be any cause to come and search for her, to call her name.

She loved me, he thinks. God.

Goodbye, Martha Jane.

Martha Jane had her share of problems, her aunt said.

Gail was her aunt's name, a woman of seventy-four, retired from the Tennessee Methodist Publishing House after thirty years of editing Sunday School quarterlies, a widow of six years now living in Rhodes because that was where her husband had been from originally, where he'd bought a house for their retirement before dropping dead in the back yard on a Saturday morning while painting a metal glider. Gail was from Jonesborough but saw no need to leave a house she'd just finished moving into and joining the Methodist church in Rhodes and adopting two dogs and a cat from the pound in Athens, and when Martha Jane took a radio job at the library and moved to Rhodes her Aunt Gail had been more than glad to rent her the upstairs of the house at a nominal price. It had worked out fine for her and she thought it had been good for Martha Jane too.

But Martha Jane, bless her heart, had problems. Aunt Gail didn't want to sugar-coat that fact.

First, it was the worthless so and so she married when she got out of college. I don't know what she was thinking when she did a stupid thing like that, Aunt Gail said. Maybe she thought he'd change when he got used to being married, stop drinking and taking drugs and going from job to job the way he did. He was, after all, from a good family in Kingsport, a preacher's boy, and maybe he would have turned out better later on, but when he got caught with his hand in the till with a whole lot of the bank's money where he worked there wasn't a lawyer anywhere that could keep him from serving some time in jail. Add that to the fact that he had this nasty habit of taking a swing at Martha Jane on a semi-regular basis, and the writing was on the wall for her to get away from him. The bad thing is a lot of his trash rubbed off on her before she could do it. You know you can't be around dirt and excrement too much without getting some of it on your own shoes.

Tom sat and listened. He was with Aunt Gail at the Waffle House in Rhodes, and it had been two weeks since Martha Jane's funeral in Jonesborough. All he is hearing is fresh news to him. He had stayed in a motel outside Jonesborough for five days, seeking out Gail and Martha Jane's other aunt who lived with Martha Jane's dad, in some vain attempt to lessen the pain of Martha Jane's death on everyone, not succeeding at all with the father, who was pretty much ready for institutional living soon, so close to losing his faculties for good as he was that Tom was not the least bit sure the old guy knew what was going on during the visitation and the funeral. Tom had met Martha Jane's aunts at the visitation, Gail knowing him before he knew her, and she had asked him to come and see her when all this was over and the two of them were back in Rhodes. Tom put it off as long as he could because he felt that as soon as the meeting took place the final nail would be driven into Martha Jane's coffin and then she truly would be gone forever.

Martha Jane was always a nervous sort of girl, Aunt Gail told him. Her mama—my little sister—died, and her father started going down right after that, and that didn't help Martha Jane a bit. She'd have spells and the headaches would come soon after, and before it all got said and done she was taking pills just so the pain wouldn't start up again in her head. I don't know if it was so much physical pain or if it was nerves from her marriage or if it was both of them put together, but she ended up having a real problem with it. She went to doctors to help her do something about it, and then there were more doctors all of a sudden than there was at the beginning, and every dern one of them were giving her pills to take on top of the ones she was already taking. I know you didn't know about any of this. Martha Jane told me how she was afraid to tell you too much about herself. She said what a nice guy you were, but how she thought you were sad and a little angry too, and how it was hard for you to trust anybody much, and how she was afraid she was going to do something to drive you away, and she didn't want anything like that to happen, how sad that would be, because you were the only nice thing that had come along in her life for the longest time. She told me all this before she left to go home. She said she wanted to try and figure out a way to make this work with you. She said she was a hundred percent certain she was in love with you.

Tom sits with his sad countenance and listens. He pays the bill and thanks Miss Gail—that is what he calls her in his oh-so-Southern polite way of addressing an older lady—and makes his way to his car. It is November, the official beginning of Fall two weeks ago, and the sky is still clear blue and every tree still the deepest green, every ray of the sun as orange/yellow as possible. And in this mid-afternoon, with Rhodes settling back into labor mode after breaking for lunch, Indian Summer appears capable of lasting forever.

But Tom Lockhart knows it is already done. Beauty is hanging by its fingernails, losing its grip with each lengthening shadow, and soon clouds will come to hide the blue and blanket the sun, will cover up what stars try to appear and tell the moon to hide itself away. He travels down South Main and runs a yellow light or two, not wanting to sit still and allow whatever is creeping up his spine to finally get its hold on him.

He has not shown up for work for over three weeks now. He has not called. He expects sooner or later Matt will call him, but he doesn't know exactly what he wants to hear or what he himself will say. Your sister is a murderer, he could say. The woman who loved me is dead, he could say. That is all he knows right now, and he is sure Matt doesn't want to discuss either one. He is certain Matt knows all about what really happened to

Garland and the way he died. There is a lot to talk about, but no one wants to say the words.

His days in Rhodes are peaceful and serene no more. The fact that he knows nowhere else to go only compounds the matter.

He sees Dewey's pickup with the tail down pulled up to the garage. The doors of the garage are open and Dewey is struggling with the RCA console—the antique monstrosity that has always been somewhere in Dewey's orb, so Tom knows this is getting to be serious business once this item starts getting transported somewhere.

"Hey," he says to Dewey when he pulls up. "I thought you were selling everything and not taking anything with you."

"Everything's already gone except for this old son of a bitch, and the only reason for that is I couldn't bear to sell it." Dewey attempts to get the front legs of the console up on the platform, and Tom steps over to help. They lift it up into the cargo area and slam the gate.

"That's about it," Dewey says. "This," he points to the console, "I couldn't let go of. I can't take it with me, so I was going to see if you wanted it. Everything works, and it opens up to store albums too. We could get rid of a few folks and stow them inside here and nobody'd ever be the wiser. I bet Doug would fit in there just fine," he smiles, "if it ever comes down to that."

"Doug? What's Doug done to get a contract put out on him?"

"Linda, my friend. You remember Linda, don't you? Linda who married Doug when she thought I was going to be crazy forever."

"Seems to me she was right."

"Allow me to let you in on a little secret, Thomas. Linda is thinking of joining me in Ireland some day in the sunny future. She just has to get a few things straightened out first. Like divorcing Doug, which is number one on the list. This is something that's been in the works for a while."

"I thought you two were history a long time ago."

"It's never over until it's over," Dewey says. "Things are always happening right under your nose just where you can't see them. You have to stay alert to the ever-changing vista."

"Don't I know it."

"Speaking of weird happenings and all, I have to say that next to dearly-departed Garland, you, old pal, are the talk of this town. I went into Thompson's for a burger the other night and I must have had ten people ask me about you. They were all wanting to know about you quitting your job with Matt and if Abigail had anything to do with it."

"I haven't officially tendered my resignation. I've just stopped making personal appearances down at the dealership."

"Well, just about everybody I talked to has you right square in the middle of Garland and Abigail. I don't think anybody knows much about you and Martha Jane, though. That seems to be a secret." Dewey lays a hand on Tom's shoulder and shakes his head. "I'm sorry about what happened. She seemed like a nice girl the couple of times I was around her. I could tell the two of you had feelings for each other."

"We did."

Dewey doesn't seem to know anything much more to say, so he reaches in and pats the RCA on the surface a couple of times.

"I generally try and not get too sentimental," he says, "but I'm going to miss this hunk of wood. We've been through a lot together over the years." He takes his keys from his pocket. There are about a thousand keys on the fob, some of them probably belonging to vehicles that disappeared years ago, but he selects the truck's key as if by feel. "You sure you don't want this contraption?" he asks. "You're about the only person I know who halfway deserves to have it. If you don't want it then I think it needs to go out in a blaze of glory."

They drive to a curb market on South Main with the table in the back. Dewey goes inside and returns with a paper bag full of Coors.

"Your favorite brand, right?" He sets the bag in the bed and gets behind the wheel. "Let's go to your place and get silly," he says, "for old time's sake. We can sit out on the balcony and get drunker'n hell and watch my old friend back there in the back get a Viking funeral as a send-off. Heck, she can't go with me, so if you don't want her she's better off dead. I refuse to let anybody else in this goddamn world touch her. Haven't seen a human being come along in a long while who deserves to hear music from a machine like this one. I think we ought to build us a funeral pyre like old Jim Morrison used to sing about and sit upstairs under the stars and watch it burn."

Tom looks over at him like there's the possibility he's truly gone loco, and Dewey laughs.

"I sold the house, Tom. In a couple of days I'm out of here. Maybe Linda's going to come join me and maybe she won't—there's no way of telling what's going to happen. I guess I forgot to fill you in on all that. I also neglected to say that you're the lucky guy who gets to drive me to the Knoxville airport. For that good deed I'll sign the title to this fine pickup truck over to you, and you can drive it back and haul trees and dirt around or sell it for some ready cash or whatever, because once I'm off the ground and in the air I'll have no further use for it. Because, I promise you, I'm never coming back. All my dough is going into an Irish bank and that's it."

Once they get to Tom's house, they unload the console with grunts and curses and mashed fingers, then push and lift and pull and drag until it's at the back of the house, where they leave it twenty yards off by itself and away from everything that might be flammable. They gather tree branches and break them up into kindling along with anything else that will burn, then Tom empties a bag of charcoal out and makes a bed under the legs and spreads a pile on top. He squeezes lighter fluid everywhere possible and hands a box of kitchen matches to Dewey.

"Here," he says. "It's only right that you should have the honor."

It takes Dewey several tries but the coals and the wood and a box of Tom's old manuscript drafts at last ignite, and the flames start licking around the console in a circle. When they're convinced the fire is not going to go out or sputter, they climb the stairs to the balcony and take seats by the railing to watch the spectacle. The console begins acquiring a red glow at its center, and flames shoot higher while dark smoke lifts skyward. Tom hopes no one calls the fire department, thinking maybe the cemetery is on fire. Also, he thinks, we don't really need Doug showing up around here right now. Don't know what he does or doesn't know about Linda and Dewey.

Screw it, he thinks, because he'll probably be leaving soon too. He can't pay the utilities without a job, and besides, why would he possibly want to stay here alone and think about how Martha Jane was once in his bed, and how she will never be here with him again.

Unless he dreams it.

It's a funny damn thing," Dewey says. "I've hung around this town my entire goddamned life, even dropped out of school to come back to it because I just couldn't see anything out there in the world worth picking up stakes for, and now here in the winter of my discontented years I'm selling everything off and burning what's left and getting out of here with practically nothing to show for anything I've done, but for some reason this is the best I've felt mentally in years. I tried never to whine about my life too much, but I haven't been too happy about very much at all for a hell of a long time now."

"Sometimes I wish I could tap my heels together and go back in time and do everything differently."

"I did things just exactly the way I pleased for a long while, and it still didn't help. Here," he says. He passes a tightly rolled joint to Tom. "We may as well get busy and smoke all my stash. It's not like I'm going to be fool enough to try and take it with me on the plane. I'm too long in the tooth to start serving a prison sentence now."

After an immense burst of flame and smoke, the console bonfire settles down into a comfortable burn, the fingers of the flame licking the sides of the cabinet, the fire in a nice circle below the turntable progressing up in a steady passage breaking through the center to float up to the sky. Tom and

Dewey watch it burn like they have never seen fire before. After a while Tom imagines Peterson Library in his head once again, the fire that burned there, and in his mind's eye he sees Faith Mercer falling to the earth below.

How many times? How much longer?

"I wish I could gather up all the negative scrapheap shit in my life with a big existential shovel," Dewey remarks, "and burn it up and cremate it all down to ashes, just like we're doing with the holy RCA there. Wouldn't that be cool? Think of it, Thomas. All the stupid crap we've carried around in our heads for years could be gone with the flick of a Zippo lighter. See all the crap you've made yourself keep remembering turn orange and go black and then just drift away with the wind, never to be reckoned with again."

"Happy trails to you," Tom says.

"I don't know if it's like this for everybody. Hell, I doubt it. It's probably just the intelligent thinking dumbasses who have to get stuck with all the mental garbage a lifetime brings, and I think it starts early. Take you and me, we're good examples of what I'm talking about. We've never really said it out loud much, but I think we can agree on the premise that at some point in our childhood and all that followed after it—hell, probably even the better part of our adult lives, we're such fools—but at one time or another we started believing what we'd read in books and seen on television and the movies and somehow came to think that life was like that to a tee, a fairy tale with a happy ending. The good guys won, and there was always going to be a beautiful princess out there who was made for you and you were made for her, so cue the swelling closing music and tell the birds to start singing and gather everybody into a circle and join hands and smile, because we bought into the idea that this was the way life worked. It was a lot more pleasant to let it take over the old cranium and never have to consider how everything you'd let yourself come to believe was actually a load of shit and you were going to learn differently and suffer greatly for the rest of your years finding out the truth."

"I found out a long while back," Tom says. His fingers burn from the hot roach in his fingers, so he lets it drop into the ashtray. "I just thought I'd ignore it and it would one day go away."

"I don't know if I ever told you this much about it," Dewey says. "Probably not, since I'm pretty sure it's been a deep dark secret since the first of Forever. The reason I left school and gave up my scholarship was all because I was afraid I was going to lose Linda and have to spend the rest of my life without my one true love. Jesus. That's the way I built it up in my mind back then. I made it seem like there was only one road I could take to lead me to the pot of gold at the end of the rainbow with my name on it, and there was just one girl in the entire universe who could make me happy for eternity. Everything was this big absolute plan all mapped out in my head, and I thought if I deviated off course my life would go to shit and all my dreams would tumble into broken pieces. I didn't think any amount of education could save me from anything like that, so I quit and came home with the idea I'd marry Linda and take my chances with the Draft and live here in Rhodes and someday write my own personal version of *Ulysses* or *The Wasteland* or something. And what happened was none of it worked out the way I had it in my head. Linda ended up marrying Doug—which I don't really blame her that much for now, since he was the wiser and more stable choice who was steady and not way out there and who'd probably be a good father and provider and shit like that—and I tinkered with about a million broken-down cars to make a living and wait for my time to come around again, memorizing Joyce and Eliot and hanging out with squirrels waiting for the day when my own divine inspiration was going to come over me, and now it's all these years later and I've come to realize that all that stuff was just filler I put in my head so I wouldn't take notice of how life was going by without me and I didn't matter to any part of it in the long run, and how all those dreams and plans and waiting for the day when it all comes together isn't going to happen, wasn't ever going to happen anywhere except in my own head where all the nonsense of great things to come had holed up and made themselves at home. So one day I started doing some spring cleaning mentally, and I found all that crapola festering there, and I had to drag it out into the light and look at it, and that's when I had my own epiphany. I saw how I'd been full of it all along, that what I believed in and thought was going to be mine was never there for me to begin with. I had to tell myself the truth. Everything I believed in was just something I made up to make me think my life here on earth was something special and not the big void that it is."

"Goddamn," Tom says. "Run in there and get my razor. Too much more of this talk and I'll be needing to open up a vein."

"And this is why, Thomas Lockhart, ye of Covington College and Chattanooga and formerly and lately of Rhodes, I am abandoning you as of one week's time, setting my status as a United States citizen aside, and leaving for a place where I'm not constantly reminded of how I have possibly wasted my life, taking off so I can perhaps find a place where I just might fit in. And be happy, Tom. With or without Linda. Let's not forget happy. Being happy is not overrated."

"Sounds like you've got it all mapped out. I'll miss you, Dewey."

"Hey, you can always come join me one of these days, when you get straight and all and not crazy as a two-dick dog. It's not like you've lost anything here."

"No. I'm a glutton for punishment. I have to stick around here until the game plays out."

"It's a hell of a game, isn't it? I haven't figured out how to win at it yet."

"Sometimes, Dewey, you never do."

"What are you going to do about your job? And that damn Abigail? You're going to have to deal with all the Lanes sooner or later if you stay here."

"I suppose I'll just keep sitting here watching the console burn."

"That's good for now, but what about tomorrow? And next week?"

"There's lots more furniture inside I can add to the pyre if I need to."

On Monday morning Dewey comes by in the truck and picks him up. A collapsible suitcase sits in the bed, that and a backpack being the sum total of Dewey's fruits and labors for three decades in Rhodes. Tom wonders if Dewey has even told Linda that today is the day he is leaving. He doubts it, since Dewey has always believed words are wasted if you say them too much.

It doesn't take but a minute to get the bag checked in, and so they stop and buy coffee and a travel book on Ireland. Can't decide whether to raise horses or be a golf pro or join the IRA, Dewey says. Need to do some studying up. Lots of opportunities for advancement over there.

"Two hours from here to Newark," he says. "Been in that airport once before. You can look out a window and see the Empire State Building off in the distance. Got an hour layover, then it's on to Ireland. Eight hours over the Atlantic and I touch down in Dublin."

"And the house is sold for certain?"

"They signed the contract Friday. I told the agent they could start moving in today. All my stuff is gone, Tom. I own nothing anymore. Scattered to the winds, best way to do it. When I croak, buddy, I want you to gather up my ashes and sprinkle them in the middle of River Road when the wild wind is blowing hard. That way I won't be stuck in one place for eternity."

"You'll probably outlive me."

"I probably will. You've got a lifestyle going on that's bound to explode one of these days."

"Have to make sure I'm not around when that happens."

"Well, it's that time, amigo."

Dewey extends a hand and Tom can't help but give his old pal a hug. About the only living soul I feel like doing that to these days, he thinks. Everybody else I can't seem to get far enough away from.

"The title to the truck is in the glove compartment," Dewey says. "I already signed it over. Take good care of it and go see the USA in it if you can, even if it's not a Chevrolet."

He waves his hand and takes off walking. Tom watches him enter the security lines and get through without getting searched or arrested. When he disappears down the hallway, Tom turns around and makes his way back through the terminal. For a minute he thinks about going to the observation deck and watching Dewey and his plane take off, but he is not Rick from *Casablanca* and there is no Louis standing by his side ready to begin a beautiful friendship. No, he is alone now, and so he walks out the doors with other strangers walking along with him, other strangers coming toward him and entering the terminal to fly away to anonymous lands. He wonders if he will ever see Dewey again, if this is just one more lesson in how the world comes and goes and sometimes is never really there at all, and he wonders too why it has taken him more than fifty years to learn such a thing. He thinks about driving back to Rhodes and how when he arrives the city will never be, without Dewey, the same place again. He wonders if Linda will be leaving Rhodes too, but he doubts it. He knows how life goes, how people fit inside it mostly. It will take a while for folks to realize that Dewey is gone, that Dewey is there no more, and when they do they will adjust to his absence. They will take their balky cars elsewhere. They will pass down River Road and not look up to see him in his chair with his glass of Mateus and *Ulysses* in his lap and Phyllis by his side. And Linda Burke can go on the rest of her life not giving much thought to the man on the hill, who once loved her as no one else ever did, who she maybe loved as she never had before and never has since, but in the end it will not matter, it will make no difference, it will all go by in the end.

And who knows, he thinks, if I'll be down River Road, inside my house of stone, watching cars and people come and go through the gates of River Grove on their way to and from the gardens and the tombstones and the vistas and all the assorted landscapes of death.No way to know until tomorrow and all the days that follow.

TWELVE

He began seeing her around town again.

The weather was still nice, sunshine and blue skies despite it being November. He'd yet to hear anything from Matt about his job, and as the days went by he began to give up on the idea of him ever calling to find out what in the hell had happened to him. Matt doesn't want to talk to me, Tom decided. He knows I might ask questions about Garland and how he could get dead all of a sudden and the person who got him that way, sister Abigail, could get an extended vacation as a result, in this town of Rhodes where memories get short and questions never get answered and a dead guy who was once hot shit around the city can get planted in River Grove and then tomorrow comes around and the sun is shining and it's a brand-new day and what happened yesterday is gone and won't ever be back.

Being as he is unemployed by choice, Tom spends immeasurable amounts of time on the balcony looking off into the woods and thickets where leaves turn gold and red and fall a little more each day. One day he is able to see the river. At first it is only a splash of gray and blue, but as the leaves thinned it became more spacious and not something anymore unseen and non-existent. At times he can hear the sound of a car's throaty engine inside the gates of River Grove with shifting gears speeding up River Road toward South Main, and he knows if he gets up and looks he would see Abigail driving off in her BMW. Sometimes eating a cheeseburger at the Olympia he sees her pass by from his table at the window, and he wonders if she is still teaching at Rhodes Middle or on a leave of absence or if having a job was something she had abandoned. Once he passed Dewey's old house and was looking up the hill to check if anyone was living there yet, and a horn blasted telling him to pay attention and stay on his side of the road. He looked to see Abigail speeding by him, passing in a flash and not recognizing who he was because he was driving Dewey's unfamiliar truck that Abigail didn't know was his yet, because she'd been out of town and didn't know Dewey was gone and the truck belonged to Tom now. Maybe she had seen it parked at Tom's house on those times when she circled by to check on him, to stalk him, but he guessed she'd not equated it in her mind that it now belonged to him.

He grew tired of eating out each night, sitting alone at some table at the Olympia or Thompson's hoping no one would come and try and talk to him, people wanting to sit down and shoot the breeze and maybe discover just what in god's name old Tom Lockhart was up to these days. Charlie called him several times; Doug would want to meet for a beer. Folks wanted to know if he had a plan or if he'd just gone altogether crazy in his old age. Well, damn if he knew. Damned if he could tell them. He didn't seem to have any fresh ideas, and he knew if he did he wouldn't tell anyone what they were anyway. He might be crazy, but he wasn't stupid.

He decided the thing to do was stock up on food and cook at home for a while, avoid the crowds and inquiring eyes, so he drove to the Polka Dot Piggly Wiggly to fill a cart. Charlie, thankfully, was not to be seen anywhere, either out on a Thursday night spree or holed up in his back-office retreat in the middle of one. Tom is on Aisle Five when he sees Abigail go by with a hand cart on her arm. A glass bottle of mixer pokes out from the top of the basket, and he watches her pick out limes from a produce bin and then go toward the office by the checkout lanes to get cigarettes. Tom deduces she is readying herself for another long night of drink and smoke, and he wonders if she's already stocked up on ammunition too, since packing her pistol will complete the trinity for her and possibly get her through this night until tomorrow.

He pushes his cart towards the front, going slow to give Abigail plenty of time to check out and leave, the front wheel on the cart making it want to veer to the left and topple a display. He lingers back until she goes out the door and he can see her get in her car through the big window at the front. She sits a minute with the top down on this November night, then backs out and drives off. He wonders where she is going, home perhaps, or will she show up at his place later this evening? Batten down the hatches, he thinks. Say a little prayer. It could be I'll be murdered myself soon.

With eyes darting back and forth and around, he walks to the truck in the possibly-treacherous Piggly Wiggly lot, unloads his bags in the bed and heads for home. He takes an alternate route, thinking if he is being followed he can lose his pursuer in a maze of streets and turns and stealth behavior. The real problem will be River Road, since there is only one way in to get to his stone fortress, but he sees nothing but a lone deer on his way down the connecting road, and the driveway is deserted, and save for the ghosts and spirits who are always around to greet him it appears he is alone. He gets out of the truck and all he can feel are the watchful eyes of coyotes coveting his groceries, a sensation he is so accustomed to by now that it is almost comfortable, because it means he is at home.

Once inside, he turns every light in the place on to see if anyone is lurking in closets or behind doors. Most spooky and perilous, he thinks, and he is thankful he has a strong heart and knows what to do in the face of impending danger. Lock the doors, he commands himself. Avast and ahoy. Get these lights off now and resume blackout mode. Up to the balcony to grill my supper. Steak and potatoes, Coors on the side. Sample some of this weed Dewey has bequeathed me. Keep an eye peeled down the road for strange cars approaching. Or maybe townspeople with torches. While paying due attention to nearby howls and scratching at the door. Who knows what may be out there wanting in to do me harm?

His phone buzzes and it's the same number again. Maribeth. Calling two and three times daily now. Unaccustomed as she is to the word no. Thinks perhaps there was more to their meeting than a couple of deep kisses for old time's sake. Doing his best not to let her know she's right. Because it's tempting, even without her enduring beauty and the fact she's wallowing in it. Money. Could come in handy. Since the only way he's surviving financially without a place of employment is from the sale of the El Camino to Doug. Who envisions it as a fixer-upper that he can turn over for a chunk of dough. Perhaps could have done the same thing but one lacks anything resembling mechanical ability. Let this phone go to Voicemail and screw up the courage to listen to the message later. Sound of her voice. But not right now. Or for a while. Martha Jane still lingering. Perhaps forever.

Wonder how it all came about. Read somewhere once that everything happens for a reason. Coincidences and convergences of fate. Go for a walk in a cemetery and run across someone who brings me back to life. Dead for so long. A flat tire makes her stationary and lets me catch up to where she is. A voice I heard that made me dream I was in love with its owner. And in a place where the shadow of death is always front and center. She gave off light. Had to shield my eyes from such brightness. Hadn't seen such a thing in so long. Forgot it was out there. Believed it didn't exist anymore and maybe I'd only conjured it up to begin with so I'd have something to believe in and not go crazy thinking how death and being alone was all I'd ever have to show for my time on earth. While everything went on its merry way. And Martha Jane that first night just went ahead and said it out loud. This is probably not the wisest thing I've ever done. But I want to kiss you. I don't even know you, but it's what I want to do. I'll tell you right off the bat that I've never been smart. But I do have this way of knowing things. And I know you already. And you know me.

It went along like that. Couldn't come to comprehend how such an angel came to me in all my darkness. Even when I told her who I was and where I'd come from. Black of heart and dark of night. Things I'd done that could never be taken back. Might as well call me a murderer. Because life ended because of me. Or so I believed. Maybe it wasn't me who caused any of what had happened, but I had murder in my heart. Inside me for a long time until I used it up. Did my best to go straight and atone for all those sins. And just when I'd think redemption was near. Here would come something else.

He doesn't know how long he has been sitting looking off into the dark horizon of the night. He remembers eating and drinking while stars shuffled along overhead, but he did not play music for fear of it being heard by possible invaders outside his door. At some point in the early morning hours he awakens from a slight sleep excursion to the sound of sirens and the intermittent whoops of emergency vehicles. He walks over to the corner rail and looks off past River Road toward South Main and sees a halo of blue and red lights reflecting through the darkness. There has been a wreck. He tries determining how many cars are involved or exactly where the accident has taken place, but he is too far away to tell for sure. He guesses he will find out tomorrow, when he watches the news or listens to the radio or goes into town. He will find out all about it. But for now it is not that important. He is here and out there is the rest of the world, and for an unspecified amount of time this is the way he wants it to stay.

He goes inside and hits the sack. A long day. He guesses his brain has been emptied of every image and instance, because for the first time in weeks he does not dream.

He hears about it on the news the next morning.

It is the first time he has turned on the library's station since Martha Jane's death, since he has not been able to stand the idea that someone else is speaking into the very same microphone or sitting in the same chair she once used. The image and idea of life going on without her has been too much for a while, and it is only in a moment of forgetfulness that he clicks on the radio this morning. He catches the gist of the report after it has been reported on a few seconds, and it rushes to his ears almost as if the information it was dispatching is growing old already and it was time to move on to something else.

"The accident occurred at approximately one-thirty this morning on the southern stretch of South Main near the Lane automobile dealership. Reports say a car crossed the center line and hit a car going north, causing it to go off the road and into an embankment. The driver and passenger of that car were rushed to Athens Memorial Hospital, where both are listed in critical condition. The driver of the car that police say is responsible for the accident suffered only minor injuries and was released. There is a suspicion of impaired driving, and an investigation is being done."

He is pouring his second cup of coffee when these words register in his head and he knows all at once it is Abigail who is involved. He is aware of this because of the danger she carries around with her, how that malevolence has incorporated itself into some form of dangerous entity that hits one first with beauty and light and lingers long enough to cloak wherever she has been in darkness, and it is hard to ignore it. He also knows she had been by his house earlier. He'd heard the sound of the BMW racing up River Road. He knows it is her who has caused this accident. Still, he makes himself stop with these thoughts and tell himself that what Abigail has done this time has nothing to do with him. He is untouched by her for once, but someone else, two people maybe, could soon be dead. He wonders if he should call Matt and see what evil she has wrought this time, if his ancient friendship with Matt should encompass such an occurrence as this.

But he decides to keep his distance, to stay away. He is poisoned enough already. He doesn't need any help from the Lane family.

Of course the driver in the wreck is Abigail, as if there had ever been any doubt in his mind.

It is four days later, while he is enjoying another in a succession of cheeseburgers at the Olympia, when Matt walks over to his table and stands before him.

"Mind if I sit down?" he asks.

He sits across from Tom and crosses his hands on the table, looks over at Tom and smiles.

"It's been a while, buddy. To tell you the truth I came down here today on purpose, just to see if you might be around. A couple of fellows from Service told me you liked to eat lunch here, that they'd seen you here a few times. This is like the third time I've come looking for you. I started to come out to your place but I thought it would be a little too pushy. I thought it might make for an awkward situation."

"You shouldn't feel that way. Probably I'm the one who should have come see you."

"Well, I suppose both of us have had a lot of things happening, most of it not very good. I know about the trouble you had with your lady friend. I was sorry to hear it. I would have called you or something, but I thought maybe it was best to give you a little space."

"I heard about Abigail," Tom says. "It sounds pretty bad."

"It hasn't been easy, but it's getting better. One of the people involved got released from the hospital yesterday, and her husband's out of critical care and into a room. So, it appears that eventually everything is going to be okay. A little healing over time. Probably I'll take care of their medical bills."

"What about Abigail?"

"Back in a rehab center again, as of yesterday. I think she signed herself out too soon the last time. She's definitely got a problem with substances, Tom, and she's having a hell of a time getting it under control."

He orders a glass of iced tea from a waitress and leans back in his chair.

"I guess you know it as well as anybody, but Abigail has been an alcoholic from the very first time she ever took a drink. You know how wild she was in high school. Man, it was everything my folks could do to keep her out of trouble even then. They finally shipped her off to a private school her senior year. You were already gone by then. She went to UT-Knoxville after that and almost made it through, but she got pregnant her senior year and dropped out and get married. That was number one, and when she lost the baby—probably stemming from too much drugs and alcohol—the marriage went under too. She went back to school and finished up, then she married a guy who used to be one of my salesmen at the dealership—the best salesman I ever had, brought in a ton of money on commissions every damn month—but that one was over in less than a year and he couldn't leave town fast enough. He even tried to sue her for damages and we had to take him to court and fight it. He finally gave up and disappeared off into oblivion somewhere, and I've never heard of him since. She started teaching and made it ten years or so, and then Garland showed up."

Matt stops his tirade and lets the matter hang in the air. He takes a sip of tea and continues.

"I actually thought it might work out with Garland. He was smarter than the two guys before him. Everything appeared to be going along nicely. It seemed like the two of them had come together after their joint domestic troubles—Garland had a bad first marriage by that time under his belt too—and the two of them seemed ready to have some semblance of a peaceful life together. Abigail was still young, and they even talked about having children in the future."

Tom considers the possibility of Abigail being a mother and the image doesn't come into focus for him, but he says nothing. Best to let Matt say his piece.

"It got to the breaking point with Garland," Matt says. "As long as I knew Garland I could never talk sense to him. I tried to tell him the way Abigail was and how to deal with it, but he just went over the edge finally. He couldn't come to grips with reason when it came to her. Abigail broke off with him and took out a peace bond and it didn't make a damn bit of difference. She always said he was going to do her harm someday, and I had to agree. With the peace bond he knew he wasn't allowed to be within a certain distance of her, but he couldn't stay away and ignored it and came out to the house that night anyway. I saw him coming in and stopped him and told him to go away, but he said Abigail had called him and invited him out. I thought maybe they were trying to get back together or something like that. A few minutes later she took her pistol and shot him right there on the porch. He was trying to kick the door in, so she shot him before he could get at her. His truck kept sitting there in the drive, and after a while Abigail called and told me what had happened. I drove over and Garland was in the yard with half his head blown off. Abigail kept saying she'd tried to make him leave, but he wouldn't. I didn't know anything else to do, so I called the police."

Tom keeps listening to more narrative of all that has gone wrong in Abigail's life and how there had not been any way this incident could have been averted, and he thinks of the night Garland approached Abigail at Thompson's. Garland was angry and out of control that night too, but he hadn't acted entirely stupid. The guy was a lawyer with a good practice, he was a councilman, he ran the Park board, he knew what a peace bond meant. He wasn't somebody who was going to travel out to Abigail's house without knowing that if he did there might be trouble. There was Abigail's statement about Garland having a gun and how it was self-defense, but in another one of Tom's psychic moments he knows Garland didn't have a gun on him the night he died. He would bet the ranch Garland's gun had been in his truck, stored beneath the seat, stashed in the glove compartment. Matt had waited to call the police, and when they arrived they found Garland's gun lying on the ground beside his body. Abigail had to shoot him before he shot her. That was her story.

And Matt had corroborated it.

But Tom knows Matt had planted Garland's gun beside him there in the yard so it would truly be a case of self-defense. He knows this as sure as he knows anything in the world.

It is like everything is coming to him sitting there at the table with Matt talking, like he is in a Humphrey Bogart movie, and he knows that what was in his head before was true. Bad things never happened to the Lanes, he remembers, they just couldn't. It was fixed so they never got the chance. That was the way it was growing up, Matt making teams when he wasn't that good and all going well and never a dark cloud overhead. He can hear Matt telling him once how he had a way of making people see his way in the end, and Tom knows this is exactly the way Matt had wanted the city of Rhodes to see it that night, a beautiful woman from a prominent family having to defend herself from a bad man threatening her and meaning to do her harm, to sweep up this mess and all the messes that follow and clean up around all the corners, offer some plausible explanations about why things worked out the way they did, spread some money around, and then in a matter of time—a short time, really, because in the end people were people and people tended to forget things—all would be forgotten. Garland could be buried and accident victims would get well and become richer and after a little time away Abigail could come back home once more, and everything would all work out the way they always had.

Tom knew different. Things only really worked out for the Lanes. That was the way it worked in Rhodes. He was a citizen here, he was the younger brother of Sam Lockhart. He knows how the well-to-do are in this town, how they've always been. He knows how it goes without being told. He doesn't need a refresher course.

Still, he makes no mention of it. He is kind and polite and tells Matt how he hopes things work out, and then he gets up to leave. He tells Matt how he is sorry about walking away from his job, how he wishes he hadn't done such a thing. But he's not sorry. The job was one of those things, like Abigail, like a lot of things he'd been a part of in his life, thoughts he'd had, places he'd been, stuff he knew wouldn't work out right from the start, that he'd known from the beginning wasn't going to be a good fit for him, but he'd jumped in the water and swam around in the muck anyway. Because, he tried to tell himself, he'd had each time nowhere else to turn. But that was a lie too. He'd let himself off the hook with that way of thinking for way too long a time now, and the truth was he'd come back to Rhodes and gone right back to being on the verge of doing the same things again.

It had been coming for a long time. He'd persisted in ignoring it because he hadn't wanted to admit there was this sort of quality inside him that chose the wrong thing to do and made bad decisions and used people like chess pieces to get what he wanted, just like Matt, just like Sam had done, like Abigail, the way everybody in the world seemed to do at one time or another. He was a part of it and he was one of those people he had always looked down upon. He was a part of the enemy. He was right there with them, in cahoots, up to his neck in a river where everybody used whoever they could to keep themselves afloat.He walked to the truck trying to escape the terrible truth of who he was.

THIRTEEN

Maribeth continues to call and text. Tom cannot understand what she wants from him, why anything can be so important or dire, so he does not return the calls or acknowledge the messages. Silence, he theorizes, and a refusal to engage will eventually dampen her interest, but every day he finds that not to be the case. There is even a handwritten letter one day in his mailbox, asking him in a polite yet demanding sort of way just exactly what it is going to take to make contact with him. He doesn't answer that either.

The second week in November a form letter arrives with his name on it, forwarded from his old address in Chattanooga. Seeing such a correspondence from the place he'd left and promised himself never to return to sends a faint chill through him, and he starts to toss it into the trash but doesn't, mainly because he knows he will die of curiosity if he doesn't open it and see what it's about. Perhaps it will be good for a laugh if someone or something from that forlorn time is actually wanting something from him, if times are indeed that desperate, and he supposes he might need to know how they ever possibly got that way just so he can take a wider berth and avoid them even more than he's done previously. He knows how bad stuff has an ugly habit of sneaking up on one and leaping out with fangs and claws when one least expects it, so best to be in the know.

Covington College, he reads, is closing its doors after one hundred and fifty-nine years. The letter is reaching out to all the former alumni it can locate to provide this information and give them time to come and visit the campus one final time before the end of the semester, at which time classes will be suspended and brought to a close and the contents of the buildings will be duly appropriated elsewhere or marked for sale before the structures are demolished for the future owners taking over the property. Tom remembers the dilapidated state of the school when he was a part of it thirty years before and wonders what could possibly be put up for sale

163

that anyone might want to own. Perhaps there are sentimentalists and folks eaten up with rampaging nostalgia who might possibly desire a desk from a decaying classroom they once sat in back in the days of their golden youths, a bed from a dorm where dreams were hatched, a book from the library that once was of great inspiration, a brick from a revered building set to be leveled. Tom thinks of Peterson Library and tries to recall if souvenir seekers had advanced on its charred ruins and attempted to salvage some essence of it for the sake of their own selves, a piece of wood or tile from one of the floors, a door handle or some broken glass from a window. He wonders if a forensic investigator had ever ambled up with a pick and a trowel and unearthed sections of the porch where Faith Mercer went splat and oozed out her vital juices.

He sets the letter down on his desk, thinking that perhaps it will get lost in the clutter there and he will never have to think about it again. Among all the other information that keeps hurtling down the road his way, falling from the dark clouds above his head, coming through the windows to envelop his memory, he doesn't need the stormy mystery of Covington College and all its roster of ghosts from the past rearing up on him now.

But it does come to him in an uneasy, plodding way that his time here in this house of stone guarding the entranceway to Rhode's dead is coming to a close. There is nothing to keep him here anymore. His immediate family is together over the hill of River Grove in Sunnycrest, and, as in real life, they do not miss him. His old friends have nothing new to tell him, and he is reluctant to rely upon their kindnesses toward him much longer, for he knows it is misguided and they are merely living in a memory of him that really never was. Abigail, who desired him for some reason, is gone. Matt is his friend and employer no more. Dewey is set loose in Dublin or thereabouts, and the only way to see him is to board a plane and make his way across the sea, and it is not in him to do that now, for it is Dewey's world there and not his. Martha Jane is no more for this world, and try as he may the memory of what sweetness they shared is fading in his waking moments; she is only his in dreams now. He knows he cannot stay much longer here in this city of Rhodes, but he also knows he cannot go backward in retreat to fall upon some former battleground and pass the rest of his days and nights in regret for what has happened that cannot be changed and may have happened in a completely different sphere than what he had supposed, and is it to be for him to give himself over as penance to a multitude of events that only happened within his scope of understanding and were never really present at all? No, he cannot go back to such a place and time and dwell there. He would never find the pieces of the puzzle that would fit and give him an image and answer for all that has passed.

But he could stop for a visit and see if there is something of himself possibly worth retrieving.

He picks up the letter from Covington and reads it through again. The last days of the college are not so far off, Thanksgiving and the week beyond; by December the opportunity will be forever lost to view the place. Four weeks at the most. Perhaps he should begin winding things up here in Rhodes so he will be free to travel back through miles and time to say a final goodbye to the old alma mater.

He takes another look at Maribeth's handwritten letter, the way her penmanship looks like it ought to be in a how-to book on cursive writing, the swirls and precise forming of each letter and word. What would it take, she has written, to see him? Is there a chance she will ever see him again?

He calls Doug and asks if he will meet him tonight at Thompson's, then calls Charlie at the Polka Dot Piggly Wiggly and asks him to come too. Doug and Charlie are not the best friends he has ever had in this world, but for the lack of any other candidates available at this moment they will have to do. It is in his head that tonight is the best time for some hails and farewells to the old hometown, because it's settled in his noggin now and there won't be any going back. This time he's leaving Rhodes for good.

Wander around this house deciding what to pack up and what to leave behind. Get Doug or somebody knowledgeable to post some items on eBay, sell them off to the highest bidder. Refrigerator, stove, sofa, bed. Donate to whoever is around being borne back ceaselessly into their pasts. In memory of Thomas Lockhart and good old F. Scott Fitzgerald. Scott with his god-damned Daisy and me with Maribeth. Her letter with my name and address on the envelope. Her name on the note with a self-addressed envelope inside. Stamp for postage. Her way, he guesses, of being a smartass. Or being in such a funky state that desperate measures are required.

At seven o'clock to enter Thompson's for probably the last time. Unless he doesn't drink enough this night and feels compelled to travel back for more. But don't think that will be the case. Because when you're done, you're done. No hanging around to see if you change your mind. No hesitating or stalling this time. No remaining in the same place when your head is telling your feet it's time to get moving.

Doug and Charlie sit at the bar, watching the door for him to come. They swivel on their stools when he arrives, handshakes and smiles and quizzical looks. Know something is in the works but not sure what just yet. Because the Tom Lockhart they know is still a fellow full of surprises. Rule of thumb is you never know what he might do next. Been that way forever. But this time there's something funny going on. Truth is the Lockhart they knew way back when is different now. Been a change in the programming somewhere, because he's not precisely who he used to be. That's what Doug told Charlie earlier. And Charlie said, yeah, but who is?

"Fellows," says Tom. "Thanks for coming."

"I was happy to get out of the store," Charlie says. "And all my employees were even happier than I was for me to leave, because if I'm not around they can actually get some work done. It's funny how I'm the only one who doesn't give the first shit what happens around there."

"The question I have to ask," Tom says, "is have you ever given a shit about a whole lot of anything?"

"Now that you've raised the question," Charlie muses, "I'd have to say the answer to that is no."

More beer gets ordered, cold draft in a heavy glass pitcher. Tom orders whiskey on the side for an added treat. Blast from the past. Boilermakers, he announces. Just to let you boys know this is a serious occasion.

He gets right to it.

"I asked you to meet me tonight for a good reason. This is no social visit to catch up on old times. I'm way past the point where I want to talk about the days of yesteryear or discuss what a frigging drag it is getting old."

A long swallow of beer. Tasty as always here at good old Thompson's. Have to give the place credit. Never had a bad beer here. Which is really saying something. Add a finger of whiskey and jiggle the mug. Makes it even better.

"I'm here to tell you boys goodbye. The conviction has finally settled in my head that there's nothing around here for me anymore. Rhodes is bad medicine for what's always ailed me, and I don't know why I ever came back and decided to stick around. I guess at the time I was desperate. Everything had gone south in Chattanooga for me, and there I was, a fifty-year old guy with no job, divorced with a kid I hardly knew, and about the only thing I was qualified for was to go get a job stocking shelves and getting drunk every night. I'd given up writing because I was damn sure there wasn't anything inside me worth saying. Sam died and I came back for the funeral—and don't ask me why I did that, because it wasn't like there was any brotherly love between us anymore—and then Matt offered me a job, and since it seemed my presence wasn't required much of any place or anybody I knew of at that moment in time, I took him up on it. For some strange reason I thought I could come back to Rhodes and make a go of it starting all over again fresh. I thought I could find myself and maybe even start writing again, how I just knew I had another book in me. I could begin a new and productive life. Boy, talk about feeding yourself a shovelful of unadulterated crock."

"There are other things you can do," Doug says, attempting to offer some common sense. "Working for Matt isn't all there is in this town. Heck, you can have a job tomorrow at River Grove if you want. You know I can't keep an entire crew. They're all the time not showing up because they're drunk or in jail or some such shit, or just quitting without notice and not even telling me they're gone."

"I'm devoting too much time to the dead already," Tom smiles. "I'm trying to get to a point where I learn to deal with the living."

"Come down to the store tomorrow," Charlie tells him. "I'll put you to work doing something. Hell, I'll make you a manager first thing. You for damn sure can be around a bunch of living people that way, although you'll probably be coming to the back wanting to hole up with me in the end. People get scary as hell after you deal with them a while."

From the corner of his eye Tom cannot help but see the table where he and Martha Jane sat during their evening of declarations not so long ago. There have been lots of times he's been here in Thompson's through the years, sneaking in for illegal beer his senior year, visitations on dark nights of those rare occasions when he came home for holiday breaks, just recently in his return to Rhodes when the siren song of alcohol bade him come through the doors again, yet none stand out like the one spent with Martha Jane. Always one moment in somebody's life, he thinks, whether it be an instant of magic with a woman or someplace where something life-altering took hold, a poem, a song, a line in a book. Things stick and never go away. He thinks of his own two books, his contribution to the artistic world, and he wonders if his words are included in someone's moment. At the time he wrote them that was what he was shooting for. He wanted to speak to someone out in the world, the universe, the night. Did this ever happen? Is he a failure? He tries to summon all the moments of his life together to peruse and decide if they are tonight what he thought they were in the way back yonder, and he thinks it is probable he will never know.

"Does anybody remember coming in here on Christmas Eve? 1969?" Tom lifts his mug and swivels the contents around, making certain the beer and the whiskey intermingle and conjoin. Because he wants to get the full effect of this right now. Tonight. The whole magilla. "I was home from Covington my freshman year. We were all still minors. We just walked in here pretty as you please and sat down at that table over there"—he points off to a corner spot beneath a glowing Pabst Blue Ribbon sign— "and some woman, looked like she was frigging Zsa Zsa Gabor or somebody, took our order and brought us pitcher after pitcher with no questions asked. Remember that? I think the only thing she ever said to us besides asking if we wanted another pitcher was to tell us it was closing time and we had to go home and go to bed so Santa could hurry up and come down our chimneys."

"I knocked down a mailbox in my Roadrunner on the way home," Charlie says. "I never told you guys about that."

"I threw up out in my driveway," Doug laughs. "I fell into the shrubs on my way up the porch steps and rested there for about a half hour. I couldn't get up."

"Everybody was asleep when I got in," Tom remembers. "The house was dark and I didn't feel like going in. I was all wound up for some reason. I walked around the block looking at all the houses with their Christmas lights glowing. There wasn't anybody out at all. I ended up going all the way over to the park where the Little League diamonds and the softball fields were, and I walked out to right field and leaned on a chain-link fence for a while looking at the railroad tracks. It was getting cold, but I was drunk and I made myself stand there and wait until a train came by. I didn't even know if a train would be running on Christmas Eve or Christmas Day or not, and I wondered if maybe I'd be standing out there in the dark and cold forever waiting for one to pass, even though it didn't make a damn bit of sense for me to be out there, but I just stayed right where I was anyway. I was shivering and shaking and thinking about everything that had ever happened to me and everything that was going to happen in all the years to come, and I couldn't decide whether to start bawling or be scared to death or laugh out loud. Finally a train came and I walked home and went to bed. In the morning it was like it never even happened. It was like the whole entire night before was unreal."

A last opportunity to glance around and take notice of certain artifacts from the past. Some of which may have shaped my future for better or worse. Old Wurlitzer (currently out of order) where numerous quarters were dropped in the slot for the sake of a song. See myself standing there before it, stoned, ghostly, hands resting on the glass studying available selections. Already memorized the contents. Chuck Berry, Linda Ronstadt, the Rolling Stones. Neon signs on the walls. Miller, Pabst, Budweiser. Ancient history too. Stroh's, Blatz, Falstaff. Frightening to think I remember those brands. Relics. Makes me old. Can even taste them now in my mind, sing all the commercial jingles. Pictures of dogs and hot rods and newspaper headlines about Kennedy in Dallas, MLK in Memphis. Neil Armstrong taking his first step. If I walked into the restroom I could spend the rest of the night reading messages written on the walls, carved into the wood with pocketknives. Who was here when and poetic philosophical offerings left behind for future perusal. This is Thompson's Tavern and always will be, but Vince Thompson has been dead since before I took my first step. Family sold it to some Krausses with enough business sense not to mess with a good thing. Leave the Thompson's sign above the door and out on the street. Not to run what regulars there were away. Escaping sobriety

*again under the same name. Abandoned my senses here many times before.
Here once more with friends who were with me then. With me now. Except for
Dewey. Gone already like I will be soon. Continuity rises up and pats me on
the cheek. Rubs my shoulder in a gentle way. Says it's all okay now. It's as okay
as it's ever going to be.*

Here's to it, he thinks, and he downs his mug. Here's to all those things
that once were and used to be and probably never were in the first place.
Down another glass. Glug glug. Preserve this moment in my saturated brain
of what this minute and others before have been. A nice place for a lost soul
to occupy.

"To growing up blind," he announces aloud. "To the beginning of time
and the end of the world. To everything we kept believing it was even when
we knew it wasn't. Especially," he adds for emphasis, "for those moments
when it wasn't there and we could see it plain as day anyway."

"Better ease off that whiskey for a couple of rounds," Charlie says.
"You're starting to make too much sense."

"Can't have that," Doug says.

Tom smiling now at these two who knew him when and still didn't
hold it against him. Must, he thinks, make sure I do something nice to pay
them back someday for their faithfulness, even when in the deep dark past
I disappeared into the beyond and had it in my head never to set foot on
this plot of earth again. Could dedicate the next book to them. To all those
who knew me when and decided to let me live anyway. Forever in your debt.
Even when it would have been better if you'd been merciful and put a pistol
to my head. For your own good and salvation, Thomas Lockhart. This will
save you a lot of time and suffering later on.

*Say my farewells and throw a hundred-dollar bill on the table. Ben
Franklin in all his wisdom looking up at us. Remember him saying beer is good
for you and a gift from God. He loves us, yeah, yeah, yeah. Old Ben was right.*

*Out the door and into the night. Fall in full earnest, stars twinkling, win-
ter soon upon me. Have this feeling everything is fleeting, headed somewhere
in a hurry. Got to give it chase or get left behind. There's the truck parked
up ahead. Don't want to drive because it doesn't feel like it's mine yet. And
inebriation. Don't forget that. Let it sit and take off walking once more, but
that's not good enough either. Too many places to be when feeling this way and
the night only lasts a short time until morning.*

Have to run.

*Down South Main at a fast clip. Not used to such a pace anymore. Could
blow a knee or tear something. Used to run like this all the time when I was
a kid. It was a way to stop thinking about crappy stuff but also a way to get
it together upstairs. Passing things right and left helps one understand how*

transient everything is. Here for a while, gone pretty damn soon. Whether you like it or not. Not to stand still and become a target for missiles and flying bad omens. Get launched your way and you're gone already and not there to be the recipient. Good plan back then and probably still is today.

Take a left.

Into the neighborhoods and down the streets. Working people mostly in bed now. Nobody out and about. Lights dim and cars cold inside garages. Dogs barking from backyards. And lots of these yards I used to cut when I was a kid. Only way I had to make money. Delivering papers and working at the Piggly Wiggly with Charlie. And washing cars. Bought a used mower and went at in the summertime. Saved my money and bought a car. Dewey and I bought our first cars together on the same Saturday at the same used car lot. An Impala for him, a Tempest for me. Waxed and washed them in his driveway, arguing all the time over who was going to drive that night. Share joints and illegal beer. Cruise the streets dreaming of girls. Both wondering when one would ever come our way. And the two of us not truly wanting for that to happen too soon. Since the girls living in our heads were so much nicer than the real ones in Rhodes.

A few more twists and turns and there's Martha Jane's aunt's house. Come to a stop to rest a minute and look up at her window. Can almost see Martha Jane looking out. But she's not there, not all of her, at least. Maybe some small part lingering still. As I say hi. And turn and run some more.

Back to South Main and I still can't stop. Have to keep churning the knees even with the breath rising in my lungs and feet screaming at me to stop. Old man, they say, what in god's name are you doing? Because I know what time it is now. This is that moment when everything inside says stop. And you know you have to keep going, because there's something waiting for you down the road, and you won't see it unless you get there on time.

No need to stop and get in the truck because there's still a lot of running left. Know better than to stop in mid-flight. Hear my feet and my breath in rhythm passing under streetlights, turning the corner into darkness down River Road. City too cheap over the years to do away with the darkness. No streetlights. Look up the hill on the left and see Dewey's old house. Still dark, like it's waiting for him to come back. Don't hold your breath. He's gone. Like most everything else in Rhodes. Dead and gone or exiled or vanished with not a trace. Everything but memory. And that's going fast too.

Past my cold stony house with every light out. People drive by in the dead of night and think it's haunted for sure. And I can't help but agree. Seen a few weird shapes and illusions around there myself. Never could decide if I brought them with me or if they were present already. Don't really want to find out this minute. Keep running and go through the gates of River Grove. Ghosts *and goblins and bumpy shades down these lanes, but I'm not worried. Can't be much worse than what I've run up against so far. Spirits and spirits-to-be in waiting. Matt, who God will surely strike with a bolt of lightning one of these days, just because he's at the juncture where what he has in the bank is all that keeps him going and makes him believe he's got sole access to all that's wonderful in the world. Doug with Linda and the semblance of a happy marriage. Dewey there in Linda's head but far away now where the two of them will never mesh and meet. But that's show biz, Thomas Lockhart. Martha Jane's flowers and gardens un-withering still, not giving in to winter's call, living on so far without her, telling me that's what I need to do too. And I think how romantic that sounds, like I am Heathcliff and Martha Jane is some Cathy lost and gone on the dark moors, and even in my state that wants to believe how tidy and satisfying such a scene as that would be to my own personal cinematic happily-ever-after fade to black among not a dry eye in the audience, it is not that way in this real life. No, old friend, it just ain't that way at all.*

Run through the brown grass beneath the moon to Sunnycrest. Dad and Mother and Sam all here waiting. A few aunts around too, an uncle or two over there. See how they've measured off where Sam's tombstone is going to be. Probably in its final stages in the masonry and soon ready for delivery and installation. Never say never, but inside I know I won't be back to see it.

And when I stop running it comes to me.

There is no place in this plot of earth designated for Thomas Lockhart. There is my mother, my dad, Sam, all of them in a neat row, the rest of the family I halfway knew scattered about. A place for Sam's wife, Janet, for later, his son and daughter and whatever children they have sired. Sister-in-law, nephew and niece, remember hardly any of the names anymore. How sad and detached. But anywhere I look I know the ground is taken and not meant for me. Life follows death in a tidy little procession. No place for me to rest among all these fortunate.

Why am I here?

Suppose it is to say goodbye. One more time to all those whom I've already said it a thousand times before. To make sure, I guess, they finally hear me say the words this last time.

Say it aloud and wonder if it matters. If I shed a tear for a family lost, would anyone really know it? If I utter a curse for all that was taken and a world of wrongs, would anyone hear it? Would they care to?

Stand here in the darkest place on earth under a moon meant just for me. Wait for an echo of all I've brought with me to come back around, and when silence is all there is to hear to turn away and go back to my own lost world of wheres and whos and whys. This time to walk. Not to run.

FOURTEEN

Arriving at the city limits this Wednesday before Thanksgiving. Montgomery, hotbed of the Confederacy. Down Dexter Avenue to see the state capital building up on a hill. Dexter Baptist Church there too, where Martin Luther King preached. Confederate White House on down the road. Tall buildings, sunshine, and history. Not too much traffic today because the Thanksgiving holiday is nigh.

Departed Rhodes early with the sun coming up behind the trees and the world turning orange and pink. Gone before it made it over the trees and the night animals went into hiding. Deer and opossums and coyotes and racoons. Always wondered if bears might be out there too. Never saw them but that doesn't mean they're not around. Lots of things I've never seen, but I know they're out there somewhere. Feel their presence and can almost hear them breathing. Like love, faith, and peace. Still waiting for them to appear. Waiting for an omen or a sign that says hello.

Search through rich affluent lanes. Instructions written on an index card so I won't get lost. Go here, turn there, turn here. Big house on the left. If you come to an intersection you've gone too far. Turn around and come back. Driveway with high shrubbery. Stone mailbox. You'll know it when you see it. Because you've been here before. And I said but it was dark that night. And I had stars in my eyes, Maribeth. Because I couldn't believe I'd found you again. But today only to talk and that is all. There's something I have to say, a word or two to make it right somehow. And she said call me if you get really lost. Wondered how I could possibly get any more lost than I've been before.

Knock on this door with the heavy iron ring. Wait for a moment looking up at clear blue skies and fall foliage abundantly dispersed at every nook and corner of this immense house. Reds and pinks, yellow mums in bloom. Way down south summer wants to linger forever. Wraparound porch here where I could sit on soft nights thinking of how the meager world is outside the gates struggling to get by. Would have to do it in my head because real life and all its toils and strife can't be seen from here. Nothing or no one of that ilk anywhere near. And off to the right a garage larger than some hotels I've stayed in. A couple of gleaming cars parked in there without a scratch, dent, or suggestion of rust. Not allowed in this place.

Door opens and there is Maribeth, resplendent in a forest green dress and a gold necklace stretching all the way down to her breasts. Take note of that for sure. Her hair that color of wheat-silk I fancied immediately in antiquity time. She smiles and brown eyes invite me in. Make sure to not go too far inside this palace if I can help it. Make a wrong turn and be lost forever. One step too many could make me a goner. Because she is Maribeth and she is still something from a dream and my hands want to be upon her. She stands on tiptoes and kisses me on the cheek. Do my best and darndest to keep hands to myself. First time for everything, I think.

"You really did come," she says, like seeing is believing.

"Did you think you'd seen the last of me?"

"I was hoping not. Have you had anything to eat? Would you like something to drink?"

"I'm fine. I had lunch along the way."

Tom looking at her, Maribeth looking back. He wonders what to say about it all when everything has been said and done and decided already. Water, they call it, under the bridge. Been rushing out to sea a long damn time now.

"I suppose," Tom grins, "you've been wondering why I finally invited myself here?"

"I was hoping it was because you'd come to your senses," Maribeth says, "but I've tried not to let my expectations get too high."

"Good sense is not something I've ever excelled in. You have to remember I've been out of my mind over you for a number of decades. It's difficult getting all my ducks in a row after they've been flying off in any direction they wanted to for so long."

"You say that like you were the only one who harbored any kind of deep feelings about what went on between us. Because that's not the truth. Maybe you're having trouble believing it, but I never quite got you out of my system either."

She inches closer and all at once is in his arms. He doesn't remember allowing this to happen, but here it is right here, even if he is wondering if this is real or not or if Maribeth McAllister-Warren is merely acting out some scene she can enjoy thinking about later. He tries to equate this instant with all the images he's memorized from the starry past, and there's trouble getting it to mesh. He wonders if his feelings are as imagined and contrived as he's beginning to think they are.

"I need to talk to you," he tells her. "Can we go for a walk or something?"

"Let's stay here," she says, leaning into him and brushing his neck with her lips. "There's no one home. There won't be anyone here until tomorrow morning. We're all alone."

It is oh so tempting, he tells himself, it is so easy he would be a fool to let it go, but he remembers when this moment he is in was the hardest thing to accomplish on the face of this planet, when it was past difficult and well within impossible, and he wonders if he has managed to learn anything from all his years, the days and nights and beds and towns, and if he goes too far this time around that there won't be any coming back. Whatever had ruled him before would have him once again. He will have to once more believe ancient promises that were never true. He will have to accept as true once more that this is the thing he has always looked for, the magical thing that he had made himself believe he has lost.

He steps back and out of Maribeth's arms and wanders off into a cavernous room. There are two sofas and numerous chairs, a table with a floral arrangement and pottery strewn around, paintings and lithographs on the walls, a fireplace with a mantle with more pictures of strange people in past lives, gifts from exotic lands. Framed photographs of children and beloved spots, shadow images of toddlers, a sculpture of the Madonna, crockery collected, all set up in locales and positions to view and recall with a smile of a life well-led. And over on the edge of the mantle, a picture of a husband, dead now, gone, yet here, the father of her children, and Tom looks at the image and sees who he was left behind for all those years ago.

Was it love or money? Was it both?

He looks at Maribeth in her green and gold, sees her standing where he has left her in this house where she's lived all these years, a wife, a mother, a member of the world time sets its mark upon, and Tom knows all the sugarcoating and fictionalizing under the sun will never change any of it, that it is there upon Maribeth McAllister-Warren and upon him too, even him, and all the idyllic dreaming and rationalizing is never going to change the facts, is never going to make it the way either of them thought it once was or had spent their lives trying to convince themselves was the way it had really been, for time had seen it there and touched it with its hand and now there was not a way of going back, no way to know what had been back then and if it was real or not, had happened or not happened, was ever truly present in the first place, or was simply something that had been conjured up beneath the sky by the light of the moon and the shimmering of distant stars.

They walk out of the house into the sunshine toward a garden with thousands of colors in the brilliance of the blue November sky. Most of the world is tinged in drab browns and shadows and dingy grays by this time of the year, but not Maribeth. No, not here in her world. Here there is light and a shining sun; this is the world she has chosen. This is a world where light will always beam, where there are no monsters hiding in dark abscesses and corners waiting to do her harm. Here it is safe. Money, he thinks. Money keeps the bad things in the world somewhere else, away from her. This is what she wanted, then, now.

"You might as well go on and tell me," she says. "I know you have something on your mind and you're determined to say it."

Yes, he thinks, this is what he's been waiting for, prepping for this moment all these thousands of years.

"When I met you," he begins, "was a year or so after my parents' funeral. I never said much about it to anyone, because I was working it out in my head. They'd died in a car wreck, and I'd gone home for a week. While I was there I came to find out that nothing was the same anymore. It wasn't my home. I was a stranger and my brother and I didn't have the first thing to say to each other anymore. I thought maybe I was imagining things, that I was just freaking out over my folks being dead, but then a little later my dear brother finagled my half of the estate away from me, just as a show of how he was the favorite son all along and he was a budding lawyer with friends and knew just how to do it, and I was nothing but an outcast, and Rhodes wasn't my home from then on. I had to start getting used to the fact I didn't belong there from then on out."

By this time they are in Maribeth's manicured yard behind the house surrounded by tall iron fencing, the kind with points on the end where marauders and usurpers impale themselves if they attempt to enter the private grounds.

"I already had it in my head how I was going to make it on my own, how I was going to be a big-time writer and abide in spacious mansions in exciting cities and spend my life stampeding through all sorts of times with women and money. I thought the best time to start was right then and there at Covington. I spent a lot of time doing everything I could to go to bed with every girl at the damn school, every female there was in that entire city of McClellan. And I did a good job of it too. I was this rare form of hot shit drinking and drugging and screwing everybody right and left while a lot of poor guys were off getting killed in Viet Nam. I even came to believe I'd forged some sort of pact with God or the Devil or somebody that gave me the right to do whatever I wanted with whoever I chose and there'd never be a word said about it. There would never be any kind of payment I would ever have to render for retribution. Then you came along and the whole world changed."

"It changed for me too," Maribeth says in a whisper, like she is in awe or shamed by the memory of it.

"I met you and all at once decided to change my ways," he says. "I thought I'd make a deal with God on your behalf, Maribeth, like if He gave you to me I'd do everything differently. I promised I'd start being a good guy again, the fellow I used to be. And I did change. I did everything I could to keep my end of the bargain I'd struck, and since I'd never known by that time in my life what it was like to come up on the short end of the stick I was convinced in the end I'd get what I asked for and all my dreams would come true. I was going to end up with you and it was going to be the classic case of everybody living happily ever after. But it didn't turn out that way, did it? You took off and left me and came back here to Montgomery and married somebody else."

"I never lied to you. I told you the way it was right from the beginning. Everything was way far along by the time you showed up. I was falling in love with you but all the wheels were already too much in motion."

"I believed you loved me. That was what made it so damn hard."

"I did. But you have to understand there wasn't any way to walk away from my life back here in Montgomery—not for some crazy wild boy I hardly knew but that every girl I knew warned me about. You had a horrible reputation at Covington back then, Tom. You have to understand the way it was."

"I was only that way until you came along, until I met you. I saw you and all that other stuff was history."

"That's what you said. And I believed you too. All the time I thought I was being a fool, believing you like that, but I couldn't help myself." Maribeth looks into his eyes like she is searching for the right switch to throw, the right button to push to get them both out of the shadowy past and advanced into the light of today. "I loved you then, that was true, but sometimes love can't change everything into what it wants it to be. Sometimes love makes no difference in what's right and what's wrong."

"It made a big difference to me whether it did or not. You left and I went straight to hell for a good while. Maybe I've got only myself to blame for a lot of it, letting myself get hurt and angry because of you and then wanting to take revenge on the whole human race, but whatever, the truth of it is for a time I did some pretty terrible things to some people who didn't deserve it. It makes it a little hard to live with now, knowing you could do things like that willingly. You start not being able to forgive yourself."

"I heard a few things. I had a lot of friends still at Covington who saw to it I was well-informed of your comings and goings. All I had to do was answer my phone and there would be another story about you."

"Probably they were all true."

"They said you blamed yourself for Faith Mercer."

"I think she jumped because of me. I think she was pregnant and the baby was mine."

Maribeth smiles and shakes her head.

"Faith was traveling down that road from the first day she set foot on Covington's campus, Tom. Everybody knew it, especially me. I was her roommate for two years, remember? I stopped rooming with her that last year because she was doing so many drugs I thought I was going to get in trouble being around her. Faith was this frail, innocent looking little girl, her daddy was a preacher, for god's sake, but there wasn't a single solitary thing she wouldn't do. Drugs, liquor, boys, you name it. And it was heavy stuff too. I'm surprised you didn't know it. She was like a legend around our dorm, going to bed with a bunch of guys, going to bed with girls, even. Drugs, drinking, and all the time stringing people along on whatever weird game she was playing at the moment. The rumor was she got knocked up and didn't want to go home and face her parents, but I think she was beyond that already. What somebody said that makes the most sense is she was tripping on acid the day she went off the balcony. Knowing her, I'd bet it's true."

"I never heard any of that," Tom says. "She was in one of my Lit classes, and I started talking to her because she sat by me and I knew she used to be your roommate and I wanted you to know about it. I was in the middle of my plan to screw every girl I came across to get the taste of you out of my mouth, the thought and notion of you out of my head for good. To me, that was the only way I was ever going to get over you." He pauses, thinking of the way he was. Is he telling the truth? Was it that real, or was he young and wanted to make sure he put on a hell of a show? "And then she died the way she did," he says. "I thought she did it because I got her pregnant."

"Shoot," Maribeth says, "you may have gone to bed with her a couple of times but you weren't the only one. I'd bet there were fifty more guys besides you. God, it was common knowledge. Any of those boys could have been the father. That's if she was actually pregnant, which nobody really knows if she was or wasn't. I don't think she was, because Faith was always too smart to let something like that happen. My bet is she was high and drunk and tripping and over the railing she went with no help from anyone at all. I think you've blamed yourself for it for all this time and there's a good chance none of it happened that way."

"It's strange to me how I didn't know any of this," he says.

"You lived off campus," she says. "You always kept to yourself. Remember? In that tiny apartment behind those run-down shops downtown?" She looks at him and gives him her wicked smile. "I remember that place very well. There I was, this innocent little coed, and you whisked me away to your cave and did all kinds of things with me. You shattered my innocence." Her eyes twinkle. "I loved every second of it."

He doesn't respond to this. He is lost in thought somewhere.

"Come on, Tom. I went with you because that was what I wanted to do. I didn't want to leave school and go home to get married until death did me part and not have anything nice to remember the rest of my life. Heck, honey, I was young back then too. I wasn't about to walk away from the chance of making love with a guy like you."

Tom studies the particular way Maribeth's lips part and her oh-so-white teeth shine. He sees the glow in her eyes and sees the expensive way her hair is cut, her clothes so perfect for a woman her age, clothes that fit her like a picture in a fashion magazine that go with her skin and the color of her hair and tell whoever is looking at her how this is a woman time has no bearing on, a woman the past holds no sway in her actions or her beliefs, and the amazing thing to him is how he can see she has not changed from that girl he knew at Covington. She is exactly the person she was those years ago, her manner, her speech, her way of looking at what is happening around her own aura. She is always going to say the correct words, do what is best, choose the right path. She is older now but still Maribeth, still beautiful, her voice full of pure honey and her eyes sparkling like diamonds, and Tom takes it all in again. She will be this way forever. She is eternal.

She has always been and is now exactly the way he never believed she was. Always he'd thought she was someone else entirely. He had gone forever and a day believing she was this person from a wonderful dream he'd been having off and on for all his life.

And now it comes to him she isn't.

"I drove all the way here because I didn't want to say it over the phone. I didn't want to goddamn text you or write you some sincere letter. I had it in my head that I owed you an explanation about who I was way back then and who I became down through the years, mostly because all of it involved you. So I get here and I listen to what you tell me about Covington and me and you and a hippy girl named Faith Mercer who either fell or jumped off the top floor of Peterson Library. And Peterson doesn't exist anymore, Maribeth, isn't that a trip, because it burned down a month after Faith died, and I think now that everything I ever thought or believed about that time and place was all just a bag of smoke I made up in my mind, and it seems to me I've been going for years now looking and waiting for a bunch of things that never existed in the first place, for them to suddenly come alive and return to me and tell me what I need to know, like that is going to take care of everything I do and everywhere I go for the rest of my blessed life."

This is one hell of a speech and quite an explanation, and Maribeth sits down at a granite table with an umbrella keeping the sun off her and looks at him like he is the bearer of some fantastical tale of whimsy she has never caught wind of before, and he thinks how this is true and she is right, so right, again. This is all something she's never been concerned with much or even thought about taking into consideration. She has been busy with her own life. There has been so much to do and so many places to go. While all the while this whole shebang has been exclusively playing out in his head.

"Sometimes," he says, "you just read the signals and the signs wrong, those directions and diagrams that life gives you, and you go the wrong way and you end up believing the wrong dogma, you read stuff into situations that aren't there, and then later on you take a look at where you've been and what you invested your trust in and you find you managed to get it all wrong. Or maybe it's not that you necessarily got everything wrong, but more a case of you were operating under rules and guidelines that didn't apply to anyone else but you. Maybe it wasn't your fault because no one ever told you or pointed out how you were going about looking for the answers to everything in the wrong way, but the bottom line is, right or wrong, educated or ignorant, you were. That holy enchanted quest you traveled on for all those years had no final destination. You were doomed to keep going and going and searching for something that never was there to be found."

"I don't really know what you're talking about," Maribeth says. "You lost me way back there."

Tom has to stop from laughing out loud.

"Of course you don't," he says. "Nobody's known for quite a while, maybe even forever. And what's funny is I don't even know myself."

It is funny when he thinks of it this way, this banana peel he's been slipping on for so long, funny the way he's thought of himself as a wild beast when truly all he's ever been is a clown in a fleabag circus, one who keeps falling down and always wondering why, a bozo without sense enough to learn that walls and locked doors can't be penetrated simply by putting the old head down and running straight ahead, a fool who ignores the signs saying *Danger* or *Thin Ice* or *No Swimming* but just goes ahead and tries it all anyway, because maybe, the clown always thinks and is determined to make himself believe, this is the time or place or circumstance where everything pursued or sought after will be there, will be revealed, will be his to keep forevermore.

Ha, he thinks.

"You know, Maribeth, if you get down to brass tacks with you and me, then it's pretty funny how God has seen fit to bring us back together through our kids. My son marries your daughter, you're his mother-in-law and I'm her father-in-law. In the tribal sort of context, I don't know what that makes us, if we're now considered family or kin or what our status is, but it seems to me like it's a third cousin bordering on incest or something. I don't know if the two of us together are much different from those hillbillies in the mountains or crackers in the deep woods, marrying each other and fostering offspring with unibrows and crossed-eyes and buckteeth. That's not exactly what I had in mind back in those days of our star-crossed speedy courtship on the hallowed grounds of Covington."

"You haven't changed much, do you know that?"

"I thought I had until lately, but yes, you're right. I'm beginning to real-ize I'm still the same old me, and it's time to start getting used to it."

It's been an arduous steep road to where he is this moment, thirty-plus years of twists and turns, so he doesn't know how to tie everything up in a bow, end it all somehow with a flourish. He stands in front of Maribeth to be close to her once more the way he never thought he'd ever be again. He takes her in his arms like he is somebody from a love song and kisses her a long goodbye. Her lips are full and sweet, and he almost thinks he should remain in this pose indefinitely, but he knows how things get sometimes when a fellow outstays his welcome, and so he lets her go and steps back into his world and leaves her in hers.

"You're leaving, aren't you?" Maribeth says. "I'm not going to see you again, is that the way it is? I hope you don't feel as bad about it as I do."

"It only hurts when I smile," he tells her. "Anyway, I'll be seeing you at the family reunions every year. I'll be the one with the Jello salad."

This makes her at least smile, which makes the sweet sorrow of part-ing easier. He circles the driveway and drives out the gate in search of the interstate. His next stop is McClellan, two hundred miles away, and if he puts the pedal down he can be there by suppertime. He will be there on Thanksgiving Eve, an anniversary of sorts.

In time to say so long.

Coward that he is, Tom recognizes how he has not graced the city limits of McClellan since his graduation. This absence has not truly been deliberate, but it is also not one of those things that just happened to creep up on him either. He has known all along he's distanced himself from the scene of the crimes of his youth, and while he has not been afraid to give the place a great deal of reflection, he's still believed it wiser to stay far away and not frequent the battleground where ghosts and dead dreams could still be waiting to leap out and reveal further intimations of regret and loss and things he's done his dead level best to repress.

By suppertime he is in McClellan, cruising down Moss Road feeling secure in the fact he is in the right place and that not much has changed since his last time here. Already the town has mostly closed up for the night. Other than the ancient Lassiter Foods grocery store two blocks up and the modern Kroger store he'd seen on the west side of town where the highway runs into what goes for downtown McClellan and then is quickly on the way to somewhere else, not much will be in operation tomorrow on Thanksgiving Day. The biggest attraction McClellan has always had to offer is Covington College, closed for Thanksgiving break now and in another month gone for good. He sees the same Walgreen's that was here before is still open, but other than that the town is dark and semi-deserted.

The Dixie Pub is a thing of the past, replaced now by a salvage store with rickety furniture and farm implements on the front porch. The Dairy Dip is still around, albeit the building's color has changed and the sign at the street doesn't advertise the World's Best Corn Dog anymore. Now it just says Open until 10 Weekends, but there's no mention of a corn dog. Because he has it in his head how he is going to undergo this catharsis and self-exorcism in as precise a manner as possible, Tom holds to the rule he has set down that any contact he has with the Covington campus must be on this day, Thanksgiving Eve, which will make the entire experience occur within the same time period as it did in the haunted past. He doesn't know why this seems to be of such importance, but it has been in his head since he departed Rhodes, and he is very much aware there's no way to get it out without following through in exactly the same vein, trying to retrace the sad steps of yesteryear with the retreads of today. What he aims to accomplish from this he doesn't know, but that's at least not a whole lot different from anything else he's found himself in the middle of all these decades.

He has to go down the road some before he finds a motel for the night. Once that's done, he leaves the truck parked and walks back to town taking in the sights he remembers and those he doesn't, trying to decide what has changed and what hasn't. McClellan seems to be much like himself; a lot of it is the same, but older, the way he feels he is, both he and the town bordering on decrepit and ancient.

Once back, he looks around for a place to eat. For lack of any alternative, he picks the primeval Dairy Dip, from which he gets two of the world's formerly best corn dogs and an order of fries, washing them down with a cup of barely-carbonated root beer while he sits at a table outside. The weather is not cold for late November, yet sitting out in the cool breeze is not his favorite way of partaking of a relaxing meal. A lone picnic table seems to be the only place to wolf down his supper, since there is no dining area inside the tiny Dairy Dip. Once more, not much of a choice.

After he finishes, he swallows his saved for this occasion hit of acid, donated to him by Dewey, further enhancing what he believes will be a spooky evening to come.

Thanks, Dewey.

He walks down a sidewalk looking for something to entertain him for a few minutes, but all he ends up seeing is a hole in the wall bar called Judy's Inn, which looks like a cabin Jed Clampett and Granny would live in, what with its clapboard walls and tin roof and a lack of windows to look outside. The door is propped open and Merle Haggard's voice drifts out into the street, pushed along by a current of cigarette smoke and wafts of draft beer.

But draft beer is exactly what Tom is looking for this minute, so he walks inside without weighing the possibility that this is a beer joint of the highest stereotypical nature and that the possibility could exist that all sorts of dangerous characters are present inside, leaning on the bar, flirting with the wives of other men, kicking the jukebox, getting altogether shit-faced and looking for trouble. What he sees when he gets inside is none of that though, but merely one man sitting on a stool behind the bar reading a Stephen King book and a man and a woman seated at one of the four available tables. Nobody stirs at his entrance, and Merle keeps saying he has Rambling Fever, which is apparently uncurable.

He sits down at the farthest corner of the bar and orders a Pabst, since there are about six signs and a neon clock advertising the product on the walls with nothing else in competition, which makes Tom hesitant to rock the boat asking for an alternative. The beer comes to him in a frosty mug and is altogether foamy and delicious, so this will do nicely for him now, and he relaxes and settles in. There is nowhere else to be right this moment but here at Judy's, so he wets his parched insides and looks up at the basketball game on the overhead TV at what appears to be Duke versus some junior high team from Paraguay, the sound turned down so he can't hear the announcers. He studies the bottles lined up behind the bar and starts playing this game in his head matching up the brand names of the bottles with incidents in his own life where something memorable took place when he'd swallowed the spirits inside the bottles he's looking at.

Smirnoff and Jim Beam and Maker's Mark and Jack Daniels. Names eliciting images of laughter and sex and hostility and deadly hangovers. Tanqueray and Bacardi and Jose Cuervo and Jameson's. Embarrassing moments and high drama and those astute instances of revelation and philosophy. Brought into focus later during mornings of regret, shame, and sickness. And joy, Thomas Lockhart. Do not forget that. Remember that joy in leaving the good earth and taking off in flights of fancy. For lands unknown. Sometimes blessedly accompanied by a woman. And, like now, drugs. Yes, the pleasure of drugs. How you would smile later when recalling what a wildly entertaining trip you and your senses had been passengers on.

Women. Fancied around with a lot of women under the guise of alcohol.

Wine. Add that to the list. Beer too. Glorious beer. Pabst and Coors and Budweiser and Miller. Lowenbrau and Schlitz and Blatz and Falstaff, beer of Dizzy Dean. Blasts from the past that made the spirit soar. Order another mug. As a matter of fact, my friend, make that a pitcher. Because I'm not driving. Mentally a box of rocks sometimes, but smart enough this night to leave the truck at the motel. Because I always know when moments like this are coming. Have learned from past experience that when confronting the haunted past and coming to close proximity with ghosts, ghouls, and goblins it is generally best to gird and lubricate oneself and insulate the brain before going to war. Because without a stiff jolt of liquid courage and added chemistry the hair might tend to stand on end. Maybe to break and run not only for one's life but because death might be soon only an afterthought.

"Well, I'm trying to mind my own business and leave you alone, but I keep sitting here looking at you and thinking I know you."

Familiar face of this bartender, standing before me with his book shut and an inquisitive look on his face.

"I think I went to school here at Covington with you," he says. "It's been a while ago, maybe a million years. But I think you and I had a few classes together."

"We did," Tom says. "Freshman English and British Lit. You're Phillip Gibson, right?"

"Right, and you're Tom Lockhart. I kept sitting over there thinking it was you, but wondering how that could be after all this time. I couldn't for the life of me figure out what you might be doing back here in McClellan sitting in the only beer joint in town."

"I'm here to pay my last respects to dear old Covington. They sent me a letter informing me it was closing."

"That's true. There's only a few more weeks to go. The place has gone broke at last and there aren't enough students enrolled anymore to afford to keep the lights on. It's sad when you think of it. Covington used to be a pretty good school."

"And you're still around? God, Phillip, I didn't think anybody actually stayed in this town after they graduated."

"I married a girl from McClellan. She was two years behind me at school. She lived at home and commuted to class. Brenda Lewis. I doubt you knew her. We got married in 1974 and still live across the street from her parents' house where she grew up. I worked twenty-five years at Chrysler Glass and then retired. I work here three nights a week because Judy is my wife's sister and she pays me a good wage to come and fill in. Some nights I even rack up on tips, but it's slow right now, what with the holiday coming up. A lot of people are out of town."

Phillip wipes at a dab of moisture on the bar with his towel.

"I remember talking to you on the night Peterson Library burned down. Me and Brenda saw it on the news and drove over to watch them fight it. You were there by yourself. Remember me talking to you?"

"Faintly. I was pretty freaked out at the time. It hadn't been but a couple of weeks since a girl I knew fell from the balcony. The day before Thanksgiving," he adds.

"Oh yeah, an anniversary tonight. Faith Mercer. I remember that all too well myself. I'd had some dealings with Faith back then, like a lot of guys did. The rumor at the time was she jumped because she was pregnant, but it turned out that wasn't true. Shit, she was just doing LSD or something and figured she could fly if she took a step off into the air. Then she fell forty feet and broke her neck."

"You knew Faith?"

"The same way a lot of guys did. Matter of fact one of my buddies was semi-engaged to her at one time, but that was never going to happen. She liked too many guys, Faith did, and she didn't mind showing it. She was into a lot of wild shit, drinking and drugs and fooling around. It was funny, in a way, because she also liked to come across like she was just a sweet little girl, daughter of a Methodist minister, who'd gone to Sunday School all her life and never done the first thing wrong."

"That's what I thought about her."

"Heck, that's what everybody thought," Phillip laughs, "until they got out with her. Then they found out different, sometimes immediately, sometimes after a while. My friend never found out about her until after she went off the balcony, but other people, like me, learned about her right off the bat. I regret that to this day too, me fooling around with Faith behind my buddy's back. He never found out and I for damn sure didn't tell him either, because it would have driven him off the deep end to know the truth about her and me. But he's dead now, died a couple of years ago of a stroke, so I guess if there's an afterlife he knows all about us by now."

Drink this pitcher down. See it disappear and have another. Phillip going on and on with stories of Ancient Covington. Tall tales and scandals down through the decades. How the facts of Faith falling to her death made her into a campus legend. The Hippie Girl Ghost. Appears sometimes in dorm rooms and dark campus lanes. Looking for the father of her baby. Because, Phillip says, in the legend it's much more romantic for Faith the Hippie Girl Ghost to have been pregnant when she leaped to her death. Abandoned and forsaken. Looking forever for her guilty lover. To take revenge for what he'd done to her.

At ten Phillip wipes the bar down and turns off the TV. Game long over. Closing up early for Thanksgiving, he says. It's been good to see you, Tom. Hope you see what you came to see. Hard to believe old Covington's closing down. The next time you come through here there won't be anything left. It will be like it was never here at all.

Out the door and into the night. God, the sidewalks here really do fold up at night. Not a soul moving. Walk down this way and peer inside windows of stores at items for sale. Hardly a thing worth having. Go a block and civilization drops off completely and there's only streetlights and asphalt. Silence of night and a stretch of road in my path. Gives me time to think. What I need this moment.

Faith Mercer no angel. That's what Phillip said. I wasn't the only one. She wasn't pregnant. Suppose I'm off the hook. Odd and strange the way I've been guilty all this time and now I'm not. Faith not offing herself for the likes of me. Not pregnant or dead on my account. Takes a little getting used to. Spent so long condemning myself to a life sentence. Hard to suddenly unlock the cell and walk free. Like nothing ever happened.

Today. An anniversary for sure. This is Thanksgiving Eve.

He begins the long walk up Rainbow Hills, taking it slow and soaking it all in on this walk to Covington, because it is not so far now to be where he wants to be, and there is still some time left on this Eve before midnight arrives, so he does not have to run and hurry, because he is due nowhere but here on this night before the holiday, he only has to be in this place where he has an appointment to keep.

Mind starting to dance.

Old residential neighborhood here, old citizens of McClellan and lots of faculty lived in this spot. The letter said some of the departments had closed already and the faculty had lost some members taking jobs at other schools and the student population had dipped dramatically once word the school was closing at the end of the semester. A hundred and fifty years and that's it. Gone. Poof, just like that. Once the bulldozers get here there won't be a sign of Covington anywhere. Whatever happened here once will be hearsay.

Married students' apartments on the right. Used to see guys walking from there to get to their classes. If they had a car they left it behind so they wouldn't have to buy a sticker and a parking pass for the campus lot. Most of them close to broke. Some of the wives working at places in town, waitressing, teaching school, babysitting, typing up term papers, but some stayed home with their kids because they couldn't afford daycare. Used to see them walking babies in strollers, young women in loose dresses trying to get their figures back. Down Rainbow Hills and stop at the Foodland. Eat at home because they couldn't afford a fancy restaurant. As if there was such a place in McClellan.

And remember one of those wives had a dog. Friendly retriever who came over and licked me on the hand as I sat on a bench downtown. Eating an ice cream cone and the temptation was too great for him to pass me by. Thought I might share. Sorry, she said. Dylan has no manners whatsoever. Did he lick your cone? If he did I'll buy you another. It's okay, I said. I was through with it anyway. So don't think twice, it's all right. Is that why his name is Dylan?

We talked for a few more minutes and I learned it was her off day. Worked at a Kmart five miles down the road. Customer service and she hated it, but somebody had to pay the bills. Husband in Business Administration, but that was a joke, she said. Because he hasn't had a job for two years now. Won't even work in the summers because he says he has to take classes so he can graduate early. Fat chance of that, she said. He'll just think of something else to help him stay an eternal student.

She was a Linda from Huntsville, and we went a couple of semesters seeing each other, at first me coming by her place in the mid-mornings when Don, her husband, was deep in academia, but later to my small alcove, because she was afraid Don might skip class one day and show up and that would be it. Although, she said, if he did how big a tragedy would that be? Because one of these days one of them was going to take off anyway, both of them knew it without saying, and sometimes it didn't matter to her who was leaving or who was staying.

She was a girl with a problem trying to figure it out, but she never asked me for advice. Which was fine, me being devoid of wisdom in those days. She wanted from me what I wanted from her, not to be alone when the crazies came calling. I didn't feel bad while it was going on, which was different, and when she told me she was leaving Don I didn't ask her to stay; we were both of the opinion that we were at a good ending point and it was a smart thing to keep it that way. And two days later I walked by her apartment and saw that her Falcon was gone.

Wonder where she is these days? Hard to picture her as an old lady, but I guess that's how it is. Hard picturing myself as ancient either, but I do slip up and look in the mirror sometimes. Who's that in there? I ask.

Come up this last hill and go between two un-demolished buildings. Don't recognize either one, but they're not new. I've been gone a long time. Some people would call it a lifetime.

Even from a mile off I can hear the courthouse clock chiming off the hour of eleven. One more hour until Thanksgiving. Give myself credit. Here like I said I'd be.

Up this sidewalk leading to the dorms. On the right are the academic buildings, the bookstore, the new library. Not so new, really. Been here at least a quarter of a century. But to me that's new.

Gazebos and a dried-up pond where goldfish used to swim. Disappear during the winter and I always wondered if somebody from Covington came around with a net and scooped them up. Took them off for safekeeping. Off in the distance the old gymnasium, vacant now, since it got to where there wasn't enough money to field athletic teams. And anyone who could play any kind of sport decided to go somewhere else.

On a bench inside the last gazebo a young woman sits with her hands in her lap. Wondering why a woman is sitting outside by herself at this time of night on a closed and deserted campus, Tom moves her way. He tries not to come upon her too suddenly so as not to frighten her, make her jump with surprise. He half-thinks he knows her, but that's ridiculous. How could that be? He is a stranger here himself.

"Are you okay?" he asks.

The woman sees him but does not speak. She is smiling though.

He wants to stop and rub his eyes to make certain he is seeing what he thinks he is. Because he is almost sure the woman is Faith Mercer.

As she has been dead for thirty years at last count, Tom doesn't have much to say at the moment, but when he sees Faith look up at him and smile again, he knows the ball is in his court.

"Faith," he says, "is that really you? Am I seeing things?"

"It's me, Thomas Lockhart," she says. "I've been waiting here for you."

"I didn't know if I was going to come," he tells her, "until just a few days ago."

Faith smiles as if she is pleased.

"I guess I need to point this out," he says, "but up until about a minute ago I had you penciled in as dead."

"I'm dead to many people, Tom, but not to you."

She stands and straightens the shawl she's wearing. There's a dress beneath it, pale white in the moonlight. It's getting brisk because it's November, but she has on sandals.

"You wouldn't let me die, Tom," she says quietly. "It was you who kept me alive all these years."

She reaches out and takes his hand, and he does not jump at her touch. Her hands are not cold like he thought they might be; they are warm, almost like she is alive.

He tries to evaluate how drunk he is from all the beer at Judy's, how far along on his trip he is from Dewey's leftover LSD, but he has made it here to Covington just fine, not staggering, not tripping, not wavering off the sidewalks and getting lost. He seems as straight as he ever is, rain or shine, day or night.

"You said you were waiting for me, Faith. Why are you waiting?"

She smiles again.

"Because," she says, "you're growing older, Tom Lockhart. I knew you'd have to come and see me sometime soon."

She waits a moment, then laughs.

"I am thy lover's spirit, come back to settle a few things once and for all. Don't be frightened. Don't look at me like you think you're going crazy."

"I might be," he tells her. "I could be hallucinating from the acid I dropped. I might be crazy drunk. Losing my mind seems like a good possibility of happening pretty soon."

"You've lost a lot of things over time," she says, "but your mind isn't one of them."

"Are you telling me you're real? That I'm not imagining this?"

"Everything you do is real, Thomas. Every thought you have is real. Nothing is imaginary that is within. It is there. If you can see and hear me then it means that I am real. Or at least I am to you."

From nearby he hears the sound of approaching footsteps. He sees Maribeth McAllister walk by on the way to her dorm, carrying a cloth purse over one arm and two books clutched in the other. She is the Maribeth of long ago, so he doesn't call to her, only watches as she passes.

"Did you see her?" he asks.

"Maribeth McAllister? Not for a long time I haven't. Not until tonight."

"It was Maribeth, all right," he says, "walking by us, twenty years old again."

"That would be right," Faith says. "That would be the way she is here. She is the way you think of her, the way you remember her being."

"She's not that way anymore," Tom says. "I know because I've seen her. She's a widow these days. She's fifty-something."

"You're older, Tom Lockhart. I would be too, if I'd made it that far."

Tom watches Maribeth fade away into the night. He hears Faith speak to him again.

"Do you know why you are here, Tom? I'm sure you have questions."

"I suppose I'm here to make some sort of sense of everything while I'm tripping."

"Do you believe nothing has made any sense yet in your life, even after all this time?"

"Not a whole lot has ever made sense to me," he says wearily. "About the only thing I've ever understood much is the fact that a lot of bad stuff happens because of things I do. I've made excuses for the way I act, but in the long run it always comes back to being my fault."

"You believed you got me pregnant. You went a long time thinking you were the reason I jumped from Peterson's balcony."

"I'm told that wasn't the case. I don't know what to believe anymore. I'm beginning to think that a lot of things that happened didn't happen the way I thought they did."

"You don't control what people do, Thomas. Do you believe that?"

"Sure," he says. "It's not me that makes the world go around."

"Yet you've gone a long while thinking that everything that transpires does so because of you."

"It happens the way I see it," he says. "That makes it real, right?"

"But I wasn't pregnant, Thomas. I wasn't innocent the way you wanted me to be. I couldn't be a symbol of both your revenge and the guilt that came afterward. The real truth was I was on my own acid trip. I didn't jump because I wanted to end it all. I just had it in my head that I might as well take flight while I could. It seemed like a good idea at the time. But you didn't have anything to do with it. Sorry, Thomas Lockhart, but you were just another boy I thought it would be fun to fuck."

"I never saw any of that," he admits. "I saw you as this preacher's girl who was on her way to someday marrying some vanilla guy she'd met on campus, and my idea was to get in your pants and mess with your mind and know when I was through with you that I'd won another victory for the old home team, which was me, playing this game I had to win at after losing so badly before, else I'd go through the rest of my life knowing I'd been on the losing side and I was always going to be a loser."

"You didn't lose, Thomas, but you didn't win either. You made sure of that in your own way."

"I guess the game must still be going on. Is that what you're saying? You're telling me the rules of the game were never what I thought they were."

"Perhaps that is so," Faith says. "That is for you to determine."

He is standing before Peterson Library now, which has not burned down but is still here this night, present and erect. He sees Faith now up on the third-floor balcony and he wants to call out to her. Go back inside. Be careful. He will get someone to come and open the door. Be patient and someone will be here with a key. You do not need to do what you are thinking of doing.

"No one made you jump," says Tom. "It was nothing that made you do what you did. You just thought it would be fun to fly."

"I was playing a game, Thomas, much like you were. Hide and seek. I was tripping and I was hiding in the library. I was going to win if nobody found me."

"It's stupid," he says. "I wish I'd had more sense. I wish someone had come and told me I was going to go through my entire life thinking you died because of me, that I'd be afraid to love anyone because I'd think I was going to ruin their life, for fear somehow I'd end up killing them too. I carried a curse and there was no way around it."

"Did you really believe that, Thomas? Or was that only a prop to justify the way you decided to hide from life?"

He hears the courthouse clock strike the half hour. In thirty minutes it will be Thanksgiving. He will never spend Thanksgiving Eve at Covington College again.

"This is where my life began. It started here at Covington. I came from Rhodes with high ideals and big expectations. I was going to do something great. I was going to write the greatest book, sing the best song. have the most marvelous life. I'd know every woman inside and out, clothed and unclothed, and in the end I would find the one who was perfect and that would be it. There I'd go, out into the real and magical world, both would be all mine forever. I was indestructible. But then everything changed."

He wants to look for Maribeth, but she is gone. Faith is standing beside him again, listening to all he says, but there is more than this, he knows. There is more to see, more to come.

"You're just another ghost, aren't you, Faith Mercer?" he says. "You're like all the other visions I've seen all my life."

"I am of your own making. I am also the Flower Child Hippie Girl Ghost of Covington College. It is good for everyone to be someone at last."

"I couldn't get your death out of my head, Faith Mercer. Did you always know that?"

"Yes, but I couldn't help what was inside you. I was already gone."

Faith Mercer died and I made it a part of me. All who have come and gone through all the years have been a part of me.

"Nothing stays the same," he tells her. "It changes and becomes something else. One day I won't notice the comings and goings anymore."

"It is always that way, Thomas Lockhart. One day you will come to understand. Nothing is ever the way you think it is. Nothing will stay the way you want it to. All this before you now has never been the way you thought it was then."

"You are a memory, Faith Mercer, from the long ago. You are a shape that passed by and touched me and then went on. You are dead and gone and you are not the same as before. Maribeth McAllister is dead to me too. I have forgotten the person I loved back then because that person became the person I know now, and she is someone I do not know anymore. I do not love her. I don't know you. I thought I knew you both for the longest time, but it's different now. You're both strangers to me. I'm a stranger to you."

"We are all strangers, Thomas Lockhart. We were always strangers. even when we touched in our secret, unknown places."

He does not know what to say to this. He has no words. If Maribeth were to reappear before him this moment there would only be silence for her too. The two of them have said all there is to say to each other. Whatever was there for them to know as lovers is vanished now.

He sees Abigail drive by in her car, motoring along to some deadly liaison on an invisible road. In wonder he sees Martha Jane tending what flowers remain in the November gardens of Covington, hears Chopin on the wind and recognizes it as a piece she loved. He remembers hearing it played on her broadcast, and now this night he hears it again. He sees Sam and his parents walking by, the three of them in steady conversation. They do not see him. Doug and Linda pass by with Charlie, the three on their way somewhere, a ball game, a carnival, Thompson's Tavern to meet others. He sees Dewey in another country. He knows as long as he is in this place where his life came into being he will see all who he has passed or have passed him by, coming and going, all gone now, lingering only in the context of a world they once existed within.

Martha Jane stops the tending of the garden and comes his way, look-ing at him and seeing unseeing him, speaking to him with no words or sound, cocking her head to hear his voice but hearing nothing, because he has no earthly words to say to her, Martha Jane, his lost love who came to him when he believed love never was to come again, who left him in a flash of metal and bade him farewell with only a memory of what might have been, a wisp of reminiscence that may have been only within his own facul-ties, because perhaps it was true that the Martha Jane DeMars he loved did not walk the same earth as he, perhaps he had made her come into being in the same way he had invented Maribeth McAllister once, his sad-tragic his-tory with Faith Mercer, the ego-driven thrusting days and nights spent with Abigail. Was any of it real? Did it all happen as he believed it had, through his eyes and his mind and his soul? Or was it all a fiction, like the books he wrote that failed because readers could in the end see his words had no basis in love or life, there was no theme, which was like his own life, made up and fictionalized through the river of himself.

He sees himself moving these minutes before midnight while the spell is cast upon him, Thomas Lockhart at age twenty, on his way somewhere to do something, to paint a false picture of himself for his own good, to lie, to speak silver words of love and mean nothing by them, to come to some sort of understanding with an imagined deity on high that he alone, Thomas Lockhart, is the protagonist of in a great panoramic life that envelops all and is at the root of all, friend, lover, writer, one privy to all the twists and turns of a world that just might not contain everything he is seeking, but having the talent and ability to fill in the spaces and the blanks where something might be lacking and make it whole, make it into a hero's life that the world might look up at the heavens and exclaim their wonder and admiration for, to say, oh my, oh my, what a life this Thomas Lockhart led on this earthly star!

He wants to yell at his figure-self going his merry and merciless way and tell him to come back, to return, to forget about the paths to be taken, forget the songs he wants to someday sing, forsake the women he wants to win and lose and carry forever in his soul.

But he lets the image vanish, disappear as if it was entering another world, knowing that no matter what he has to tell it it will come to nothing in the end, will not change the way things have been or the way they are at this instant or will be in the days to come. He hears the courthouse clock mark the arrival of midnight, Thanksgiving Day, and he knows that all he has seen and touched and believed in up until this flash and slice of time, this singular beat of his heart, is gone from him now forever.

He walks Covington once more, another round, a final time. In the black of the night, in the darkness, he sees more clearly than he has before.

Faith Mercer enters a still-standing Peterson Library amid Confederate architecture and statues and musty books. She glides through the doors like she is late for some meeting, and climbs the flights of stairs, foregoing the small elevator in the lobby, a picture of health and energy, her eyes glancing his way as she makes her way to the third-floor. She has business there, an appointment to keep, and soon she will assume the mantle of the ghost she has spent her short life preparing to be. It is something that was always going to happen and he had no bearing in it.

Dewey and Phyllis are by Gibbons Auditorium, Dewey in his lawn chair with his Mateus and his copy of *Ulysses*. He asks if Dewey has started writing his own book now, but Dewey does not hear him. Phyllis is not aware of his presence. Dewey is in another country. Phyllis is dead.

It is not autumn anymore; now it has turned into winter.

The wind blows and snow falls on Covington, and he sees River Grove those miles away in a blanket of white. He is walking up the rise, and he looks back and sees the caretaker's stone house and realizes he is the caretaker there no more, nor the tenant, but only a figure visiting from another land and time to see the remnants of what had once been conjured for him. There are his parents entering into their plot, Sam his brother waiting for them to descend and then follow. He wants to go and ask what it had been that kept him from being one of them, for living a life outside their horizons that had taken him running from Rhodes to a far corner of a distant state so he would be one of them no more, and he sees himself running back in Covington making certain the distance grew larger with each step in his gait, his feet churning and his eyes looking ahead and never back from where he'd come, from whom he had once been a part of. He sees the faces of teachers, students, women he has touched with his unholy hands and possessed only for the time he wished.

He hears voices asking questions.

"What are you looking for?" It is Faith's voice again. "What are you wanting to find?"

"Answers," he replies. "I want to know why everything is the way it is. Why it worked out that way."

"You were at the bottom of it," Abigail says. "It was you who caused it to happen."

"No," he tells her. "It was not me. It was you who had no dreams in your being. You were not like me at all. You cared for nothing of what I believed. We did not want the same things."

"You were always a fool," she laughs. "You are a fool to keep looking for something that is not there."

He sees Martha Jane in her funeral dress, the one she is buried in, her cheeks red once more, her lips glossy, her eyes with one last dance left in them, moving over him, seeing him again.

"What was it with you and me?" he asks.

I could never be the great love you wanted me to be, she says with her eyes. There was too much time between us, too many mistakes that couldn't be fixed.

"Where do I go without you? Where am I supposed to look to find you once more? You are dead and gone, while I am left to go on without you in this world, only to hear your voice and feel your touch in the parameters of my mind. What is there left for me to search for? To find?"

"You may find me somewhere," Martha Jane says. "But it could be we will never meet again."

"I've spent a lifetime, it seems, trying to find what I am looking for."

"Perhaps it is because what you seek does not exist."

He sees it is he and Martha Jane alone now, away from Covington and Rhodes, separate and alone above the swirl below them, and when he reaches out to touch her he finds no trace of her there. She is gone.

From this starry place on high, he stands and studies the disappearing lands below, the books he's written, the cities where he's lived, the women he perhaps loved, watching it all go away from him, going up in smoke and vanishing into a mist and being no more of the earth as the night falls away. He sees his life waning from this time and place he is in, and he knows when the sun rises he will be the person he was no more. All will be different. All will be changed.

He strains his eyes and finds he can see nothing. Is he blind? Is there nothing left behind and below for him to see?

"Am I an old man now?" he says to no one. "Is this an omen and a portent of the end to come? Is there nothing left for me in the wake of all my banished dreams?"

"Don't make it out to be so bad," Maribeth's voice tells him. "You were always the one for that. A mountain from a molehill, that was you. You raised the stakes so high, turned up the volume so you couldn't help but hear every single note. Your fur so thick and your cry so loud. You were one and all inside yourself while everyone else was only along for the ride. You spoke of faith and love and how someday you'd find it, but everybody knew—everybody—that you'd run away if it ever got too near where you could see it up close. You didn't want anyone to tell you how love is never quite as lovely as it seems from where you are, how nothing is ever what you truly want it to be once you actually hold it in your hand."

She kisses him on the cheek and squeezes his hand a last time.

"Goodbye, Tom Lockhart," she says. "I loved you the best way I knew how, but I was never who you thought I was. No one is, dear one. There is no one."

Maribeth is gone.

All of them gone now," he says aloud, the sound of his voice all that is audible after the courthouse clock finishes its twelfth chime.

Were any of them ever truly present? All moved on now and can't ask if they actually existed at all? Maybe they were extensions of faces and spirits I made up to accommodate myself, for amusement, inventions of my own choosing to make certain my life would be magical? Whether they were real or not made not that much of a difference?

He stands in his darkness and sees as if for the first time the world he has created; the faces and figures before him, fables and myths and tall tales of a life that wanted nothing less than a series of spectacular moments.

"Maybe the whole of you were not real, maybe this life is all a screenplay for the movie wherein I am the star with top billing. It could be those moments in the dark, the caresses and whispered vows, the songs of love and declarations to the heavens were of my own devising, but I take no fault from this day forward for what was not there for me to find when I was looking for it so desperately, when I desired it so and needed for the sanctity of my soul and being for it to appear. I am blameless for believing all I heard or for memorizing the lyrics of sweeping songs or wishing on the moon for my life to be such as all that. I had no grasp of circled orbs. I was only a believer wishing for it all to be true. My visions were starry and nothing less."

There is no treasure to discover. Perhaps that is true.

And he thinks of it all from the beginning and through all the doors and portals of his time on the land he'd come from, and he sees old houses and familiar roads and sacred sites and Lynda with a Y and Mitchell who is possibly his son and Chattanooga and all he had lost and left behind.

And Rhodes rises and falls before him, Matt and Abigail and Thompson's with his friends at tables, standing at the bar, the music from the juke-box, the walks home down River Road with the coyotes barking in the night and the deer running out of the darkness in fear of the danger within him coming near to them.

Still, as he feels the morning's approach, it comes to him how night will never be the same for him again, how there will be no more visions of a Maribeth or a Covington or Faith Mercer falling from a burning Peterson. There will be no Martha Jane DeMars at Rhodes for any more visitations, but there will be, he thinks, another road for him to travel soon, another land where magic dwells if he can find it, for he knows the way it is in this life, how nothing is ever completely the way it appears, how nothing can be realized totally in the fiction of the mind, but he knows he can continue in his own way to look for it and to wander until he comes across something close to it one more time, because that is fine, that is the way he is, he is Thomas Lockhart and he will live on as himself and not ever be one among all the rest, those faces all lost out there and estranged from the world of enchantment, those souls milling in their realities and living out their lives as if they were dead already.

Madison, TN 2019–2021

CPSIA information can be obtained
at www.ICGtesting.com
Printed in the USA
BVHW081407130521
607269BV00011B/2053